SECRETS, LIES AND LOVE

MARCIE STEELE

B R
BOOKS

For my best friend, Alison.

CHAPTER ONE

Sophie Wheldon turned over in bed and faced her sleeping husband. Hands tucked under her chin, she stared at his familiar face. It wasn't as if she didn't love Reece anymore, but lately something wasn't working. She didn't know whether it was because he worked away during the week and she'd got too used to a single life or if it was something deeper than that. Reece was a steady, reliable man and not everyone could keep the passion alive for so many years, surely?

Watching someone sleep should be so romantic, she thought, holding in a sigh in case she woke him. In his day, he'd been the proverbial tall, dark and handsome man that everyone wanted. Even with age taking away most of his hair and adding a few weather-worn lines, he didn't look a day over twenty-eight when in reality he was pushing thirty-six.

Reece had been the school heart-throb. Sophie had thought he was lovely from the minute she'd noticed him hanging around with her friend Beth's brother, Ryan. One night, the two of them had sneaked into the local pub, all eyeliner and lip gloss to make them look eighteen, even though they'd barely reached sweet sixteen, and Sophie got chatting to him. She'd seen him around for as long as she could remember, but hadn't really spoken to him until then.

They'd been together for two years before marrying when she was eighteen. Now she couldn't recall a time when Reece hadn't been in her life. Yet ...

She closed her eyes, trying not to liken him to Damien Wilshaw, the man who could make her knees quiver with one smile. On Friday morning, he'd stopped at her market stall to talk to her again and she'd been so tongue-tied she'd had to resort to a nod, feeling the mortification as her cheeks reddened. Damien had noticed too and had flirted with her, making her blush even more.

She thought back to when she'd first noticed him a few weeks ago. Sophie had inherited a thriving fruit and veg business when she was eighteen, after her dad had died. Damien had called at one of the stalls opposite hers in the indoor market and bought a mobile phone. Surreptitiously, Sophie watched him from a distance. He caught her looking a couple of times but she'd been quick to hide behind her own customers.

Moments later, he'd walked across to her stall and bought an apple. Sophie was sure it had been meant as a symbol. It was the forbidden fruit: he obviously knew she was married. Well, that and the fact she was wearing a wedding ring.

It had been a one-off meeting, or so she thought. Damien had called at the stall the next day and the next, so much so that Beth and her sister Nicci, who worked on the stall too, had started to rib her about him.

Yet when he'd caught her away from the stall and asked her to join him for coffee at the café on the next aisle, she'd found herself saying yes. Even though she knew they shouldn't, they'd swapped phone numbers and so the texting had begun.

Damien had made it perfectly clear from the moment they'd shared that first coffee that he wanted her. There was something that she wanted from him too, but she was married. Good girls didn't have affairs, did they?

But the more she thought of him, the more she wanted a little excitement in her life. It was sorely missing right now.

Reece stirred, stretching his arms above his head. Sophie felt the guilt almost immediately.

'Morning,' he smiled.

'Morning.' She stayed huddled under the covers, hoping her body language would be enough to stop him reaching over to her.

They lay in silence for a moment before Reece threw back the duvet. He kissed her lightly on the forehead before jumping out of the bed.

'I'd better make a move. I'm meeting Matt for a run before I head back to Sheffield. I reckon a ten-miler is on the cards today.'

It took all of Sophie's strength to smile. But she needn't have bothered, because Reece wouldn't have noticed anyway. It had been a long time since Reece had noticed anything that Sophie did – or said, for that matter.

She pulled the duvet over her head to block out the day. Already she was counting down the hours until Reece would be leaving. After lunch, he'd pick up his bag of freshly washed clothes that she'd ironed while catching up on Saturday night television after their customary takeaway.

Where were they heading, her and Reece? They'd been married for the past sixteen years. Did he feel as bored as she was? They were definitely stuck in a rut but they had been happy once. It was just that things had gone stale.

Sophie craved excitement, passion, all the things that she should have been getting from Reece. And even if she wasn't sure that she loved him anymore, she wouldn't cheat on him. Would she?

She let out another big sigh. No wonder Damien Wilshaw was filling her thoughts.

Beth Pellington lifted her head from the pillow, slowly opened one eye and promptly closed it. She turned onto her side, pushed her hair away from her face and huddled in the foetal position. She felt dreadful after last night's shenanigans. Hadn't she made a New Year's resolution ten days ago not to drink too much? A tear trickled from the corner of her eye and onto the pillow.

"Too much alcohol will limit your life," she'd read somewhere in her daughter's magazine. Charley Pellington was fifteen and the old head of the family, as she often told her mother when Beth wasn't keen to act her age of thirty-four.

It all boiled down to loneliness. On a regular basis, Beth wished she could find someone dependable like her friend Sophie had. She felt as if she was past her sell-by date already.

All those thoughts of big weddings and happy-ever-afters that she'd dreamed about as a child had accounted to nothing. She had got married but it had left her a lonely divorcee who now couldn't get a civilised man whatever she tried. And Beth knew that if she carried on like this, by the time she found anyone half-decent she'd be too reliant on alcohol.

Why couldn't her marriage have survived the early years? But then again, her ex-husband Brian had never really accepted her daughter. Charley had been a toddler when they'd met and he'd been fine with her at first. He'd take her out to the park, showing her off as if she were his own flesh and blood; buy her presents, spoiling her at Christmas and birthdays. But the older she grew, the more he said she reminded him that she wasn't his daughter. And the fact that she wouldn't tell him who Charley's father was became another bone of contention.

Come off it, she scolded herself inwardly as she rolled over onto her back. Brian leaving hadn't been anything to do with Charley. Beth had thought that by marrying him and providing Charley with a father figure it would be the fairy tale life she'd dreamed of. She'd got her man, and she had her daughter, but she hadn't been happy. So in true Beth style, she'd nagged at him, constantly winding him up. It didn't take long for them to start living separate lives before eventually he left altogether.

How had everything gone so wrong? Was it life that had got in the way, or was it something to do with her? Because right now, Beth wasn't feeling particularly proud of herself.

CHAPTER TWO

After Reece returned from his run, he and Sophie had wrapped up warmly and decided to go for roast beef with all the trimmings at a local pub. It had been quite pleasant and they'd bumped into a few friends who had popped in too. It meant that Sophie didn't get to chat to Reece much, which was good and bad because sharing a lunch would have given them the opportunity. Pretty soon it would be time for him to get back to his digs in Sheffield.

Their house was a small semi-detached in a quiet, leafy street only five miles from the city centre of Hedworth. Sophie's market stall was located on the high street in the suburb of Somerley, a ten-minute walk. Martin Smithson, Sophie's dad, had died of a heart attack when he was thirty-six. It had been sudden and brutal and she would never forget the horrifying image of him collapsed on the kitchen floor right in front of her. A post mortem had revealed a faulty valve in his heart. It had also left her an orphan, as Sophie's mum, Angela, had died of a brain tumour when Sophie was four.

Both Martin and Angela had been only children, so

Sophie had grown up very much the centre of their world. There were no aunties, uncles and cousins and both sets of grandparents had gone by the time she was fifteen. So it had been the two of them for years, and one of the reasons why she only had a few close friends. She didn't let people in easily.

During her teens, she'd become really close to her dad. He'd been there for everything: laughing with her as he'd tried to help out with her maths homework, watching over her when she was sick, looking out for her when she was upset about something.

Before his death, Martin had worked hard to improve the house, which Sophie inherited too, so she was in a more fortunate position than her friends. Having added her individual style to it for the past sixteen years, their home now had a modern feel with wooden flooring throughout, chromes and bright colours. It was also her sanctuary at the end of a day spent on her feet.

After they returned back from lunch, Reece dropped his bombshell. Sophie noticed he'd been a bit quiet on the drive from the pub and had put it down to his usual tiredness after his long week at work. But even back at the house, she'd seen him glancing at her a few times, studying her, as if he wanted to speak to her but didn't know how to start.

The conversation came when they were in the living room sorting out his things. Sophie was squashing rolled-up socks down one side of his holdall.

'Would it bother you if I didn't come home for the next few weeks, Soph?' Reece shoved in another pair of jeans, studiously not looking at her as he spoke.

Oh.

Well, would it?

A sense of dread rippled through her. If she was honest, she knew how she *should* feel but it wasn't necessarily how she *did* feel. But that was more of a problem than she would care to admit.

'Why? You're not planning on doing a runner, are you?'

Reece's laugh was a little awkward. 'Some of the lads have been offered a job in Germany. It's only for two months, three at tops. I thought—'

'Two or three months?' Sophie put down a box of mince pies left over from Christmas. Her shoulders dropped.

'It's good money,' Reece added. 'I could make double what I do on the site now.'

'Money isn't everything. It's not as if we need it.' Sophie glanced around the room with the best of everything in it – leather settees, a few expensive figurines and photographs, all the latest gadgets for cinema-style television viewing.

'I know but ...well ...'

Sophie sighed, realising that was why he was packing more than he normally would. It was obvious he'd already made up his mind and she definitely didn't know what to think about that.

'If you want to go, I'm not going to stop you,' she said. 'But it's a long time not to see each other.'

Reece shrugged. 'It's probably going to be no more than two months. And it's not as if we see that much of each other anyway. I'll be back before you know it.'

Sophie's mouth hung agape. He didn't seem bothered at all. But part of her didn't really care either way. She *was* used to not having him around.

Yet the other part of her wanted to scream out to him. *Don't leave me, not for that long. I'm lonely and I can't trust myself. I need you to stay. I want you to love me. I want to feel like you still need me.*

'You'd better bring me back something nice,' she told him instead with a wag of her index finger.

As Reece moved towards her and kissed her on the cheek,

Sophie pondered on this new revelation. Looking on the bright side of things, it wouldn't be that long without him. He was right; they didn't see that much of each other now so it wouldn't seem too different.

Besides, all of this fantasy thinking of Damien Wilshaw could be harmful to her marriage. She owed it to them both to give the relationship the go it needed. After sixteen years together, all the ups and downs, she had to try to get their marriage back on track.

CHAPTER THREE

Sophie stood outside Beth's house, stamping her feet to keep them warm as she waited for her to come out. She was about to ring her when her front door opened. Beth rushed down the path towards her.

'Sorry! Late as usual, but don't tell the boss.'

'I'm going to start docking your wages one of these days,' she chided.

'No, you're not.' Beth grinned and linked her arm through Sophie's. 'So what did you and Reece get up to yesterday? Anything interesting?'

'The usual.' Sophie didn't want to share the conversation she'd had with Reece yet. They walked along the pavement. 'What about you?'

'Same old, same old. Saturday night in the Hope and Anchor; Sunday lunch with the family. I thought you two might have popped over.'

'We went for a drive.'

The lie rolled off her tongue before she had time to stop it. Why did she feel the need to fib to her best friend?

'In this weather?' Beth eyed her with incredulity. 'You must be mad.'

'It was something to do.'

'Is Reece home next weekend? Because if he isn't, I could do with a good night out with my bestie.'

'You make us sound like we're teenagers.' Sophie's voice was wistful. 'What about Charley?'

'She'll probably be staying over at Sarah's and if she isn't, Matt will look after her.'

'Have you asked him?'

'There's no need. He's always around for us.'

Sophie looked at her pointedly. 'You take him for granted, you know.'

'I *do* know, yes. But he's a darling and he adores Charley.'

'Actually, it's you that he adores but I'm not going to labour that point again.'

'That's because it isn't true. Matt is just a friend.'

Beth and Matt had dated during their last year at high school but things had fizzled out within a matter of weeks. Afterwards they'd kept in touch as friends, even when Beth had found herself pregnant with Charley when she was seventeen. But things had petered off slightly when she'd met and fallen in love with Brian.

There had been no double wedding as they'd dreamed about when they were teenagers. Beth's wedded bliss had lasted five years, followed by a messy divorce. Matt went on to have two long-term partners, but Sophie suspected he'd always have a soft spot for their friend. Even his latest relationship was off more than it was on.

Matt was always there for Beth and she didn't appreciate how much. He spent most of his free time at her house. Charley got on really well with him and loved it when her mum went out and Matt came round to babysit.

'So what do you think?' Beth pressed her.

'It's Monday morning,' Sophie stressed, 'and you're already thinking about Saturday?'

'Live for the weekend, you know that's my motto. I suppose Reece could come too, if he's around. At a push, I could deal with that.'

'I'll think about it. How is my goddaughter, by the way? Still being hormonal?'

'As ever.' Beth pouted. 'I can't believe how she's changed over the past couple of years. The minute she turned into a teenager, she's been nothing but moody and stroppy. I wish I knew what she was getting up to. I've been searching for her diary but I haven't been able —'

'You've looked for Charley's diary?' Sophie raised her eyebrows.

'Of course I have. I had one at that age.'

'Yes, but Sandra didn't read it.'

'My mum would never have found it, the amount of times I had to hide it because of my brother. I also know that she'd have gone mad if she had read it. I know what I got up to at that age, so I worry about Charl.'

'You did all right.' Sophie wouldn't let Beth become the martyr, as she was prone to doing.

'Yeah, sure,' Beth scoffed. 'Single mum at eighteen. That's a fine example to set. I don't want her getting caught like I did.'

Sophie pressed the button on the pedestrian lights and waited for them to change.

'I know she added a lot to my life,' Beth continued, 'but you know what I mean. If I hadn't had her when I was so young—'

'Stop moaning. Charley's a good kid. She won't make the same mistakes as you.'

Beth's head turned ninety degrees sharply. 'Well, thanks for the vote of confidence.'

'Well, thanks for confiding in me.'

'Oh, don't start that again.'

Beth and Sophie had been friends since their first day at nursery school. By the time Beth had hung her coat up on the peg with the white star sticker next to Sophie's green pear, they'd already formed a friendship that would take them through the next thirty years. Yet there was one secret between them. When Beth became pregnant, Sophie supported her through antenatal classes, labour pains, Charley's terrible twos and beyond. But Beth never told anyone who Charley's father was. Over the years, Sophie got used to not knowing but still she didn't like it.

'Anyway,' Beth added. 'I feel like I'm seventy-four not thirty-four. I'm so bored. A night out will do me the world of good.'

'You do that every week.' Sophie lowered her voice. 'I don't mean to be all preachy, but I worry about you.'

'I know, and I love you for it, but really, I'm okay.' Beth nodded her head vehemently. 'So, how about it?'

Arriving at the market, Sophie pushed her keys into the lock on the front doors.

'I don't know if I'm up to it,' she replied.

Glancing in the mirrored panels inside the doorway, she noticed how pale she looked. It was only her short, red hair flicked under at the ends and framing her face that gave her some much needed colour. She wore mostly neutral make-up, the heavy lids above blue eyes denoting her lack of sleep. She hoped she wasn't wearing her heart on her sleeve, worrying about Reece's sudden need to leave her for longer than a week at a time.

'You're not coming down with anything, are you?' Beth put a hand on her arm. 'You do look a little peaky.'

'Actually,' Sophie fibbed, seeing this as a way out of a long and lengthy marriage guidance session if she did spill the beans. 'I do feel a bit meh, if you must know.'

'Don't worry. You'll be fine by Saturday. Do you want to get ready at mine? Shall I book the taxi for eight?'

Sophie sighed as they went inside. Sometimes she wished that Beth would think about someone else for a change. Charley was far more well behaved for her years.

But then again, perhaps it was time to worry about herself more. The fact that she was starting to preach to her best friend about her going out too much made her own life seem boring in comparison.

CHAPTER FOUR

As soon as the door shut behind her mum, Charley Pellington dived back into bed. She reached for her phone to text her friend Sarah but there was already a message waiting from her.

'What were you up to on Sat night? You never told me what you did when I saw you yest. x'

Charley sighed. That was all she needed, rumours going around the school that she was frigid. On Saturday evening, Matt had called round to look after her because her mum was going to be out late. Charley didn't need a babysitter as such but her mum preferred someone to be around if she was going to get home later than midnight. Besides, Charley adored Matt. He was part of the furniture at their house. Often he'd take time out to chat with her about school and TV programs. She could ask him advice about most things too.

Charley had told him she and Sarah were going to the shops and she'd be home by ten. Well, she wasn't lying about the shops. But she didn't tell him they were meeting up with some of the lads from school. She'd hooked up with Aaron Smythe.

Nothing had happened though, but Aaron had been really annoyed when she'd stopped his wandering hands, and then he'd gone off in a strop. It was one thing to try it on, but to persistently continue when she'd said no, and sulk when he didn't get his own way?

She'd decided yesterday she would finish things when she saw him next. There was no way she was putting out to someone who didn't care about her.

She texted Sarah back.

'Didn't do anything. Come round. Coast clear. x'

Ten minutes later, the two of them were in the kitchen. Charley made coffee for them both. Even though she was still in her dressing gown and pyjamas, her hair had been straightened and she had added a bit of make-up; lippy, eye shadow and mascara. If she had been ready for school, she would have looked like a mirror image of her friend, with their slight frames and long legs that were perfect for skirts rolled up at the waist. When they were out together, they looked more like twins than friends.

With a sigh, she flopped down at the table, pushed into a corner that was barely big enough for it. Although Mum tried her best to keep on top of everything, and the house was always spotless, the kitchen in the terraced house was in need of a good lick of paint, the years old lino flooring in bad need of replacement.

Sarah was dressed in school uniform, a striped tie hung down in front of a V-necked maroon jumper, short navy skirt and thick black tights worn with Dr Martens. She shrugged off her coat and turned towards her friend.

'So tell me, Charley the tease. Did you or didn't you?'

Charley looked on in disinterest. 'Did I or didn't I what?'

'You haven't got a clue, have you?' Sarah covered her

mouth with a hand. 'I thought you'd have had at least one text message from someone other than me.'

'I was listening to music this morning,' Charley sighed in exasperation. 'What is it I'm supposed to have done this time?'

'Aaron's telling everyone that you gave him a blow job.'

Charley nearly fell off her chair. 'He said what! When? But ... how do you know all this? I only saw you last night and—'

'Never mind that.' Sarah pulled out a chair. 'Why didn't you tell me? I was —'

'I didn't tell you because nothing happened!'

Sarah looked up to see Charley's distraught expression. 'I know,' she said quickly. 'It was a joke. Sorry.'

'I would have told you,' Charley said. 'Especially if I had done *that*, you know I would. I mean come on, you think I'd put my mouth around Aaron's ... yuck. I would never. Not yet, anyway.'

'Aaron Smythe is an idiot,' Sarah retorted. 'Don't worry. It'll blow over soon.'

Both girls burst into laughter at Sarah's unfortunate choice of words.

Charley stood up. 'Give me five minutes to get changed. We'd better get going or we'll be late for school.'

Sarah nodded. 'You can tell me about Alex too. I want to know all of the gossip.'

Alex was a boy Charley had met online about a month ago. They'd started chatting and last week they'd exchanged WhatsApp messages. She looked forward to every one of them.

And she bet he would never spread lies about her.

CHAPTER FIVE

Somerley Indoor Market was set back off the high street. In front of the red brick building, a wide area of paving slabs ran its length, large stone plant pots dotted here and there for extra colour. In summer, when the flowers were in bloom it was a beautiful place to relax and have a sandwich at lunchtime. In winter, its shadows were long but it never looked dull in the dim light.

Monday mornings were always manic. Sophie loved the hustle and bustle. Bang on the dot of eight, her delivery would arrive and they'd start to stock the shelves. She had a walk-in booth, twice the size of the original one that she'd inherited from her dad. Back then the stall had been one tiny table in the far corner. Over the years, she had expanded and now stocked organic food and exotic fruit as well as her normal range.

A framed photo of her parents took pride of place on the back wall, moving with her several times as she had relocated to larger stalls. This booth was in the middle of an aisle, in prime position, and she had two full-time staff, Beth and Beth's younger sister Nicci.

'Morning Sophie. Grand day again,' Duncan Tamworth greeted her as he carried in trays full of bananas and apples. He placed them carefully on the floor before standing up and rubbing his back. His small and portly frame wasn't really meant for lugging heavy items around but he had been young, slim and far nimbler when she'd first got to know him.

'You need to get that seen to.' She pulled back the tissue paper to inspect her merchandise. 'It'll only get worse lugging all this about. Beth, give Duncan a hand, will you?'

Beth, who was making a hot drink, put down the coffee jar with a sigh. 'I'm coming, Mrs slave driver. Since when did anyone start the day before drinking at least three mugs of coffee?'

Sophie ignored the comment. Beth always had some excuse not to get going the minute she walked through the door. Even though she'd been working on the stall for the past seven years, she never failed to realise that if she got all the sorting finished for eight thirty, they could sit down for a coffee in peace. Sophie needed everything shipshape for when the first customer was let in. From nine a.m. every morning, it would be manic until around two o'clock when it would start to die down a little. At least the morning rush gave her no time to think about Reece.

Once Duncan had gone and apples and oranges and bananas were on the shelves, along with sacks of potatoes and carrots, and every imaginable salad vegetable had been placed in their baskets, Sophie finally felt herself relax. She checked her watch. Now it was time for coffee.

'Tell me more about Saturday night,' she encouraged Beth as she flicked on the kettle. She grabbed three mugs from the wooden rack Reece had put up in the tiny partitioned room at the back of the unit. 'Were the usual crowd in?'

Beth pulled her hair into a ponytail and fastened it back with a covered elastic band. 'Yes, which was the problem really. Everything is the same old, same old.' She sighed dramatically. 'Which is why I drank too much.'

'You always drink too much.' Sophie passed a coffee to her.

'I do not.'

Sophie stared at her pointedly. 'Well, that's what you keep telling me.'

Beth waved her hand around, as if batting away the comment. She was about to continue when her younger sister saved her from another lecture.

'Good morning, lovelies.' Nicci Pellington squeezed herself into the room. 'How goes it on this fine day?'

'Fine day?' Beth shook her head. 'It's brass monkey weather.'

'It isn't that bad.'

'Always the optimist, my sister.' Beth rolled her eyes at Sophie.

After Nicci had taken off her coat, Sophie passed her a mug too.

'Thanks.' She took it from her. 'So everyone happy today?'

'At least I see one of us had a good weekend,' Beth muttered.

'Yes, I did.' Nicci grinned. 'We had a cosy night in on Saturday, if you catch my drift. Then a long lie-in on Sunday morning—'

'Oh please,' Beth complained with a grimace. 'You're my baby sister. That's too much information.'

'Jealousy will get you nowhere.' Nicci wagged a finger at her. 'Anyway, I'm not sad and single, nor married, so I get lots of loving.'

'That puts me in my place, too,' Sophie laughed. She

picked up her drink and moved past her, leaving the sisters to it. For all their bantering, they got on really well.

Beth was the middle child of three. Her brother Ryan was thirty-six. Nicci was twenty-seven and often told everyone that her mum said she was the best mistake she'd made. Beth had been seven when Nicci was born and her status of youngest child disappeared overnight. From the first day Nicola Pellington arrived home from the hospital, Beth seemed to develop middle child syndrome. To this day, Sophie didn't think it had left her.

Just as Charley looked like her mum, Nicci was practically a double of her older sister. The years between them only showed up Beth's wrinkles. Both women had naturally dirty brown hair like their dad: both of them had it dyed chocolate brown every few weeks. They were the same height at five foot six apiece and apart from a stone in weight could hardly be told apart when seen from the back. Many customers mixed their names up – much to Beth's delight, and Nicci's dismay, over the years.

While Nicci checked her make-up in the small mirror above the sink, Sophie pulled the final few boxes out into the aisle. She threw out her hand and caught an apple as it tried to escape her stall. Carefully she put it back before glancing around at the place she knew so well that it could be her second home.

She had grown up with most of the stallholders. Many of them had known her since she'd been born and had tales to tell of how she'd sat in her pushchair while her parents worked around her until she was old enough for school. How shocked they were when Angela passed away so young. How devastated they were when Martin died suddenly too.

There were twenty-eight stalls in total, fourteen stalls in their aisle, for most occasions and needs. Make-up, haberdashery, knitting, clothing, underwear and car accessories.

Cupcake Delights sold the most heavenly cakes that none of them could resist come three p.m. Geoff Adams sold the best home-baked scones and flat breads she'd ever tasted. Then there were greetings cards, a fancy-dress stall and a T-shirt printing stand. At the back of the market were all the food counters. Across from them, Ryan and Matt sold mobile phone accessories.

To her right, Sophie caught Malcolm Worthington out of the corner of her eye. A tall and thin man with short grey hair, Malcolm and his wife, Maureen, sold sweets. Sophie knew Nicci hoped that someday in the future they'd be her in-laws when she married their son, Jay.

She checked her watch. Nearly opening time. She ran her eyes over the stall. Everything was looking perfect. Let another week begin.

But then, she noticed there was some kind of gathering going on along the aisle.

CHAPTER SIX

'Who's that?' Beth asked as she drew level with Sophie. She'd spotted Ryan and Matt talking to a young woman. 'Does she look familiar to you?'

'I recognise her vaguely,' Sophie said.

'Oh, no. Please tell me it isn't.'

Both Sophie and Beth turned as Nicci joined them with a groan.

'It's Jay's sister, Jess,' she explained. 'She must be back from London.'

'Ah, the prodigal one,' Sophie said. 'She's a bit of a black sheep.'

Nicci nodded. 'She moved to London a few years ago after being caught having an affair with a man she was working for.'

'Didn't you know she was here?' Beth asked.

Nicci shook her head. 'Jay told me she was thinking of coming back, but we had nothing more concrete than that.'

All three women stood in a line watching Jess busy flirting and pouting at Ryan and Matt.

She was tall like her father, and skinny like her mother. Her dark hair hung down in waves, the expensive cut of her jeans accentuating her long legs. Above them, a thick Aran jumper and a multi-coloured scarf with fingerless gloves to keep her hands warm and her fingers free to work.

Beth puffed and folded her arms to show her disgust. 'If she pushes her chest out any further, we'll be able to have a feel from here.'

'She's really pretty, though, isn't she?' Sophie was still looking over at them.

'Let's go and see what she's here for.'

Although Jess loved the attention she was getting that morning at the market, she would much rather have been in London. At eight forty-five, she would be coming up from the Tube at Paddington Station and grabbing her daily coffee and blueberry muffin. She would be making her way to the offices she worked at, to the desk where she would open her emails and check Laurie Porter's appointments for the day.

She would have been doing all that if Laurie hadn't decided to finish things with her the minute she told him her news.

Jess had worked at Porter's Finance as Laurie's personal assistant for the past four years, and for three and a half of those years she'd been sleeping with the boss. It was the reason she'd wanted to stay in the job for so long. The pay wasn't much but the joy she received as his bit on the side had been worth it. She'd played the game well, or so she'd thought.

Now she found herself back in sleepy Somerley, although she was trying to keep a low profile this morning. Attention to the stall would bring Nicci across to question her and that was another thing she was dreading. Nicci and Jess had been in the same year at high school. They hadn't liked each other then and the bad feelings had escalated even more since Nicci had become an item with her brother.

She smiled, bringing herself back into the conversation as she heard laughter. Although she hadn't seen either of her brother's friends in a while, Jess knew them well. Ryan and Matt had often been in her home when she was younger. Now they reminded her of the Mitchell brothers from EastEnders – all clean shaven and muscly, with hardly a hair on their heads between them. Ryan oozed a raw sex appeal like Ross Kemp. Matt wasn't too far behind either.

'Hiya, Jess.' Sophie came up beside her, closely followed by Beth.

Jess smiled widely at her, ignoring Beth. She'd always got on well with Sophie when she'd seen her out with her husband. But she had never been much for Beth, and she was glad that Nicci hadn't come across too.

'Hi, Sophie,' she said. 'How are you?'

'Good, thanks. What brings you back to Somerley? I thought you were settled in London?'

'Got another guilty secret?' Beth asked snidely, before Jess could reply.

'Wouldn't you like to know?' Jess chided. 'Actually, I needed a bit of space so I thought I'd help out on the stall. It gives mum and dad some spare time if I'm here, doesn't it, dad?'

Malcolm Worthington beamed at his daughter. 'It certainly does, love. We could always do with an extra pair of hands.'

'If you need any help,' Sophie pointed down the aisle, 'we're not far away. You know us all, and I'm sure Nicci will be across to say hello soon.'

'I doubt that very much.' Jess pulled her face at the impending argument. Later that morning she was going to ask her dad if he would speak to her brother and see if she could stay with him and Nicci for a while. For the past few nights she'd been at her parents, but recently they'd downsized to a bungalow and there was hardly room for the two of them, never mind Jess and all her belongings.

'Why's that then?' Beth asked. 'Got something to hide?'

'Mind your own business.' Jess gave her a filthy look. 'You're only after finding the gossip and I'm not going to give it to you.'

Beth shrugged her shoulders. 'It'll all come out in the wash. Nothing stays secret around here for long. You should know that after the last time you left.'

'That has nothing to do –'

'Blimey, is that the time?' Malcolm Worthington pushed past them with an armful of boxes. 'Don't you lot have anything to do before we open? Come on, away with you.'

Jess went back to the stall, annoyed by the way she'd been greeted by Beth. But then again, she only had herself to blame for that.

CHAPTER SEVEN

Once the morning rush was underway, all thoughts of the weekend had long since been forgotten. Sophie waited for a lull in trade before making a list of items they had run short of. Since being left on her own at such a young age, she had become organised. It was one of the reasons she'd been able to hold down the stall and the house.

'We need some paper bags.' She ticked off things with her fingers. 'And some yellow stickers. Oh, and a roll of Sellotape. Anything else while I'm there?'

Beth and Nicci couldn't think of anything, so she set off for the stock room at the bottom of the market. The aisles were full of regular shoppers and it took her a good ten minutes to get through them as some wanted to chat. It seemed rude to tell them she was busy as she knew some never saw anyone unless they came into the town. So she always stopped when approached.

In the stock room, she located the items she required, popping one box on top of the other before heading back. She was nearly at the door when she spotted Damien Wilshaw walking right towards her.

Her heartbeat quickened at the sight of him. He wore a long black coat over tailored, pin-striped trousers, slick square-toe boots and a red woollen scarf. Sophie cursed the fact she hadn't made more of an effort to conceal her lack of sleep. But with no mirror she didn't have time to check her appearance. Her jeans, thick jumper and bodywarmer would have to do as well.

Deliberately, she pushed the boxes further up so that he couldn't see too much of her face.

'Hi,' she managed to say, feeling the heat of an emerging blush. 'This is staff only. You really shouldn't be in here.'

Damien smiled warmly. 'I was passing ...' He removed the top box and placed it on the window ledge next to them. Then he grasped the other box but, instead of taking it from her, he pushed Sophie gently until she felt the wall behind her. His face was inches from hers, only the box now separating them, as he gazed into her eyes.

'I want to see you,' he spoke softly.

Sophie gulped. It was hard to do anything else in close proximity to the man of her fantasies when he was staring at her intensely.

'I'm married.'

'But we shouldn't let that stop us.'

'St— stop us?'

Before she could protest, he leaned closer and kissed her gently on the lips. He pulled away, gazed into her eyes for a long second. Then he kissed her again, enough for her to ache for more.

'Someone might see,' she whispered afterwards without meaning.

But Damien pushed his chest forward. The flimsy cardboard box between them began to shudder. At least it was covering her breasts, Sophie mused, feeling no less safe as the box began to collapse in on itself.

She prayed that the exit door leading to the public would stay closed for ever as Damien kissed her again. This time he kissed her properly. Tenderly, he nibbled her bottom lip before easing her mouth open again with his tongue.

Eventually they broke free.

'You are one sexy woman.' He looked from her eyes to her chest and back to her eyes again. 'What's a man got to do to get some time with you?'

'I can't. You know that I'm –'

'I have to see you.' Damien's hand moved to cup her chin.

She swallowed down the feelings erupting inside her. She hadn't felt this way in a long time with Reece. This was so wrong, yet ... so right.

The door crashed open and Mike Sharpe pushed a trolley full of rubbish through it, cursing loudly. Damien moved away and Sophie stooped to pick up the box and its contents that were now strewn across the floor.

'Bleeding trolley,' Mike grimaced as he walked past them. 'Wonky wheel, if you ask me but will the council shell out for a new one? I don't think so. Sophie, Beth told me to tell you to hurry up and get yourself back to the stall.'

'I'm on my way.' Sophie reached up for the box on the window ledge and piled it on top of the other one, hoping to hide her blushes.

Once Mike had disappeared, she looked at Damien. They burst out laughing, Sophie with relief that they hadn't been caught.

'I feel like a love-struck teenager.' Damien placed a hand on Sophie's bottom as they walked back towards the door.

Sophie took a step away from him. 'Don't do that.'

Damien raised his hands in mock surrender. 'I can't help it.'

'Well you'd better stop because that will have to be your lot.' She tried to talk with her head and not her heart. 'You shouldn't have kissed me and I shouldn't have kissed you back. I don't think we—'

Damien pressed her up against the wall.

'No, this is wrong,' She pushed him away gently, grabbed the boxes and rushed back to the safety of the stall.

CHAPTER EIGHT

'Sorry!' Sophie said as she arrived at the stall all hot and flustered. 'I couldn't find what I was looking for.'

'We've been rushed off our feet. And Damien came by about ten minutes ago.' Beth lowered her voice as she weighed out a kilo of apples for a young woman. 'He was asking after you.'

'I never saw him,' Sophie practically shouted.

Beth quickly finished serving and turned back to her with a frown. 'What's going on?'

'Nothing.' She handed a box of bags to her. 'Pop these behind the counter, will you?'

Sophie sought refuge in the staff room while she tried desperately to control her reddening skin. But every time she thought about what she'd done, it caused her to blush even more. Had she really kissed another man? At first, Damien's lips had barely touched hers, as if he knew how anxious she was at the thought of what it might lead to. Then she remembered his mouth, his lips, his tongue ... She fanned her face with her hand.

'Coffee?' She held up the kettle in front of her face as Beth walked in.

'Please.' Beth nodded gratefully.

Sophie turned her back and busied herself adding coffee to their favourite mugs.

'Come on, spit it out,' Beth said eventually when Sophie wasn't forthcoming with any chat. 'What's happened?'

'What?'

'You're blushing.'

'It's hot in here.'

'No, it isn't.' Beth folded her arms and stared at her.

Finally, Sophie gave in.

'Damien came to find me in the store room and he—he kissed me.'

Beth covered her mouth with her hand for a moment. 'What did you do?'

'I kind of kissed him back.' She closed her eyes momentarily, trying not to think of the man who could make her knees quiver with one smile.

'You've gone off in a daydream.' Beth waved a hand in front of her face. 'I wasn't expecting that, though.'

'Please don't make a big fuss about it,' Sophie begged her. 'It was only a kiss.'

'*Only* a kiss? Don't you realise that can be more intimate than sleeping with him?'

'You must have read that somewhere.' Sophie batted the comment away with her hand. 'It won't happen again. I told him to—'

'Sophie.' Beth snapped her fingers. 'Look at me. No, actually, look at you! Your eyes are shining and you're virtually hyperventilating. Tell me what happened.'

'One minute I was talking to him and the next he had me pushed up against the wall kissing me with a passion. Honestly Beth, he's made me come alive, more than I remember feeling for a long time. But I'm married. I shouldn't be doing this.'

The look on Beth's face was comical.

'I don't know whether to shout at my best friend or give her a high five.' Beth pushed the door to when she saw Nicci coming a bit too close as she added more stock to the shelves. 'What happened after he kissed you?'

'He kissed me again and I was all in the moment. If Mike hadn't interrupted us, I don't know what would have happened.'

Beth raised her eyebrows in comical fashion. 'But was he good?'

'I'm in the middle of a crisis and all you want to know is if he's a good kisser?'

'Well—'

Sophie handed a mug to her. 'It was exciting and dangerous ... unlike everything else in my life. But it was so wrong. I shouldn't have done it.'

'I thought things were all right between you and Reece.'

Sophie didn't want to tell anyone that Reece had left for Germany, and there was obviously no point in saying it right then either. Somehow she thought Beth might not believe her, thinking she was saying it as an excuse. Instead, she babbled.

'I don't know what came over me. Damien appeared out of nowhere and the next minute we were kissing. I didn't know he was going to show up. It wasn't as if I planned it to happen.'

'But you wanted it to?' Beth probed.

Her words hung in the air for a few moments. Sophie could hardly breathe, let alone speak.

Several customers approached the store at once and they went out to help Nicci. Sophie grabbed Beth's elbow.

'This goes no further than the two of us,' she said. 'I don't know what to do right now, okay?'

Beth nodded. 'Of course I won't say anything.'

Left with her thoughts as they went back to work, Sophie struggled to think about anything but the touch of Damien's lips on her own. Feelings of guilt, exhilaration and yes, a little bit of lust, combined to make her utterly confused.

What was happening to her? And more to the point, what would happen to her and Reece if she let it continue?

CHAPTER NINE

That evening, Charley Pellington lay on her bed trying to concentrate on the magazine article she was reading. She wondered whether it would be wise to stay off school tomorrow, following the numerous messages she'd received. Charley hated being the source of gossip. Her Facebook account had a stream of comments on it. Some of her friends wanted to know if what Aaron was talking about was true. Some of them – especially the boys – wanted more details of what had happened. Some of the girls she didn't know so well took the opportunity to call her names.

Aaron didn't have to live with all the name calling. She bet his friends probably thought he was a super stud. She thought he was a rat.

She'd written a message on his wall, asking why he had lied, knowing that everyone would see his reply. So far, he hadn't answered it. One thing was certain though. Every boy in the school would think they could try their luck with her now. And it wasn't as if she was the only female virgin in their year. Sarah was too.

If truth be known, Charley reckoned most of the girls

were all talk. There were the odd ones who seemed to be working their way through the boys' surnames in alphabetical order, so frequent were their escapades, but really they were far and few between.

Fear flooded her. There was no way she wanted to end up like her mum, pregnant at seventeen. Maybe it would be worse if she didn't go to school though. The rumour then would probably be that she'd had sex with Aaron five times, hung from the living room lights and been taken over the kitchen table afterwards before jumping into her mum's bed for a final fling.

She flipped open her laptop and looked to see if Alex was logged in. Over the past few weeks, she'd found she could always talk things through with him, even though she wouldn't say anything about this in detail. But then again, he would see all the comments left about her.

CP: Hey.

AL: Hey, I've just come online. How are you?

CP: Not good. I've had a rumour started about me today and I wanted to let you know that it isn't true.

AL: Oh? What about?

Charley paused for a moment. If he saw her page, he would know, so she might as well be honest.

CP: Some boy at school says that I did stuff with him, but I didn't. He sent messages to a few kids in my year and they've been calling me names.

AL: Idiot! What did he do that for?

CP: I don't know – attention, I guess?

AL: I wish I was there. I'd be able to reassure you.

CP: Thanks, but I'm okay. Just wanted to tell you, that's all.

They moved on to general chit-chat for a few minutes and then said goodbye. Charley checked out her Facebook page again and sighed. There were more comments so she logged off.

Her eyes filled with tears. Why did it have to be her that everyone was talking about? Most of the time she enjoyed school. She had a good bunch of friends as well as Sarah and was quite popular. But it only took something like this to lose everything. How she reacted now would always be remembered.

She wasn't going to make a fuss. She would ignore it until it passed. And perhaps once it was over, she may be able to sort out her real friends from the ones who sided with whoever was the most popular.

'Charley!'

Her mother nudged her and she removed her earphones.

'I've been shouting you for ages.' Beth put a mug of tea down onto the bedside cabinet. 'I bought you some biscuits too.'

'I'm not hungry, thanks.'

She pretended to flick through her magazine, hoping that her mum would go away.

But Beth sat down beside her. 'Are you okay, love? You seem quiet tonight. Have you fallen out with Sarah?'

There was no way Charley would share what was happening with her. So she nodded.

'What about this time?'

She flicked another page of her magazine over. 'Nothing, really.'

'That's all right then. You'll be friends again tomorrow, knowing you two. Especially if it's over nothing. You'll see.'

Charley prayed her mum wouldn't see the tears running down her cheeks. She tried to wipe at them discreetly.

But Beth did notice. 'What's the matter? I don't like to see you like this.'

Charley said nothing. Maybe if she didn't look at her, she would go away and leave her alone.

'Charl?' Beth rested her hand tentatively on her daughter's shoulder.

'Leave me alone.' Charley pushed it away. 'I'm fine.'

'I'm only trying to help.' Beth sounded hurt. 'Why won't you talk to me?'

'Because I don't want to.'

'But—'

'Can't I have any peace?' Charley pushed herself up and ran from the room. She found sanctuary in the bathroom and sat down on the side of the bath. As she looked around at the peeling wallpaper above the white tiles and the make-up and body lotions lined up untidily on the rickety shelf, she wished she didn't have to go to school any more. If she didn't have to face all those losers, everything would be much better.

Not for the first time, Charley wished her life away. She couldn't wait until she was older and able to fend for herself, earning her own money. Then she'd move out and get her own place. Somewhere she could be by herself whenever she felt the need. Where she could cry in peace and not have to explain how she was feeling; be whoever she wanted to be.

She heard her mum shout her name again and decided to run a bath. She'd stay in here all night if she had to, rather than discuss it with her.

CHAPTER TEN

Beth sat on the edge of Charley's bed, wondering what to do. She tried to put herself in her daughter's position. Could she remember what it was like at fifteen, with hormones determining your every move? She'd been a handful for her parents, that was for sure.

It wasn't unusual for Charley to stay in but usually Sarah would be here too. Beth hoped they'd make up tomorrow. In so many ways, they reminded her of when she and Sophie were younger and thick as thieves. When they had shared dreams of double weddings and having babies at the same time. How far from the dream they were now.

But if she hadn't had Sophie, things could have been much worse for her. Sophie had been her stalwart throughout her life. She'd got her through a bad marriage, a divorce, and she was always there to look out for her and Charley.

She recalled the emotions when Charley had been born. Sophie had been there at the birth, holding her hand, tears pouring down her face as she watched Charley emerge into the world. In a way, they were barely adults themselves, yet

Sophie had been her rock, stepping into the role of big sister as well as best friend.

But even though Sophie had been hurt and angry when she'd refused to tell her who Charley's father was, how could she have shared that information? She would have lost Sophie's friendship, and she wasn't sure she could have coped without her.

Beth shook her head. She was doing it again. Why did she always think of herself when she should be worrying about Charley? This wasn't about *her* ideas and dreams going wrong. This was about her daughter trying to find her way in an often lonely and cruel world.

Charley and Sarah falling out would hopefully only be a tiff; they bickered more than once a day and stormed off in opposite directions. But a text message would always have them running back. They were good friends, just like she and Sophie were at that age. Sophie and Beth: Beth and Sophie. They came as a pair, sharing everything.

Maybe she should speak to Sarah; see if she would tell her what was wrong with Charley.

No, Beth decided, standing up now. She should at least try and talk to Charley again. If she could get her to open up with a few simple questions, then she might confide in her mum without feeling that she'd been badgered into anything.

She walked across to the bathroom door and knocked gently. 'Charl?'

'Go away.'

'I only want to talk. I know there are some things that you can't chat about with Sarah. But maybe I can help. I was your age once. I know what it's like to—'

'You haven't got a clue how I'm feeling.'

'But I might be able to—'

'Leave me alone, will you? I don't want to talk to you.'

'Fine. Have it your way.' Beth shouted through the bathroom door. 'But when you finally do show your face, you can tidy that room of yours. It's like a pigsty in there.'

Beth groaned as she marched off. Why had she ended the conversation like that? If there was something seriously wrong, Charley would never open up to her if she didn't show any sympathy.

She stormed downstairs in a mood with herself. Not only did she feel that she had to be mum to Charley but she had to be dad too. And it didn't seem that she was any good at either.

Nicci was sitting in the kitchen with Jay, eating dinner.

'Dad rang me this afternoon,' he said, putting down his cutlery. 'He says they're struggling for room now that Jess is staying over. I said she could stay here for a while. That's okay, isn't it?'

Nicci turned to him with wide eyes that showed it clearly wasn't.

'It's only for a few weeks, until she finds her own place.'

She watched as he fidgeted in his chair, purposely not catching her eye. Then she waited until he looked up.

'Jay, we're a team. You should have discussed this with me before saying yes.'

'But you would have said no.'

'Too right. Jess is nothing but trouble.'

'She's not that bad.'

'You can tell her that she'll have to make alternative arrangements.' Nicci scraped her chair on the floor in her haste to get up. She shoved it noisily back under the table and leaned on it.

'I only did it to help Mum and Dad out,' he complained.

'I don't want her here. She'll cause an atmosphere.'

'Don't be so dramatic, Nic. She's my little sister. I can't turn her away.'

Nicci sighed. If she didn't love him so much, she could murder him on the spot. Jason Worthington was a gullible fool but he only did things like that because he had a heart of gold.

Jay gazed back with a puppy dog expression. 'I'm sorry. I didn't think it would be such a big issue. I'll ring her and let her know.'

'Why do you have to be such a nice guy?' Nicci shook her head. 'Okay, she can come and stay,' she relented. 'But I'm doing it for you – and not your sister.'

CHAPTER ELEVEN

It was closing time at Somerley market, and it was minus two degrees outside. Beth wanted to get home as quickly as possible and close the curtains on the dark and cold night. It wasn't fit for anything else. But Sophie had no intention of going anywhere fast and Nicci was rinsing out the coffee mugs before she headed off for the evening.

'Come on, you two,' Beth cried impatiently as she wrapped herself up to brave the elements. 'I have a date with my settee, my jim jams and a bottle of wine.'

'I'm not looking forward to going out into the cold,' Nicci moaned, wiping her hands on a tea towel. 'Still, Wedding Belles is on tonight so I do have something to look forward to.'

'I don't how you can watch that programme. Love's dream never runs its full course.'

'It will for me and Jay.' Nicci nodded at her sister. 'Not all marriages end up in divorce like yours.'

'Not all marriages end up like you think they will, either.'

Beth shook her head. Nicci was always going on about

weddings. It drove her mad, each mention reminding her of her own failing.

'You need to find the right man,' Nicci added, not put off by Beth's exasperated tone.

'I've got nothing to rush home for either,' added Sophie.

'Cold or not, I can't wait,' Beth said.

'That's because you have a bottle of wine,' Nicci chided, pulling on her coat.

'Precisely.' Beth ignored her sarcasm. 'Which is why I'm inviting you both back to mine for a drink right now.'

'I've got work to do here first,' Sophie said. 'I'll probably leave when Mike locks up.' It was Mike's job to check everything was secure before leaving at six thirty every evening.

'You work too much.' Beth wouldn't let it drop. 'I'll even cook something specially for you, if you like? One of your favourites, if I have everything in.'

'I'll take a rain check, if you don't mind.'

'Okay, but don't stay too late. See you tomorrow then.'

'Night.'

Once she was alone on the stall, Sophie's shoulders dropped in relief. After the hustle and bustle of the day, she loved to sit in the silence when most of the stallholders had left for home. It wasn't as if she had anything to be there for right now, and even an evening with Beth, which she usually enjoyed, wasn't exactly appealing either.

She hadn't told anyone about Reece yet and didn't want to slip up either. It wouldn't make any difference, she supposed. But she kept a lot of things to herself. Beth was the outgoing, loud one. Sophie preferred to stay in the background as much as possible.

An hour later, she heard the jangle of keys as Mike came to lock up. She grabbed her bag and threw on her coat before he came to check their aisle. She liked Mike but she wasn't in the mood for small talk. Half wishing she had taken Beth up on her offer now, she let herself out into the chilly evening.

She stepped out onto the pavement and heard someone shout her name. Busy with her hand in her bag, she looked up to see Damien in the distance. Her heart lurched when he started to slip and slide towards her across the icy road. He looked totally different wearing chunky beige work boots, jeans and a black parka coat, with the same red scarf knotted at the neck.

She hadn't seen him since their illicit rendezvous three days ago. But she hadn't stopped thinking about him, nor the kisses they'd shared either, and it worried her.

'Hey there.' Damien's smile widened as he drew level with her. 'I thought you might like to grab a drink somewhere before you leave?'

'I'm on my way home.' Sophie tried hard not to get caught up in the lust she could see reflected in his eyes. 'I've got so much paperwork to do.'

'That's a pity.' Damien grinned at her. 'Maybe I could join you?'

'Maybe you couldn't!'

He laughed, causing Sophie to blush.

When Beth had asked her about Damien, she'd been truthful. Sophie wouldn't have an affair. She wasn't about to chuck everything away for a quick fling with a man she hardly knew, no matter how much her feet were telling her to run to him.

But now he was standing in front of her, all floppy blond hair, little boy lost and so appealing, she could see why men and women got themselves in trouble.

Damien held up his index finger, bringing her back to reality. 'A hot toddy won't hurt, to warm us up?'

Sophie raised her eyebrows. Really? Could he see no harm

in that? But she found herself nodding, all the same.

'Go on, then,' she gave in. 'Only the one, mind.'

CHAPTER TWELVE

Jess sat on the sofa, staring at the television but not actually watching it. Before flicking over to another channel, she glanced around the room. Her brother had done well for himself by meeting Nicci. A woman's touch was evident by the faux leather cushions on the coffee three-piece suite, the fluffy scatter rugs that warmed up the polished wooden flooring. Five church candles stood in a row on the top of an Adam fireplace, the marble hearth holding bowls of fragranced balls and petals; their faint aroma mixing gently with the scents of the plug-in air fresheners.

Whereas Nicci was a stickler for cleanliness, Jess was a slob. She was perfectly turned out, but wherever she laid her hat was her hovel. Strangely enough, she found the room calming, homely and extremely pleasant. Alas, she knew she wasn't welcome.

Jay and Nicci had gone to the Hope and Anchor. Although Jay invited her along, Jess could see by the caustic look on Nicci's face that it was a no-no. She knew the pub from old, it being everyone's hang out when they were first legal to drink. It would have been nice to go and see if any of her old gang were in there. Instead she'd changed into her sweats and slouched on the settee as soon as they had gone, the weather outside completely matching her frosty mood.

She was trying desperately not to think that she could have been having dinner at an expensive restaurant with Laurie before they'd go off to have sex in a hotel nearby. Even though he was fifteen years her senior, Laurie had been an exceptional lover, thinking of her pleasure as much as his own. What had started as a fling had grown into something much more for her, even though when he had ended it, she hadn't shown him her true feelings.

Jess missed him so much and not being able to talk about him to anyone made her sad. Although he technically wasn't her man, she missed the intimacy; the feeling of belonging to someone, yet still being her own person. Now she kept wondering if she'd done the right thing by leaving London so quickly. Maybe she should have stayed and fought for him, even though he'd made it obvious that would have been tough.

As it was prone to doing, her mind slipped back to that fateful night. It had been late, about nine thirty. They'd been out for a drink and decided to get a takeaway and go back to the office. All evening Jess had been priming herself, knowing she should tell him her news, but she couldn't get the words out.

In the end, he'd asked her what was wrong. And when she told him she was pregnant, he'd flipped. It was one thing to have a bit on the side, he told her cruelly, but he would not have a woman with a child. He accused her of sleeping around, refusing to believe it was his and saying that she was trying to trap him. She'd rushed out of the building in floods of tears after he'd hurled more abuse at her.

Back at her flat she'd sat and cried, unsure what to do next. She received her answer the following morning, by text message. Laurie told her, in no uncertain terms, that she wasn't welcome back at the office.

Not one to give up without a fight, Jess went in to face the music. No amount of pleading with Laurie would change his mind. It was then that he'd given her a cheque for £5,000 to move on and forget. She took it and, once she'd ensured it had cleared, she'd booked a train ticket back to Somerley to stay with her parents. The money would help until she found her feet again and decided what she was going to do next.

She'd only been at her parents' home for a few hours before she realised it wasn't the right place to be. Jess had left home at nineteen and hadn't ever intended to come back. The first night there reminded her why. Her mum, a natural fusspot, followed her around like she would a toddler taking its first steps.

"Are you sure you're okay? You do look a little peaky. Shall I get you an aspirin?"

"Do you need anything washing or ironing? Shall I hang your clothes for you?"

"Did you sleep well? The room wasn't too hot – or too cold?"

To save herself from explanations, Jess told her that she'd been dumped and was feeling a little sore about it. It had backfired hugely as Mum then had to do what mothers do best. She mothered her – or was that smothered her?

Maureen had always been over-protective toward her, but it was too much for Jess. The last straw had been when she'd waited for her on the landing before she went to have a shower and pulled her into her arms. "We'll spend the day together, you and me. We'll go shopping, and then have coffee and cake in Somerley at The Coffee Stop."

It had been seven thirty in the morning. Unable to stand the thought of what lay ahead, she'd struck a deal with her dad to help out on the stall and was on her way to work with him by eight. And then she badgered him to ask Jay, if she could come and stay with him and Nicci for a few weeks.

It was far from an ideal situation, however. It was one thing to have her mother looking out for her every need, but it was another to be ignored and spoken to only when absolutely necessary by her brother's girlfriend. From the minute she'd arrived, Nicci had made it perfectly clear that the stay was to be a short one. She'd also taken a great interest in helping Jess look for a flat share.

But much worse than that was, being at their home she could see how much they loved each other. And it hurt. Over the past couple of nights, she'd walk in the room and they'd be kissing or groping each other. Sometimes they'd stop what they were doing; sometimes Jess would leave the room. How long had they been together now? Three years? How did they manage to keep the passion alive?

She flicked her legs up onto the settee and reached for the remote again. There must be something decent on to watch. A few minutes later, bored of channel hopping, she moved to the window.

Staring out through open curtains into the dark night, the cul-de-sac outside was quiet. There were only a few houses, gardens all covered in snow that had yet to melt from two weeks ago. Not for the first time, she wished she was married and living in suburbia with two point four children.

She hugged herself, wondering what Ryan would be doing right now. From the moment she'd started to work on the stall again, he'd taken a personal interest in her welfare. He'd bought her a bacon buttie on Monday morning, coffee the next, a Danish pastry yesterday and coffee again today. And he was buying lots from the stall. One hundred grams of aniseed balls, two twenty pence mixtures for his twin five-year-old girls, cola bottles and humbugs for him and Matt.

Today he had bought two sherbet dib-dabs, given one

back to her and they'd dunked in their lollipops as they'd laughed together about Jay in his younger days. All the same age and inseparable unless there was a girl involved, Ryan, Jay and Matt had been known as the Three Amigos at school.

Jess already had a feeling that Ryan would be up for more if she was interested. Maybe it was time to find out how far he really would go. He would be hers if she played her cards right. He'd made enough remarks and instigated enough chats for her to know.

But did she want another married man?

If she couldn't find one of her own, she'd settle for someone else's to pamper her, make her feel special. It was the way she was, finding comfort in being told she was beautiful and feeling desired. It was what she needed. Where was the harm in it?

Besides, if it stopped her worrying about her future, then that was good too. Because right now she had a potentially heart-breaking decision to make. One she wished she didn't have to do by herself.

CHAPTER THIRTEEN

Despite the icy conditions, the roads were clear so Damien drove them out of Somerley where they found a pub a bit off the beaten track. The drink turned into two, albeit soft ones. At first they stood up at the bar. Then they ordered chips and a burger apiece and found a quieter spot to eat.

'I love this,' Damien said, once they'd eaten and the plates had been cleared. 'You and me.'

Sophie looked away from his intense gaze, pretending to be more interested in the chalk menu behind the bar. Because she was enjoying herself too. And she shouldn't be. She should be at home, safe from temptation of the Damien Wilshaw's of this world. She sighed inwardly. Why was this so wrong if she was relishing this so much too?

Damien reached across the table for her hand and gave it a squeeze.

She saw the face on his watch and gasped. 'Crikey, it's nearly nine o'clock.'

'Time always goes quickly when you're having fun.' Damien rubbed his thumb back and forth across the top of her wrist. 'We could always grab a coffee at mine, if you like?'

She'd walked right into that. Damien was fabulous company. He laughed in the right places, never mentioning Reece, only to figure out the minor details. He'd even kept his lips to himself. Sophie hoped she hadn't led him on because she wanted to be with him.

'I can't,' she replied, regret clear in her tone.

'I know. It's just so hard to leave you. I've ached to kiss you again. I've thought about you constantly since Monday. You have too, haven't you? Thought about me?'

After a moment, Sophie nodded.

'There's a spark between us. You can't deny it.'

'But there shouldn't be. Can't you see what you do to me?'

'If you were happily married, you wouldn't be here.'

'You're right.' Sophie pulled her hand away. 'But it's because I'm married that I can't see you again. I'm sorry.'

They were silent for a moment amid the general noise from the pub. A group of men laughing and joking standing up at the bar. A couple with three children a table away. Two women heads together, cutlery being put down between their chatter.

Everyone going on with their lives, oblivious to her trying not to take the biggest gamble with hers.

'You do understand why?' she said to him.

'Unfortunately, I do. But it only makes me want you more because you're so warm-hearted.' Damien pulled back his chair. 'Come on then. Let's get you home.'

After parking at the front of her house, Damien grabbed the collar of her coat, pulled her towards him and kissed her briefly on the lips. Even the lightness of his touch made her cheeks burn.

'Go,' he said, 'before I change my mind.'

Her feet refused to move for a few seconds before her brain engaged. At the front door, she turned and waved and watched as he pulled away. It had been a lovely evening but it had to stop at that. She wouldn't be the wife who had an affair. *She* would be the wife who told her husband before she did. Inevitably it would lead to the same conclusion. She had some thinking to do.

Once inside the house, she raced upstairs for a shower. Unable to wash away the feel of Damien's hand on hers, his lips on her cheek, she stayed under the water for a long time.

Tears of frustration stung her eyes and she squeezed them shut to stop them falling. Spending time with him made her realise what a sham her marriage was. No wonder Reece worked away; wanted to spend time in Germany under the guise of earning some extra cash.

It shocked her to think how easily she could have been led astray. She realised the invitation wasn't for coffee. If she'd gone home with him, she wouldn't have been able to resist him.

Was her relationship – her marriage – to Reece in that much of a mess? Maybe she needed to spend her time thinking about that rather than Damien Wilshaw.

Changed into pyjamas, hair still wet, it was ten thirty when there was a knock on the front door. She peered through the living room window to see Damien on her doorstep.

Shit! What had he come back for?

But she knew as she went to let him in. She opened the door and, without a word, he pulled her into his arms.

'I can't help myself,' he whispered, his lips leaving hers for the briefest of moments.

Sophie responded before she had time to think. Damien's hands found their way inside her top and she gasped at the touch of his fingers on her bare skin. His lips moved over her neck and down towards her chest.

You have to stop, said the voice in her head, but she

ignored it. Right now, Sophie didn't care about Reece. It was all about her.

She bit down hard on her lip as his hands explored her body. Damien Wilshaw was making her moan in ecstasy ...

Hearing herself brought her back to her senses and she pushed him away. 'No, please.'

Damien had a look of concern. 'Are you okay?'

She shook her head. 'I'm sorry,' she said. 'I can't.'

'But I thought you wanted to.'

'I do – I did! Oh, I don't know. I feel so mixed up.'

'It's okay. We can wait.' He pulled her into his arms and held her.

She wanted him to leave, before the passion rose again and it became too late. She had never felt so at odds with herself for a long time.

Ten minutes later, Sophie sat alone in the living room. She felt weak. But more than that, she was scared by the intensity of her feelings.

What had gone on back there? It was one thing to want to be kissed by someone else, to enjoy a show of affection, but to let another man touch her like that? That was wrong.

How could she have done that to Reece? She'd always prided herself on being a good girl and had laughed along with Beth – not at Beth – about her colourful antics since her marriage collapsed. But she had never, ever – even in her wildest dreams when she was so annoyed with Reece that she didn't want to be in the same room as him – thought that she would come so close to sleeping with another man while she was with him.

And what would have happened afterwards? There would have been no going back. Things like that couldn't be swept under the carpet. It wasn't a mistake. It would have been a decision that had consequences.

Sophie pulled her knees up to her chest and hugged herself as the tears fell. She had never felt so lonely in her life.

CHAPTER FOURTEEN

Beth and Nicci were on the stall before Sophie the next day. As was usual some mornings, Sophie was coming in late after catching up on paperwork. Beth was telling Nicci about her daughter's recent behaviour. Since they'd had words, Charley had spent every spare minute she was at home upstairs in her room.

'Maybe you need to be more forceful with her,' Nicci said, taking the opportunity to dunk a chocolate biscuit in her coffee while there was a lull in customers. 'Charley needs boundaries. You let her get away with too much at times.'

'She's nearly sixteen. You should try setting them with someone that age. She has a mind of her own. I tell her to do one thing and she does another.'

'Sounds like someone else I know. Like mother, like daughter, obviously.'

'That's precisely the reason I'm worried about her.' Beth reached for a biscuit. 'She seems really upset about something. On Monday night, I sat outside the bathroom door for fifteen minutes after she'd stormed off in a huff but she still wouldn't come out and talk to me.'

'I don't see why you think she would. You wouldn't have said anything to Mum when you were fifteen.'

'But it's different nowadays, isn't it?' Beth ate a bite before replying. 'Daughters trust their mums with more information. They go shopping together, they lunch together. They—'

'Since when have you two ever lunched together?' Nicci raised her eyebrows. 'Or shopped together for that matter? You and Charley are like chalk and cheese.'

Beth shrugged. 'I really want us to be friends. It would be nice to go home and have a chat with her, rather than hear her music in the distance because she's shut herself in her room. It's like living with a stranger at times. I'm sure she tries to make things awkward between us.'

'Do you remember what we were like when Mum asked us any kind of question?' Nicci rolled her eyes.

'Don't I just.' Beth laughed. 'It's a good job I had you as a sister to look out for me. You got me out of lots of things. Speaking of sisters,' she pointed along the aisle to where Jess was serving on the sweet stall. 'How are you getting on with the prodigal one?'

It was Nicci's turn to look exasperated. 'She's really getting my back up, if you must know, with all her sarcastic remarks and all her bragging about her life in London. And she's so untidy. I end up clearing up after her all the time.'

'She can't be that bad.' Beth hurled a full sack of potatoes to one side and sat awkwardly on it.

'But we can't get any privacy.'

'So that's what's eating you up? Haven't you had a cuddle since baby sis turned up?'

Nicci tutted at the insinuation. 'Of course we have. But she always seems to come in at such inappropriate moments. Take last night. We'd come back from the pub and were in the kitchen when she walked in and interrupted us. She said she wanted a glass of water. Can you believe that?'

'Yes,' Beth said.

Nicci ignored her and continued. 'Imagine if she'd come in two minutes later. You never know –'

'You mean Jay lasts longer than two minutes?' Beth laughed. 'You jammy sod. You don't have anything to moan about.'

They served a few customers before speaking again.

'Has Sophie said anything else about Damien?' Nicci kept her voice low. 'I haven't seen him around for a while.'

'She said she'd sent him a message asking him not to visit the stall.' It wasn't Beth's place to say anything more.

'So that's why he's keeping away.' Nicci nodded.

'Yes I suppose so. But it must be flattering for her. He's really good-looking. And let's face it, she hardly sees Reece.'

'Do you think they're drifting apart?'

'I'm not sure.' Beth gnawed at her bottom lip. 'But I'm sure she'll tell me when she's ready.'

Sophie appeared on the stall a few minutes later. Both Beth and Nicci were serving customers.

'Morning, ladies.' She smiled at an elderly woman who was filling her tartan shopper. 'Hi, Mrs Madison. How's little Percy this week?'

'Oh, he's not doing bad, thank you. I'm sure he's going to outlive me. I've never known anyone who's had a cat for nineteen years. I don't know what I'll do without him.'

'Aw, but you've given him the best life possible. He was lucky to find you.'

Mrs Madison beamed at her. Sophie waited for the customers to be served and on their way.

Beth came over to her. 'Get warmed up last night, did you?'

Sophie froze. 'What do you mean?'

'I bet you went home and got into a hot bath. Am I right?'

'Oh. Yes, it was heaven.' She rushed into the staff room before her reddening cheeks gave her away again. Friends or not, there was no way she was telling Beth and Nicci anything about what happened last night. The guilt she was feeling wasn't for sharing.

Besides, it wouldn't be a case of problem shared, problem halved for her. Beth had known Reece for as long as she had. It didn't seem fair to talk about Damien as if Reece no longer existed.

And it had made Sophie wonder, through the long and lonely hours of the early morning as she'd tried desperately to drift off to sleep, if Reece had stayed faithful to her why he'd been working in Sheffield. It would have been far easier for him to do the dirty because he was away from anyone who would see him.

Sophie had sat up in bed at that point, suddenly panicking in case she had been seen by anyone she knew. She and Damien hadn't done anything untoward in the pub. But had anyone been able to tell what they'd wanted to do? And what happened if any of the neighbours had seen her invite him into the house?

Even now, she was wondering how she was going to face Reece when he finally came home. What a cow she was for allowing herself to fall under Damien's spell. She should have been strong enough to knock away his advances and talk to Reece about their ailing marriage first. This wasn't like her, not at all. In fact right now, Sophie didn't know what to think of herself. She was so embarrassed by her antics.

But she had enjoyed them. Was that so wrong?

'Something up?'

Sophie came out of her trance to find Beth standing in front of her. She shook her head.

'I'm fine,' she replied.

'No, you're not. I know when there's something on your mind. Is it Damien?'

'I told you, I haven't seen him since Monday.'

'He hasn't rung you – or texted you?' Beth probed.

'No – I –'

The conversation was dropped as several customers trooped in one after the other. But Sophie's mind wouldn't settle. Twice she gave out the wrong orders before heading to the safety of the back room with more paperwork. She was better off on her own for now, praying her secret wouldn't get out.

Beth gave out a sigh as she watched Sophie disappearing.

'Be gentle.' Nicci nudged her when Sophie was out of earshot. 'You don't know what it's like for her.'

'What do you mean?' Beth slapped down the card she was marking up with a two-for-one offer. 'I've been on my own for years now because I can't find a decent man. I'd love to be in a relationship again but who'd have me, with another man's child?'

'Everyone has excess baggage nowadays. That shouldn't stop you. But Sophie's had to be by herself while Reece worked away.'

'He didn't have to leave her alone for so long,' Beth protested.

'She says it's not forever. He'll be home for good in a couple of years.'

'I have a feeling she won't be sitting around waiting for him then. Don't you?'

'Maybe,' Nicci agreed.

'I'll take her for a coffee, see if she'll open up to me. Will you be okay if we go to the café?'

Nicci nodded. 'Go easy on her. She's been a good friend to

you over the years. And whether we think what she did with Damien was right or wrong, it's really none of our business.' She held up a hand as Beth went to object. 'Nor mine. I don't like what she's doing either but it might not evolve into anything more than a few sexy feelings coming through.' She turned to the woman standing in front of her with a cabbage. 'Seventy-five pence to you, my love.'

Beth stood in silence for a moment. Nicci had always been the level-headed one of the Pellington children. Even now she spoke common sense. She wondered if that was who Charley took after. Because try as she might, Beth couldn't be the sympathetic person she yearned to be.

Sophie came out on the stall again an hour later.

'Fancy grabbing a break at the café?' Beth suggested.

She shook her head. 'I'm okay, thanks.'

Beth glanced surreptitiously at Nicci before turning back to Sophie.

'Are you still coming out with me tomorrow night? Or is Reece coming home this weekend?'

'No, it seems I might be free.'

'So it's a date then?'

Sophie nodded. She hadn't got anything else to do and she'd only spend the evening worrying about everything. About how she had to end this fling before it became more serious. That was, if she could end it. If her feelings for Damien would let her.

'Fabulous.' Beth said. 'What are you wearing?'

Sophie relaxed as Beth went through the clothes in her wardrobe, ticking off on her fingers her many outfits. At least for now she'd managed to keep things to herself. But she wouldn't be able to hold out on Beth about Reece for long.

She was her best friend, after all. Maybe she should confide in her soon.

CHAPTER FIFTEEN

That afternoon, Sophie spotted Charley and Sarah walking along the aisle. They were bundled up in thick coats because of the weather.

'Hey, ladies,' Sophie greeted them as they got to her stall. She came around to the front. 'What do you know?'

Charley shrugged. 'Nothing much.'

'School okay?'

'Glad it's over for the week. You coming to ours tonight, to have something to eat with us? Sarah's coming too.' She looked across the aisle. 'We're having curry, aren't we, Matt?'

'We sure are,' he shouted over. 'All cooked by my hands too.'

'No. You overcook everything.'

'I do not.' Matt shook his head in denial.

'He even burns pizza and all you have to do is shove it in the oven,' Charley laughed.

Ryan whizzed round to face Matt. 'Do you fancy a quick jar in The Hope beforehand, mate?'

'No can do.' Matt shook his head. 'Got to take these two home.'

Ryan pressed together his thumb and index finger. 'Just a small one?' he pleaded.

'I'll come.' Jess sidled across to join them. 'I could murder a drink rather than go home with the loved-ups.'

'The loved-ups?' questioned Sarah.

'My brother and his girlfriend. They can't keep their hands off each other.'

'Jay and Nicci,' Charley explained to Sarah. 'This is Jess, Jay's sister. She's come back from London.'

'Cool,' Sarah said. 'What was it like?'

'Oh, it was great. Busy, though.'

'Sophie?' Ryan shouted across the aisle. 'Are you coming to the pub for a quick one or are you going back to Beth's?'

'I've got things to finish off first but I'll try and catch you later.' She looked at Charley. 'Nicci has gone so why don't you find your mum and tell her that she can knock off, if she likes? She's in the stock room.'

'I'd rather wait for you to come with us.'

'I have some orders to process. It may take a while.'

Just saying that made Sophie think of the night before. Her cheeks flushed at the thought of what she'd done with Damien.

'But you're always telling me I'm only young once,' moaned Charley. 'And you work too hard. Please. Come and have some fun.'

Sophie was shocked to hear that. Beth was right: Charley seemed so mature at times. She always seemed to be looking out for everyone else.

She checked her watch: it was just after five o'clock. If she closed up on her own it wouldn't take long to do everything.

She nodded to Charley. 'I'll see if I can make it in an hour, okay?'

Beth appeared then and Charley told her of Sophie's plans to join them.

'I bet you won't come,' Beth sulked.

'I'll try my best,' Sophie said.

That brought a smile to Beth's face. 'Can you finish now, Matt?'

'Sure can.'

Sophie watched as Matt came over, giving Charley a shoulder hug while Beth gathered her belongings. All the time she could see Beth glancing at him, almost shyly. He was taller than her by a few inches, a strong slim build with his hair cut to almost not there. His smile was always welcoming, never half-hearted. He'd be a catch for someone if Beth didn't hurry up and let him know how she felt about him.

When half past five came and she and Nicci had locked up the stall, Sophie decided she would go to Beth's after all.

'Impeccable timing, as ever.' Beth let Sophie in. 'We're dishing out the food. Come on through to the kitchen.'

Sophie shimmied out of her coat and threw it over the banister before following the sound of laughter. There was something about coming to Beth's home; it was good for the soul. It always felt warm, inviting, homely. Noise erupted at every second, unlike her house which was deathly quiet at times.

There were piles of shoes at the bottom of the stairs and coats stacked up underneath hers on the banister rail. Magazines spread out on the coffee table in the living room: cushions scattered everywhere.

In the kitchen, Matt was having his usual banter with Charley and Sarah as he spooned rice on to several plates.

'You cheated!' Sophie pointed at the takeaway cartons strewn over the table.

'You didn't think we were going to eat a curry Matt had made, did you?' Beth joked.

'Hey.' Matt slapped Beth's bottom as she sidled past him. 'I'll have you know I am a man of many talents. It's just that cooking isn't one of them.'

'Talents?' Beth laughed. 'Someone's been winding you up.'

Matt feigned a hurt expression, his bottom lip protruding like a scolded child. Charley gave him an impromptu hug.

'You're lovely, though.' She smiled up at him. 'I want to marry someone like you when I grow up.'

Matt hugged her back, raising his eyebrows at Beth. 'See, someone loves me.'

'*I* love you, you great big idiot,' she said.

Sophie was surprised when Beth came over to hug Matt too.

'Stop it,' she cried. 'Or me and Sarah will join in for a group hug.'

'Hugs are only for my special ladies,' Matt explained. Then he pushed them both away gently. 'Food. Come on, I'm starving.'

With a sigh of gratitude, Sophie flopped down at the kitchen table. It was barely big enough for them all. She smiled at her friend as she passed her a plate of food. Beth was a good mum, no matter what she thought of herself at times. Which made Sophie hope she might get the chance to be a mum herself one day.

After the meal, she insisted on doing the dishes and shooed them all into the living room. She hadn't even finished running the hot water before a word popped into her head.

Adultery.

It brought tears to her eyes. Reece had always been there for her and she'd let him down. When her dad died, it had been Reece who had held her together through it all while she'd been afraid for her future.

She remembered how well he'd got on with Martin. Often she'd left the two of them watching football or some violent action film while she and Beth went out shopping. Often she'd come home to see them fast asleep in the living room after it had finished, no matter what time of day or night.

Even before Martin died, Reece had been part of the furniture. He'd been there to step in and become her family when she was left with no one, and for that she would always be grateful. No one except Reece and Beth knew how close she and her dad had been.

When Martin died, it was as if Sophie's heart had been ripped out and he'd taken it with him. She couldn't ever explain how she felt to anyone else. Losing her mum at such a young age had made her more dependent on her dad. They'd been a team. Even when he'd moved Shelley Williams in for six months until their relationship had burned to a frazzle, she'd still been close to him.

Sophie had thought Reece was her soulmate. After they married, their relationship went from strength to strength but then they'd started to take each other for granted. And when they found it impossible to conceive a child, they'd drifted apart.

She had fought hard to find the closeness they once shared. But when Reece had decided to work away for the best part of each week, well, that had been the final nail in the coffin.

Would they ever get back to how they were, or was this the beginning of the end?

CHAPTER SIXTEEN

Nicci was in bed with Jay. Nothing unusual in that, except it was seven thirty in the evening and they'd only just eaten. Jess had gone out to do a little late-night shopping so they'd spotted an opportunity to be alone. Honestly, it felt like going back to being a teenager again, waiting for her parents to go to bed before she could have a quick grope with a boyfriend. It didn't feel right getting down and dirty when you knew your partner's sister was in the next room and could probably hear everything.

She and Jay had been a couple for three years now and had lived together for the last twelve months. They'd bought a town house around the corner from her parents and a few streets away from Beth. For Nicci it was the closest she could get to wedded bliss, yet she still wanted the marriage ceremony. She'd been waiting ages for Jay to pop the question but so far, all her hinting had been in vain.

'I wish she'd hurry up and move out,' Nicci said as she ran a hand lazily up and down Jay's chest. 'As much as I can be quiet, I'd rather be noisy.'

'Yeah, me too. I love it when I make you moan.' Jay gave her a quick squeeze. 'It won't be for much longer now.'

Nicci sighed. 'Are you sure about that? She looks as though she's settling in.'

'Give her a break.'

'But I like it better when there's only you and me.'

'Me too, babe. Me too.'

Nicci could tell he was falling asleep. She nudged him. 'Really?'

'Yeah.' Jay yawned. 'It's you and me to the end.'

She turned towards him and propped herself up on her elbow. 'Then let's get married.'

Jay's eyes shot open. 'What – where did that come from?'

'It came from the heart, silly,' she said, although embarrassed she had blurted it out. 'I know we've discussed marriage before and you've always wanted to wait because of the experience with your ex-wife, but, well, I think it's the right time now, so I thought I'd ask you.'

'Oh.' Jay laughed a little.

Nicci lay back down, as the atmosphere in the room became loaded. She didn't want to hear Jay say no but she had to be sure. Now that she'd broached the subject, she might as well find out the reasons why.

'Don't you want to marry me?' she asked quietly.

'Of course I do. I'd like to get some money behind us first.'

'But it doesn't have to be expensive. I don't want a big church do, or a reception at a castle or stately hall. I want –'

'Do ordinary people get married in castles?' Jay broke in. 'I mean, isn't it celebrities who do that?'

Nicci slapped his chest playfully. 'I said I don't want a castle, you dope.'

'That's okay then. For a moment I thought you were

going to get me dressed up in some medieval gear and demand a banquet.'

Even though he was making a joke of things, Nicci relaxed a little as he pulled her into his arms again.

'It might be good fun to eat from the plate with my hands, though.'

'Huh,' Nicci snorted. 'That's nothing new.'

Jay rolled on top of her, she thought with the intention of tickling her, but instead he stared at her for a moment. Then he smiled.

'I love you, Nicci Pellington.'

'Then marry me,' she repeated.

'I will, just not yet.'

She pouted. 'It –'

'What do I have to do to shut you up?' He kissed her gently on the lips to stop her from complaining anymore.

But it didn't stop her from worrying. She'd said she didn't need anything expensive so why was he so reluctant? He loved her; she was sure of that.

Maybe in time he'd come around. She had sprung it on him. Besides, she'd made a promise to herself that she never wanted to end up as lonely as her big sister.

Jess was trawling the shops at a late-night retail centre a few miles from Somerley, trying to find something to cheer herself up. She picked up a silk, plum-coloured bra and brief set and located its price tag. It was more than she'd normally spend but she felt like treating herself. And she was sure she'd be showing it off to Ryan soon.

She paid for the item, already dreading going back to her brother's house as she put away her change. She wasn't sure she could stand another night with Jay and Nicci cuddled up together on the settee while she sat on the armchair like a gooseberry.

As she made her way into the next shop, her phone beeped. A text message. It was from Ryan.

'Great to see you today. You were looking hot as usual!'

Jess giggled. Men, they were so gullible at times. She had him right where she wanted him.

CHAPTER SEVENTEEN

After the meal, Sophie insisted on doing the dishes and shooed them all into the living room. Once the kitchen was spotless, she made her excuses and left. She had only been home for a few minutes when the doorbell rang. She opened the door to find Reece standing on the step.

'Hi, what are you doing back so soon? Are you okay? And why have you rung the bell?'

Reece looked a little nervous as he stayed outside in the porch. 'I'm not entirely sure is the answer to all those questions,' he said.

'But I thought you'd gone to Germany.' Sophie closed the door behind him when he finally came inside. She followed him through to the living room, staying in the doorway as he perched on the edge of the settee.

'I can't do this anymore,' he said. 'You and me. The marriage thing. It isn't working.'

'But it was your idea to go away for so long.' Sophie frowned.

'Really?' A pained expression crossed his face.

'You haven't exactly rushed home lately. You've stayed

away more than you've been here. I thought you needed a complete break from me.'

'No, Soph. What I wanted was for you to fight, argue, scream and shout, beg me not to go. But you didn't.'

Sophie almost laughed. It was exactly what she wanted from Reece.

'We've practically lived apart for the past few years.' She sat down beside him on the settee. 'I thought you didn't want to be with me anymore.'

'Then why didn't you ask me to stay?'

Sophie paused to collect her thoughts. 'Do you mean that this was some kind of test?'

Reece nodded, looking sad. 'I'm not going to Germany. I just thought I'd see if you cared enough to stop me.'

'That's really sneaky.' Sophie gasped at the unfairness of the situation. Why would he do that to her? More to the point, it showed that both of them were lying to each other about various things. How had it come to this?

Reece ran a hand over his chin. 'It told me what I needed to know.'

'No, it didn't.'

'Then tell me you want me to come home on a permanent basis and I will.'

'You mean back to working in Somerley?'

Reece nodded. 'There are a few apartment blocks being built in Hedworth, near to the city centre. I've been offered a twelve-month contract if I want it.'

Sophie gnawed at her bottom lip. What a mess. Reece must feel like he didn't belong here now. She cursed herself inwardly. Had she been inattentive to him when he came home at the weekends? Not making him feel welcome so that he'd gone to seek solace elsewhere, treating his work colleagues as his family and following them around the country and overseas?

Reece stood up, and for a second she thought he might leave.

'I'll make coffee,' he spoke softly. 'Would you like some?'

Sophie nodded slightly. She watched him walk through to the kitchen and then flopped back onto the settee. If her mind had been in turmoil earlier, it was in a complete state now.

Reece had tricked her? Had he been so miserable that he'd felt the need to test her? Maybe it was sly but if it was the only way he could get her to admit her feelings for him, then that was wrong. She had to tell him that they were stuck in a rut, and see if the situation could be sorted. Perhaps if they got onto some sort of even keel, things could turn around.

The doorbell rang again.

'I'll get it,' Reece shouted through.

Sophie hardly ever had visitors, unless it was Beth – and it probably wouldn't be her as she had just left her house.

She sat up quickly. It couldn't be ...

She heard the door open, and then everything switched to slow motion.

'Hey, gorgeous. I –'

Sophie ran through to the hall to see Damien standing on the doorstep, holding a bouquet of the most beautiful flowers in the crook of his arm.

Reece looked from Sophie to Damien and back to Sophie.

'So he's the reason why you didn't care if I went to Germany or not?'

'No, Reece ... I. No.'

Sophie wanted the floor to open up; she would have preferred to be anywhere else other than here. As her heart reached out to the man she'd betrayed, she tried to find the right words to explain her actions.

She said the best two she could think of.

'I'm sorry.'

Damien grimaced. 'I take it this is a bad time.'

'You could say that.' Reece kicked the door shut in his face before turning to Sophie.

Sophie watched Damien's shape disappear from view through the glass panel in the door.

'No wonder you didn't want to fight for me,' Reece seethed.

'It's not like that,' she insisted. 'I would never do anything to hurt you.'

'And you expect me to believe that?'

'You have to. I never meant for it to happen.'

Reece's shoulders rose, as if he was ready to take whatever she said with dignity.

'Never meant for what to happen?'

Sophie faltered. What was she going to say to that? 'It's not what you think.'

'You have no idea what I'm thinking. No idea what I'm imagining.' Reece went to speak again but changed his mind. Sophie would never know what he was about to say because he opened the door.

'Reece, wait!' She grabbed his arm. 'Please don't go.'

But Reece pushed her hand away.

'Reece!' Sophie followed him a few steps down the driveway before stopping. She stood in the cold and dark of the night as she watched him disappear.

Tears poured down her cheeks. She wished she had the courage to go after him. But it was too late to make amends now, even if that had been remotely possible in the first place.

Her phone went off and she picked it up, greedy to see if it was a message from him.

Sorry about that - bad timing. Call me tomorrow. Dx

Sophie switched off her phone. She couldn't deal with Damien. She couldn't deal with *anything* right now. That had been one of the most embarrassing moments in her life. Seeing the hurt on her husband's face as he put two and two together and came up with five.

She may not have slept with Damien but her betrayal to Reece felt as if she had.

CHAPTER EIGHTEEN

'Sophie isn't coming in today,' Beth told Nicci the following morning as she pushed up the metal shutters on the stall. 'I've had a text from her to say she's not well. I'll pop around at lunchtime, see if she needs anything.' She sighed. 'She was supposed to be coming out with me tonight.'

Nicci fastened the straps on her overall and began to fill the till with coins. 'You can't expect her to go out if she's ill.'

'I know that. I'm feeling sorry for myself.'

'It won't hurt you to stay in for one weekend.'

'Of course it won't. And I'll be there if Sophie needs me today.'

The Saturday morning rush to the stall began. Beth wasn't feeling too well herself, if truth be known. She'd had too much wine the night before. After Sophie left, and the girls had gone up to Charley's room, she and Matt had shared a bottle of red. When he'd fallen asleep on the sofa around ten o'clock, she'd opened another bottle, only now regretting it.

She tried Sophie again and when she didn't answer, she sent a message asking if she needed anything. When a reply came back after ten minutes to say she was fine but a bit ropey, Beth realised that if Matt was babysitting, then she might as well make the most of it and go out on her own. There was always someone she would know.

It was lunchtime and Sophie still hadn't changed out of her pyjamas. The look on Reece's face kept flashing in front of her eyes every time she closed them. Hurt and humiliation, mistrust and rejection. If she ever had the chance to explain, he'd never believe she and Damien weren't an item – although Damien had certainly got under her skin in the few hours she'd shared with him.

If only they both hadn't turned up unannounced. She could have talked things through with Reece and decided where they were going first. Then she could have dealt with Damien, either telling him not to pursue things, or giving him the go ahead. Or indeed, waiting because she was so unsure about either.

She swore out loud. How could she feel sorry for *herself*? She'd let Damien smooth talk her without a second thought for her marriage. Okay, she could blame some of it on loneliness but that didn't mean she should have acted inappropriately with another man to make herself feel better. What she'd done was unthinkable and no matter how much she cried, it wouldn't change the past. She'd let Reece down. Their marriage was over, even if she didn't want it to be.

And Damien, what was she going to do about him after sending him away? At least he'd taken his flowers with him so that she hadn't got a constant reminder of how everything had gone wrong in a matter of minutes. He'd sent several messages but she hadn't replied to any of them. Even if he rang, she wouldn't answer it. She couldn't speak to him right now.

The tears started again. What was she going to do? She

needed to talk to Reece, explain what had really happened. She reached for her phone and dialled his number.

But there was no reply.

'It's ringing but she's still not answering,' Beth told Nicci two hours later. Her fingers and thumbs flicked over the keypad of her phone. 'I'll text her, see if she'll call me later. But it looks as if I'm going out on my own again.'

'You should stay at home with Charley for a change,' Nicci chided as she weighed out two kilos of potatoes for an elderly gentleman and popped them into the bag he was holding out. 'You don't exactly set a good example for her.'

Beth looked on in horror.

Nicci placed half a white cabbage on top of the potatoes. 'She's not a child anymore. She can see why you drink so much.'

'Oh, don't start that again.'

'You need to be careful that she doesn't get the idea that it's okay going around doing that, because it isn't. That's £1.72, Mr Austin. Ta very much.'

'You make it sound much worse than it is,' Beth objected.

But her younger sister shook her head.

While she served the next customer, Beth mulled over what Nicci had said. Was she a bad influence on her daughter? Would Charley grow up to think that it was okay to get drunk every weekend on a night out? If she did, then yes, it would be her fault.

She stared ahead, noticing that Jess was chatting to Ryan, over on his stall again. They were whispering together like a pair of kids. Matt was showing a customer a few phone covers, but looked like he was trying to listen in on their conversation too. Beth saw him glancing over while trying to keep his customer interested in a sale. Even when he'd popped one of the covers in a bag and rung it up on the till, Ryan and Jess were still talking.

'Matt.' She shouted over the aisle to him. 'I'm not going out with Sophie tonight as she's ill so I don't need a babysitter anymore.'

'Right, okay,' he shouted back. 'I might nip along to the Hope and Anchor. Do you want to come along too?'

'I think I'll stay in with Charley.'

'Okay. But let me know if you change your mind.'

Beth heard her mobile phone beep. It was a message from Sophie, saying she definitely wasn't going to make it tonight. She hoped there wasn't anything else wrong with her friend. Even before this, she seemed completely out of sorts but seemed unable to talk about it.

All she could do for now was give her another ring later.

'So you're off out tonight then, Matt?' Jess queried, wrapping her hair playfully round and round her index finger as she stood next to him and Ryan.

Matt nodded. 'You can join us if you like.'

'I'd rather eat my own vomit,' she muttered.

'Pardon?'

Jess stifled a giggle. 'I said I might do that.' She turned back to Ryan. 'Will you be there?'

Ryan huffed. 'Me? I doubt it.'

'Why not?'

'Because he stays in with his wife,' Matt said pointedly.

Jess knew he was trying to warn her off, but she ignored him.

'Why don't you come out on your own?' she asked Ryan. 'Are you under the thumb?'

'No, I'm not.' Ryan sounded a little offended. 'I do go out

some weekends, but not all of them. The twins take up a lot of our time.'

'I might have to babysit for you one night,' she whispered to him. 'Then you could give me a lift home. I've seen the films; the babysitter always gets the husband.'

Ryan nearly choked with laughter. He spluttered, patting himself on the chest.

'Something stuck.'

Jess noticed him glancing at Matt and Beth but they were deep in conversation. She laughed to herself. No one had heard what she had said to Ryan. Their secret was safe for now.

The tension on the stall when Ryan and Jess were together was more than electric. It was primal. Matt frowned as their heads bowed together again and Jess began to giggle. He had to do something to split them up.

'Ryan, we need some batteries fetching from the stock room,' he said. 'Size AA and AAA. I'll watch the stall while you fetch them, if you like.'

'There's enough under the counter for now,' Ryan said, never taking his eyes from Jess.

'Jess,' Malcolm shouted over. 'I need a hand over here.'

Jess sighed. 'Another day, another dollar. I'll catch up with you later.'

Ryan grinned. 'You can count on it, my lovely.'

Matt shook his head in annoyance. Ryan was such a snake at times. He wished he would realise how lucky he was to have a wife like Cassie, and two lovely little girls. The fact that Ryan seemed willing to throw it all away again was beyond his comprehension. He had covered for him before and felt bad about it. He wasn't going to do it again.

CHAPTER NINETEEN

Charley was in the living room when Beth got home from work and if she wasn't mistaken, had actually run the vacuum cleaner over the carpet. She eyed her daughter suspiciously, wondering what she was after.

'You okay?' she asked as she shrugged off her thick fleece. 'Thanks for tidying up.'

'Well, you work hard so I should do my bit every now and again.'

Beth paused, momentarily lost for words. She wanted to ask Charley if her daughter had been abducted by aliens and replaced by a goody two-shoes clone while she'd been at work.

'Have you eaten?' she asked instead.

'No, but Sarah is coming around later. We could nip to the chippie, if you like? Oh, you're going out, aren't you?'

Ah, that explained everything. Beth assumed she and Sarah wanted some time to themselves. At least they were back on speaking terms again. She sat down beside her on the settee.

'I was going out, but Sophie is poorly.'

'Oh.' The look of disappointment on Charley's face was clear.

'What are you up to, Charley Pellington?'

'Nothing,' Charley answered quickly. 'We were going to watch a DVD, that's all.'

'Sounds like a good idea.' Beth thought a little teasing was in order first. 'If I stay in with you, we could order in pizza and make it a real girls' night.'

'Cool,' Charley said.

Beth laughed as she stood up. Her pout said anything but.

'I suppose I'll crash Matt's night out and give you some peace. I'm only going to the Hope and Anchor, mind. I'll be back around eleven so you won't be on your own for too long. Would Sarah like to sleep over?'

Beth watched as Charley tried to hide the grin spreading across her face.

'I'm only down the road if you need me,' she told her.

'Mum, I'll be fine. I'm not a kid anymore.'

'I still worry, Charley. I'll always worry.'

She gave her daughter a hug, feeling pleased when it was reciprocated. Then she went to get ready.

When Beth went out with Sophie, she tended to dress more conservatively. On one occasion she'd worn a really short skirt, low cut top and the highest strappy sandals she could find while Sophie had worn jeans and a simple white top. Sophie looked like she was going out for a meal rather than a good drink and dance session and it had made Beth feel rather tarty.

But no matter what, she always had a laugh with Sophie and was desperate for a night out with her again. It had been an age since the last time, just the two of them.

She arrived at the pub to find Matt and his friends already

over in the far corner. She waved as he caught her eye, and he held up a glass of wine she realised would be for her. Easing her way through the crowd, she said hello to everyone and sat down beside him.

The Hope and Anchor – known locally as 'the hope and grope' – was on the corner of Somerley High Street and Hope Street. It was modern mixed with traditional. Creams and beiges, the odd flash of yellow and orange. Circular tables with stools; rectangular tables with chairs,

The pub was inviting, and full of regulars that were always up for a laugh. At least here she didn't have to queue to use the loos – unless it was New Year's Eve – she could get served at the bar after only a couple of minutes and it was a place where she'd often be bought drinks without feeling the need to return the favour – not that she ever took advantage.

As usual it was busy, the regular disc jockey playing the same records as the last time she'd been in. DJ Dave was big into Northern Soul and Motown, which meant that everyone else had to be too. Fortunately for Beth, she was quite partial to most of the tracks that he played. 'I Get My Kicks Out On The Floor' was a particular favourite, as was 'Ghost in My House'.

'Have you heard from Sophie?' Matt asked.

'She's still ill but a little better,' Beth replied. 'Anyway, why are you out on your own on a Saturday? Had a row with the Mrs?'

Matt had been seeing a woman called Lorraine for about four months now. Not that Beth was counting or anything, but after a while she'd started to panic at the length of this latest relationship. Their friendship hardly ever got questioned, unless Matt went out with someone for a long time. It wasn't as if Beth was involved with him romantically but because he was often around her house, some of his girlfriends over the years had ended up complaining about it. On the odd occasion, he'd told her he'd had to choose between her and them. She'd laughed it off, but was secretly delighted when he'd said she had won the toss up and no woman was going to come between him and his friends.

She glanced over at him now as she settled in and took off her coat. He winked and she grinned back. She was so lucky to have Matt.

'So?' she said, after taking a large gulp of wine. 'You haven't answered my question.'

'Night off.'

Beth nodded slightly. She knew him well enough to know when he didn't want to talk about something. Instead she turned to Amy, who had slipped in beside her after arriving with her husband, Tony.

The next couple of hours went quickly as Beth chatted with Matt and his friends. Besides Amy and Tony, there were two more men, Harry and someone called Griff, and another couple, Emily and Sean. Emily had recently given birth to a son and this was their first time out since Marco had been born four weeks earlier. Already, Emily was looking at her watch and fidgeting in her seat.

'He'll be fine.' Beth saw Amy place a comforting hand on her arm.

'Course he will,' Beth said. 'Although I remember when I first left Charley with my parents, I was so pleased that I could go off and dance all night without worrying about her. But I still came home early. It didn't feel right for ages.'

'You were only eighteen, weren't you?' Emily said, a little too sharply for Beth's taste. 'I feel like I've lost my right arm.' She caught her breath, tears welling in her eyes as she tucked blonde hair behind her ears.

'It will get better, I promise,' Beth said. It wasn't the time to snap back.

'How old is Charley now?'

'Fifteen going on fifty.' Beth rolled her eyes at Emily.

'When Marco is fifteen, I'm not letting him out of my sight,' Sean said. 'I remember what I used to get up to at that age.'

'Charley's a good girl,' Matt told the group. 'I wish she was my daughter.'

Beth smiled, feeling all warm inside. He really did care for her.

'You should have children of your by own now,' Sean added. 'You don't want to get involved with anyone else's.'

'Oi,' Beth snapped. 'There's nothing wrong in this day and age with bringing up someone else's children as part of your own family. If it was a problem, the world would be full of single-parent families.'

'Look around you. The world already is.'

'Do you want a family, then, Matt?' Emily butted in.

Matt laughed. 'I need to find a decent woman first.'

'What about Lorraine? I think you make a lovely couple.'

Yes, what about Lorraine? Beth held her breath as she waited for his reply.

As all eyes fell on Matt, he sat back in his seat. 'What's with the Spanish inquisition all of a sudden? Stop looking at me. I'm not going to comment!'

Saved by the sounds of DJ Dave as he started on his second set of the night, Matt went to the bar for the next round. Beth joined him, slipping an arm around his waist.

'If I were Lorraine, I'd feel very lucky to have you,' she shouted to him.

'What?' Matt indicated that he couldn't hear her.

Beth sighed. It had taken all her courage to say it once. She didn't feel brave enough to repeat it.

'I said, make mine a double,' she yelled.

CHAPTER TWENTY

While Beth became more and more inebriated as the night wore on, Charley was having the time of her life. She and Sarah been watching *Bridesmaids* when there was a knock on the door signalling the arrival of Connor and Owen. They'd given them some money earlier that day and they'd arrived with a bottle of vodka and a few cans of lager. Connor passed for eighteen easily, especially with his older brother's ID.

Now it was half past eight and she and Connor sat side by side on the settee, his arm draped casually around her shoulders. Across the room, Sarah was squashed in next to Owen on the armchair.

Charley couldn't believe that she was sitting with Connor. Despite liking Aaron before the blow job saga, she'd fancied Connor for months now. Most of the girls in her year at school did. He was such a catch and even nicer close up. He had a slight bit of stubble on his chin, a silver chain around his neck and the smell of something gorgeous wafting from him. His eyes were dark and moody, his lips unbelievably kissable and, even though it made her think of Alex, she thought maybe it would be okay if she had a bit of fun with him.

She glanced over when she heard a slurping noise. She squirmed. Owen was snogging the face off Sarah. How embarrassing, especially while she sat in the same room next to Connor. She knew he'd heard them too, as his head had turned at exactly the same time. He glanced at her and they both grinned. Then he moved towards her slowly, his hand at the back of her neck. At least Sarah's slurping had been of some use.

She gasped when his lips met hers, but not due to passion. Connor's kiss was all tongue and she could hardly breathe as he tried to ram it down her throat. She moved away slightly but he took this as a cue and pushed her back into the sofa. With his weight pinning her down, Charley thought she might as well try and get into his kiss. He'd slowed down the exploring with his tongue. That's because his hands had taken over.

'Erm.'

Charley glanced up to see Owen and Sarah standing up. 'We're going to get a drink from the kitchen,' Sarah managed to say before Owen dragged her away by the hand.

Once they'd gone, Connor kissed her again and she relaxed a little. It was one thing to want to share details with Sarah but she didn't want to do anything at all in *front* of her.

The feelings jiggling around inside her felt so good, like fizzy sweets exploding inside her tummy. She kissed Connor back, using her tongue to flirt with his now while she ran her fingers through his hair.

Without warning, they lost balance and rolled onto the floor with a thud. 'Ow,' they both said in unison before laughing. Then the kissing began again. For a few minutes, it was fine but with more room to manoeuvre, Charley felt Connor's hand beneath her rib cage. It lightly brushed her breast before falling on it and squeezing. Trust her to put on a dress, she cursed inwardly, pushing his hand away. Now he wouldn't be able to get inside it without going all the way up.

It didn't deter Connor. She felt his hand move down over her dress, trying to find the hem. He slid his hand up her leg, further, further, not stopping with his lips on hers for a second. She froze for a moment when he reached the side of her knickers. But his hand continued upwards, up and over her ribs to rest on her breast. She gasped as he touched it, gently at first, then again a little too roughly. She wanted to tell him it wasn't an orange but he seemed oblivious to her. And then she felt it, his *thing* hard against her leg. She pulled away for a moment.

'What's up?' asked Connor abruptly.

'Nothing.' Charley shook her head quickly. 'I thought I heard something.'

'It's probably those two in the kitchen.'

Connor kissed her again. His hand was still inside her dress, but she moved it down as he squashed her breast again. But then his hand moved lower and she realised he'd taken it as a sign that he could touch her. His fingers found the front of her knickers and slid over the material. She froze again, this time out of curiosity as he moulded his hand around her. After all the vodka she'd drunk, she felt slightly light-headed. Warm feelings were flooding her body, things she'd never experienced before. It felt really good as he moved his hand back and forth over ...

She sat upright and pushed his hand away. 'What are you doing?'

'Well, you've never had that done to you, from what I hear,' Connor replied shortly.

'What – what do you mean?' Charley could hardly speak.

'After what Aaron said, I know this is our first date but I thought if I got you off, you'd do the same to me.'

Charley pushed Connor away, stood up and straightened

her dress. She could see herself through the mirror above the fireplace. Her face was flushed, her neck too. Her eyes shone underneath far too much make-up. But inside, those first feelings of passion had disappeared entirely.

'You came for a bet, didn't you?' she said quietly.

'No, I didn't.' Connor lay back on the carpet with a sigh. 'I do like you, Charley. But I did want to see if the rumour was true.'

'And I suppose you're going to make nasty things up about me too and spread them all around the school, aren't you?'

When Connor shrugged, Charley wished she had the nerve to kick him where it would hurt him the most.

'There's nothing to tell anyway.'

Charley was close to tears now. 'I want you to go.'

'But we've only just started.' Connor grabbed her hand and tried to pull her down again.

She snatched it away sharply. 'No. Sarah, where are you?'

A moment later, Sarah came rushing into the room. She was tucking in her T-shirt, lipstick smeared all over her face. Owen followed close on her heel, fastening the buckle to his belt.

'What's up?' she asked.

Charley didn't know what to say now that Sarah had come in to help her. But Connor was done. He got up from the floor.

'Don't worry, I'm going,' he said. 'No point wasting time on a dick tease like you, anyway.'

Charley waited for them to leave before sitting down and bursting into tears.

'What happened?' Sarah sat down next to her. 'Did he push you too far?'

Charley opened her mouth but no words came out. She was unable to explain. Why had she stopped him? Why had she been so frightened? She'd wanted Connor to touch her. Why couldn't she let herself go?

She looked sheepishly at Sarah. 'Did I ruin things for you?'

Sarah sat beside her and gave her a hug. 'Course not. There'll be plenty of other opportunities. He had a big willy though.'

Charley laughed. She couldn't help it.

Sarah laughed too. 'To be honest, I was a bit scared that if he tried to put it in, he'd split me in two. So I'm glad you shouted when you did.'

Charley laughed at this even more. She grabbed the bottle of vodka, pleased to see it was half full.

'Let's get wasted,' she said, mirroring her mother's words without knowing.

CHAPTER TWENTY-ONE

Sophie opened her eyes to Sunday morning with a heavy heart. She'd been trying to ring Reece all day yesterday, but with no answer from him had gone to bed quite early the night before. It had taken her ages to get to sleep and then she had woken up numerous times before catnapping and waking for good at six a.m. It had given her ample time to think things through and now she realised that Reece turning up unannounced on Friday evening might have been the best thing that could have happened to them.

It was the same old, same old. Sophie loved Reece but wasn't sure she was *in* love with him anymore. Even though a part of her was relieved that she wasn't going to break his heart by ending the marriage, it didn't make her feel any better knowing that Reece probably felt the same too.

They'd been together since forever. Sophie couldn't help thinking that if they'd managed to have a child, maybe things would have been more solid. Ideally they would have been a family now, but after trying to conceive for five years they'd decided to let nature take its course. Unfortunately, nature never had and as well as having different interests, the lack of children had made them grow apart rather than bring them closer together. And that's why, for her, it was better for Reece to work away than to be here all the time, constantly reminding her of what they should have by now.

Sophie was always looking at children in the ticking-biological-clock kind of way. She'd smile at babies in super-markets and feel herself being pulled towards the rows of tiny newborn clothes when she went shopping in Hedworth. Thirty-four was still young to have a child nowadays, so she had time. And although Beth's life had been hard as a single parent, it had hurt Sophie to watch her bring up Charley, envying her having a daughter of her own.

Secretly she'd wanted to broach the subject of adoption, see what Reece's reaction would be. But as they grew further and further apart, it hadn't seemed appropriate. Yet another weekend had gone, and then another, and another. And now she doubted if he'd ever come back, apart from one last time to collect his belongings, maybe tie up loose ends.

Because Reece must have come home to hand her his keys. That's why he hadn't used them and had rung the bell. If Damien hadn't been there to put the nail in the coffin, she could have fought for him and he might have been willing to try again. But now it was too late.

She sat up in bed and hugged her knees, deciding that she wasn't going to give up on Reece. They had been together for eighteen years; he was worth fighting for. She'd ring him again later to see if he'd answer this time. She had to try and make him see that she hadn't cheated on him. That she'd stopped things from going too far with Damien because it was him that she loved. Their marriage couldn't be over. Could it?

Beth woke up at ten thirty. Her head felt like someone was repeatedly hitting it with a brick, her mouth dry and smelling nasty. She looked around the room, her clothes and shoes thrown anywhere as she'd removed them quickly to climb into bed, to stop the room from spinning.

Like a good girl, she'd stayed at the pub with Matt and his friends until eleven as planned and then he'd insisted on walking home with her. She recalled messing around with him – at one stage she'd pushed him into someone's hedgerow, laughing loudly as he'd bounced back at her. She recalled singing with him, and checking on Charley once she was home, finding Sarah top to toe in the bed next to her.

She remembered getting out a bottle of gin.

After showering, she went downstairs. Charley and Sarah were sitting at the kitchen table, both still in their pyjamas. Charley looked a little green, her head resting in her hands.

'You look like I feel,' Beth said to Charley, after flicking on the kettle. 'What's wrong?'

'Nothing.' But Charley winced as she'd moved her head slightly.

'You're not coming down with something?' Beth reached over and placed a hand on Charley's forehead. 'You're not hot.' She sniffed, then drew her head back as she smelt a familiar smell coming from the two girls. 'Have you been drinking?'

'We had a little bit last night,' Charley said.

'Of what? And where did you get the money from?'

'It was me, Beth,' Sarah said. 'My mum gave me some money and I – I bought a bottle of vodka.'

'Vodka? Where did you get it from? You're underage, and everyone knows you in Somerley Stores so you wouldn't be able to go in there.'

'I used my sister's ID.'

Beth's face was like thunder as she stared at them both in turn. 'Girls, I am so annoyed at you.'

'We're nearly sixteen,' Charley retorted.

'You're still children! And you'll do as you're told in my house, both of you.'

'It's not your house. It belongs to the bank until you've paid off your mortgage.'

'Don't be cheeky – and stop trying to change the subject. Have you any idea how much trouble I would be in if you were caught with alcohol underage?' She paused. 'Was there anyone else here with you, last night?'

'No!' Charley sat upright. 'It was just us.'

Beth pointed a finger close to her daughter's face. 'If I hear from any of the neighbours that you had boys around, Charley Pellington, I'm going to –'

'We didn't, did we, Sarah?'

'No Beth, we didn't.'

'Drink and boys at your age don't mix,' Beth addressed them both. 'I should know.'

'Yes, *you* should know.'

'You might think I'm being unkind watching out for you like this,' she said, 'but I'm not. I don't want you making the same mistakes that I did.'

'Like having me,' Charley said.

Beth sighed in exasperation. 'You know I didn't mean it like that.'

'Yes, you did,' she snapped. 'Just because you got pregnant when you were young doesn't mean that I'm going to. It's not the law.'

As Beth stood with her mouth open, Sarah jumped up. 'I think I'd better be off,' she said. 'I'm sorry, Beth. I'll see you later, Charl.'

Beth was too angry to address Sarah so she let her go. She finished making coffee, slid the one she'd made for Charley across the table and sat down in the chair that she'd vacated.

'That was a bit below the belt, don't you think?'

When Charley said nothing, she continued.

'I only say these things because I care.'

'Yeah, right.'

'I want you to see a bit of life before you settle down. I want you to do well at school and explore the world, see where the day takes you. I don't want you to be stuck in Somerley like me.'

Charley started to speak but Beth went on. 'You may think you have it hard but believe me, life gets harder. Mistakes made now will haunt you forever.'

'I had a drink, Mum, not a baby like you.'

Beth slapped the palm of her hand on the table. 'I had a drink and look where it got me.'

'You had *me*, remember.' Charley's eyes filled with tears.

'No, Charl. I didn't mean—'

'I was the mistake you made.' Charley prodded herself in the chest. 'How do you think that makes me feel when you go on all the time about never having any chances in life? That you never made it any further than living in a tiny terraced house? It makes me feel guilty, especially as you've never told me who my father is, denying me the chance to get to know him. I have a right to know who he is but you—'

Beth leaned across to touch her hand but Charley pulled it away abruptly. She stood up, scraping the chair across the floor. 'I hate you. You're so selfish I'm surprised anyone would want to spend time with you. No wonder you're lonely.'

'I'm not lonely.'

'Yes, you are. And I'm actually better behaved than you because you drink too much. You should give me credit for not doing that.'

Beth looked up as Charley stormed out of the room. She jumped as the kitchen door banged shut, closed her ears to the thunder of feet going up the stairs.

'Another conversation that went well, Beth,' she spoke to

an empty room before raising her mug into the air in a silent salute.

What Charley had said brought tears to her eyes when all she'd set out to do was forget about her miserable life and have a bit of fun. Yet Charley was taking in everything that she did. Beth wasn't setting a good example. Calling her a mistake was wrong, for starters. She wasn't a mistake, nor a burden, but sometimes she wished Charley had come later in life, when she could have been more mature about motherhood.

Beth ran a hand through her hair, holding in her tears. She wouldn't swap her daughter for the world. Maybe she needed to show her that.

Charley ran upstairs and threw herself onto her bed. Sometimes she hated her mum so much that she couldn't find the right words to express herself. What was it with her? She got a little bit tipsy on vodka and mum thought she could lecture her, when she came home drunk most weekends. Charley wished she was like normal mothers. When was the last time they went anywhere together? She sat and thought about it but couldn't remember.

She was right about one thing, though. Charley didn't want to have a baby tying her down. As soon as she was old enough, she was leaving Somerley and going to London. She'd get a job on a magazine, become a writer. She'd make something of herself, even if her mum hadn't.

A message pinged in on her phone. It was from Alex.

AL: How goes it, C?

CP: Crap as usual. I hate my mother.

AL: I hate my dad too. Got told off for not doing my chores again. What are you doing today?

CP: Not sure. Might hang around the shops with Sarah. You?

AL: Not much to do here either. Wish I could come and see you. We could hang out together.

CP: Me too. I wish you weren't so far away.

Charley sighed. She did too. She wished she could see Alex, chat to him face to face. Maybe he would understand how she was feeling. Lonely, abandoned and hurt. But Alex lived in Wales, so there was no way they could meet. They could chat on FaceTime if she had an Apple product but her phone was only a cheap model. Alex had said he didn't want to Skype in case his younger brother came in while he was on his computer.

They had to be content with messaging – at least for now.

CHAPTER TWENTY-TWO

Nicci's mind had been in turmoil. Since blurting out her innermost thoughts to Jay, she'd thought of nothing else but the wedding. She hadn't told anyone that she'd proposed to him but she couldn't help thinking that if they didn't get married soon, they'd never do it. There would always be one more thing to get in their way. Would they ever have enough money? Would one of them lose their job? Would one of them become ill?

But then she'd got to thinking that maybe Jay was scared of the whole idea of arranging the big day. Nicci had seen some of her friends being swept away by the romance of the wedding and spending thousands of pounds on their dresses alone. Although she was a romantic at heart, she didn't want any of that splendour. She wanted to marry the man she loved in front of her family and friends. If Jay was scared of the cost of it, she could easily get it done on the cheap.

So when she'd started to search online – to have a little check on the prices of venues and cakes and flowers – and she'd seen the number of things on offer to make that special day perfect, well, she'd got a bit carried away. In fact, she'd clicked on a few buttons, purchased a few items and found she couldn't stop. And when she saw a hotel with a cancellation for a weekend in March, in no time at all she'd convinced herself that it was what Jay wanted.

After all, she was only making life easier for him, wasn't she?

After what happened with Damien and Reece not answering his phone, Sophie hadn't expected to hear from her husband until some time had passed. So it shocked her when she received a text message that Sunday afternoon to say he was on his way over to see her. She quickly tidied herself up, putting on make-up even though her eyes were red and puffy from crying.

She opened the door to him, feeling nervous, not knowing what to expect. From the bags under his eyes, he looked like he'd had no sleep either.

He entered and paced the hallway until she'd closed the door. They stood in silence, neither of them knowing what to say.

'I didn't think you'd want to see me so soon,' Sophie started.

Reece shrugged. 'I've stayed at mum and dad's since Friday.'

'Oh.' Sophie had thought he'd gone back to Sheffield after their row.

'There was no way I wanted to stay here after ... why did you do it, Sophie?'

Sophie cringed inwardly. 'What exactly do you mean by 'it'?'

'Do I have to spell it out to you?

'Not really, but you need to know that I didn't do what you think I did.'

Reece looked confused.

'I didn't sleep with Damien.' At the mention of his name, Sophie saw her husband flinch. Tears welled in her eyes.

'Then what did you do with him?' he asked. 'Those were some flowers.'

Sophie's bottom lip started to tremble as she saw the pain in his eyes. 'Shall we go and sit down?' she suggested.

They went into the kitchen, she made coffee, and they sat in the conservatory. The winter sun streamed in. With a pang of regret, Sophie realised they should have been out somewhere enjoying it.

She closed the blinds, sat down and began to speak.

'So you only kissed?' Reece asked afterwards.

'Yes.' She left out the part where Damien had slipped his hand inside her pyjama top. Reece didn't need to know every detail.

Reece looked her straight in the eye. 'You hurt me so much.'

'I never meant to.' Sophie cursed as tears poured down her face. She hated crying when she was in the wrong. It made her feel weak. But she truly was sorry for what she'd done to him.

'What would have happened if I hadn't come back?' he wanted to know.

'If I was going to do anything, it would have been by now,' she said truthfully. 'I'd been having doubts about us and he – he was there to give me what I needed, I suppose. I know it was wrong, but I wanted some affection. I missed you being around, and I wasn't sure that you even wanted to *be* around anymore. When you did come home at weekends, it wasn't right, was it? We'd become like strangers and it hurt. And even though I want to make it better between us, I don't know how to.'

'So you thought sleeping with another man would do the trick?'

'I didn't sleep with him.'

They were silent for a moment, each lost in their own thoughts. Sophie studied Reece while he stared through the window, working out what to do next. Would he accept the job in Hedworth and come home or would he leave for Sheffield and not come back? She could almost see a pendulum in his mind swinging backwards and forwards. Yes. No. Yes. No.

'Let's see if we can work things out,' she said.

'I don't know. I —'

'I'll never hurt you, but don't you see? We've both let things slip. You've been such a huge part of my life. You were there for me when my dad died, but I've been lonely for so long and our marriage has become stale. I was upset that maybe it was me who couldn't give you children, that maybe we would have been closer if I had. My attraction to Damien was because I want to feel desired after so long of being part of the furniture.' She paused. 'I— I really do love you.'

Reece swallowed. 'I'm not sure that I trust you now.'

'That's a bit unfair.' Sophie frowned. 'I've had to trust you when you've been working away for all these years. Don't tell me there haven't been any women who attracted your attention over in Sheffield?'

'They haven't exactly been falling at my feet.' He gave a weak smile.

'You know what I mean.'

'I know that seeing him on our doorstep, thinking that you and him... It made me so angry. You're my wife.'

'Then come home.' Sophie reached across to touch his face, wiping away the lone tear that trickled down his cheek. 'Can you at least think about it?'

CHAPTER TWENTY-THREE

The next week went past without any incidents and soon it was the weekend again. Sunday lunches at the Pellingtons were a real family affair. Once a month, they'd all gather at their parents – Ryan, his wife Cassie and their twins, Abigail and Amelia; Nicci and Jay; Beth and Charley, and Matt often tagged along too. Sometimes Sophie and Reece came.

After the meal, Beth slipped to the bathroom. When the door opened, she jumped when she spotted Nicci sitting on the bottom of the stairs. She held her hand to her chest.

'You gave me a fright sitting there. What's up?'

'I need some advice.'

'From me?' Beth laughed. When Nicci didn't follow suit, she sat down next to her sister.

'Whatever's the matter?'

'I asked Jay to marry me.'

Beth let out a squeal and then clasped her hand to her mouth.

'So why the long face? He didn't say no, did he?'

Nicci shook her head.

Beth gave her a hug. 'Ohmigod. My little sister's getting spliced at last. Have you set a date?'

'Yes, March 30.'

'Well, that gives us plenty of time to prepare. We can —'

'This March.'

'But that's two months away. Don't weddings have to be planned at least a year in advance?'

'As long as the venue is available, anything else can be worked around,' Nicci explained. 'There was a cancellation so I went for it.'

'Really?'

'Really.'

Her tone was defensive but Beth could barely contain her excitement. 'This is fantastic.'

'You can't tell anyone.'

Beth frowned. 'What do you mean?'

'Well ... we didn't exactly agree on that date.'

'Did Jay want to wait a bit? Because if he did, don't worry about it and get it booked. Men don't like weddings and—' Beth stopped when she saw Nicci's face. 'What?'

'I haven't told him. I want to surprise him.'

Beth whistled softly. 'Wow, that's a brave thing to do. Have you really thought this through?'

Nicci nodded. 'What do you think?'

Beth paused. 'Don't you want Jay to get involved in anything?'

'Men don't want to know the intricacies and arrange-ments. I thought it would be a nice thing to do for him. Show my gratitude.'

'Show your— you're marrying the man, not thanking him for putting up with you.'

'I think it's a bit of both.' Nicci grinned. Then she whis-pered. 'I'm getting married, Beth. I'm going to be Jay's wife!'

Beth hugged her sister. 'It is exciting news, even though it's all so secretive.'

'Will you be my chief bridesmaid?' Nicci asked.

'I'd love to!'

As Nicci smiled at her, Beth hoped it would all work out okay. If Jay found out what Nicci was doing, he might be mad but it was Nicci's wedding day too.

'Tell me what you've planned so far,' she said.

'I've booked a hotel for the reception.' Nicci's eyes were wide like a child's. 'I went to see it and it was so beautiful. You remember when we used to talk about weddings as children? When I wanted a big hall or a marquee? Now that the law has changed and we don't have to get married in a church, this place is just what I dreamed of instead. And I've seen a gorgeous dress. It's off white, with a fitted bodice and ...'

Beth watched her sister light up as she ran through everything she had planned. She hoped it would work out okay. She deserved her happiness and she would love to have Jay as a brother-in-law.

But a secret wedding? She wasn't sure that was ever a good idea.

As Nicci told Beth about her big plans, Jess stood behind the kitchen door. She'd heard everything. How pathetic that Nicci had to plan a wedding in secret just to get someone to marry her. And to deceive her brother? Well, it wasn't on.

She'd have to tell Jay. There was no way she could let him be tricked into getting married.

As she heard the two women moving, she slipped back into the living room unnoticed. Ryan was chatting to Jay so she went over to them. But Ryan hardly looked at her.

'Oi.' She prodded him sharply after a few minutes of being ignored. 'Aren't you speaking to me?'

'Course.'

But Ryan still wouldn't meet her eye and Jess knew why. His wife was sitting no less than three feet away from them. Jess studied her out of the corner of her eye. Cassie sat with her mother-in-law Sandra while her daughters played a game on the floor in front of them. She wasn't a yummy mummy but neither was she a slummy mummy. She wore clothes that matched her age, which Jess reckoned was near or the same as Ryan's.

Her daughters shared her blonde hair, blue eyes and dimples either side of their mouths. And she hadn't let herself go, which had been Jess's first thought when Ryan started to pay her attention. She was glad now that she had manipulated her brother into getting her invited for lunch. It served Ryan right for feeling uncomfortable with her here.

She watched as Nicci joined them, giving Jay a quick peck on the cheek.

As they cuddled up and started to chat, Jess leaned into Ryan slightly. 'No one will guess what we're up to if you act natural.'

Ryan baulked. 'How can I act natural when you're here and my wife is over there? I feel like a right bastard about what we're doing.'

'Don't worry, babe,' she whispered. 'We're not the only ones with a secret. And ours is nothing compared to what I've just heard.'

CHAPTER TWENTY-FOUR

Jess decided to leave before Jay and Nicci, on the pretence that some exercise would do her good after the amount of food she'd consumed. If truth be known, she'd found the atmosphere stifling after a while. All those people paired off and playing happy families wasn't quite her thing.

As she walked, she thought about the conversation she'd overheard between Nicci and Beth. It was sneaky and the more she thought about it, the more she knew she should do something to stop it. By the time she got back to the house Jess had convinced herself that it wasn't fair to Jay if she let it go ahead.

She took off her coat and went upstairs into their bedroom, searching for clues. The room was red and black, cushions piled up on the bed. Photographs that looked like they'd been taken by a professional photographer were spread across one wall. Tasteful but sexy images, she realised. Peering closer, she laughed at Nicci's attempt to appear sultry, before grimacing as she saw her brother's bare chest on show in one of them.

On a makeshift desk over in the far corner, Nicci's laptop

was open. Jess wiggled the mouse to find it was still on, but it was password protected. After trying a few names, she gave up. She glanced around, wondering where Nicci would hide something. She tried under the mattress. She looked in the wardrobes, even inside shoe boxes and handbags. But she couldn't find one single list or wedding magazine or anything that would incriminate her.

Disheartened, she went downstairs but could find nothing in the living room. In the kitchen she made coffee, her eyes scanning the room. It was then she spotted a notebook with a bright pink spine, tucked in between the cookery books on the shelving. Jess got it down and opened it. Bingo. Written on the first page was 'Nicci and Jay's Wedding Planner.' Nice one, Nicci, she thought, smiling to herself. Jay would never find anything there.

She sat down at the table and looked through it. Nicci had certainly been hard at work. There were cuttings of dresses and flower arrangements shoved in the front pages. Printed details from the internet of wedding fancies and shoes. She found details of the hotel that she'd heard Nicci talking to Beth about. A note by the side of it read:

'Sent deposit £200.'

Next were caterers: 'Sent cheque £234.'

And cars: 'Sent deposit £250.'

Underneath those entries were written a number of things that needed to be sorted out, along with some rough estimates of prices. Jess quickly totted them up in her head. They came to nearly £5,000. Wow. She'd heard Nicci say it was going to be cheap, and low key too. Not at these prices, it wasn't. Although, she mused, how would she know what a wedding would cost these days?

She paused for a moment. Since she'd been back, Nicci hadn't been nice to her. And after what Jess had gone through with Laurie, having to move back from her glamorous life in

London to a shabby sweet stall in Somerley, she didn't want to see someone else being happy. Perhaps her brother would tell Nicci to cancel it all. And maybe he'd see her for what she really was too; a scheming, devious cow who was after his cash. She must be creaming money off their joint account at this rate.

Forty minutes later, the front door opened. Jess jumped up and stood on the chair she'd pulled across from the kitchen table in readiness, then reached up to the shelving where she'd put the notebook back. As Jay and Nicci burst into the kitchen, laughing, she made it look as if she'd slipped and knocked it off the shelf.

'Oh, sorry,' she said, raising her eyes to the ceiling. 'Clumsy me. I was after a cake recipe. Thought I might do a little baking. You wouldn't mind, would you?'

Nicci paled as the contents of the notebook scattered over the kitchen tiles like confetti.

'Those are *mine*.' She dropped to her knees, trying to gather up as many as she could. Jay bent down to help her. He picked up a brochure, an invitation sample and a pile of hand-written notes, handing them to her before picking up some more. He was about to give her that pile too but pulled back his hand and studied the top piece of paper.

'What's this?' he addressed Nicci as he held up a photo of a model wearing a wedding dress.

'It's a— it was going to be a surprise.'

Jay flicked through a couple more.

Nicci glared up at Jess, who was smirking.

'Oops,' she said all innocently. 'Is that a secret notebook? What's in it?'

'You cow!' Nicci shouted before bursting into tears. 'You've ruined everything.'

'I was only after a cake recipe.' Jess held up her hands in mock surrender. 'What's that you've got, Jay?'

Jay was flicking through the notebook, his expression hardening by the second.

'Will you give us some space, Jess?' he managed to say eventually.

'Of course.' Jess got down from the chair and left the kitchen, inwardly congratulating herself. She hadn't even got to the top of the stairs when she heard raised voices. She grinned, thinking, *Bang goes the secret wedding.*

Downstairs in the kitchen, Nicci couldn't believe what had happened.

'You had no right to do this,' Jay yelled at her.

'It was a surprise,' she sobbed. 'I was going to tell you as soon as it was all organised. I know how you'd hate all the planning so I thought if I did it for us then all you'd have to do is turn up and—'

She stopped talking. All the colour had drained from Jay's face, and his shoulders drooped. He looked like he was going to pass out. Panic set in.

'I thought you wanted to marry me,' she whispered.

'I do, but—'

'There shouldn't be a but!'

'We don't have the money right now.'

'We can save it by then. I haven't spent that much.'

'Really?' He chucked the book at her. 'Have you added all that up? It must come to a small fortune.'

'I had to pay more for short notice.'

'Have you ordered everything?'

'Not yet, but—'

'Then don't.'

'I—'

'And see if you can get those deposits back.'

Nicci shook her head. 'No,' she told him, knowing that if

she cancelled everything there would never be a wedding this year. She'd have to call his bluff. 'It's all done.'

'Then you'll have to undo it all.' Jay threw the book onto the table and walked out of the room.

'Wait,' Nicci shouted after him but he kept on going, out into the hallway and through the front door.

Knowing there wasn't any point following him, she let him go. Running upstairs to have it out with Jess, she stormed in her room to find it empty. So too was the rest of the house. Jess must have slipped out while they were arguing. Wait until she saw her. She wanted her out of their home now.

In the kitchen again, she flopped into a chair, covered her face with her hands and sobbed. What had she done? Even though she had ignored the nagging voice inside that said she was getting carried away, she'd thought she was doing the right thing.

Now it seemed as if she'd ruined everything.

CHAPTER TWENTY-FIVE

Sophie's weekend had been a quiet one. And a lonely one too, even though she'd received a few text messages from Damien. He wanted to meet up with her again, despite her replying to previous messages to say that wouldn't be right.

Reece had rung on Friday night and told her he wouldn't be coming home that weekend, or the next, as he wanted to finish off the job he was contracted to do. Sophie knew it was probably more to do with him needing more time to think, and that was fine with her. If he did come back, it had to be the right decision for both of them.

By the time Saturday evening had rolled round, she still hadn't shared the details with anyone. Earlier in the day, she'd bought a cheese-topped bloomer and a large cream cake from Mr Adams's stall. She took it home and gorged herself silly on toast topped with more cheese. Simple, stodgy comfort food was what she needed.

On Sunday, the usual routine had kicked in – washing, cleaning and ironing. By mid-morning, her chores were done, her house was shining and her mind still refused to switch off.

Would they be doing the right thing if they started again –

was it what they wanted? Was it really going to work? They'd never know until they tried, she supposed and she had missed Reece being at home. But people could still be lonely in a relationship.

After worrying about it for the rest of the day, by Sunday evening as she settled down to watch the TV, Sophie had convinced herself that she wanted to be part of a couple again. She craved to experience the butterflies that Damien gave her with Reece again.

And that couldn't be a bad thing, could it?

On Monday morning, Charley had climbed back into bed as soon as her mum left for work. She wasn't sure if she could face school again because of the rumours. They had escalated when Connor had added his version of what happened when they hooked up. She was still getting messages and comments left on Facebook about what she'd supposedly been doing.

Why did her so-called friends want to ruin her life? No one was saying nasty things about Sarah. It was always Charley. She knew girls her age, sometimes even younger, who had sex and she couldn't see what all the fuss was about.

She sent Sarah a message to say she wasn't going to school. She couldn't face all the teasing again. Everyone would be staring and laughing at her, wondering if she really did put out like Aaron and Connor had said. She wasn't the guilty party but they wouldn't care.

Her message was returned, letting her know that Sarah was on her way over anyway. It was five to eight, so she logged on to Facebook next. Ignoring the comments that people had left about her, she noticed a smiley face by her reply telling one of them to go stuff themselves. It was from Alex.

She'd been mortified when she'd thought of him reading all the abuse after what had happened before with Aaron, but he'd been fine and they'd chatted it through within a few emails. He'd told her to ignore them all, not once questioning if any of it was true.

Now she couldn't believe it was still going on and prayed that Alex didn't begin to believe the lies. She clicked on to see if he was online but he wasn't there. He must have gone to school.

When Sarah arrived, Charley made them both tea and toast before sitting on the settee next to her. They sat in companionable silence while they ate, watching some house renovating programme.

'He's such a cool guy.' Sarah sighed longingly as she ogled the presenter. 'I think I'd like to date an older man.'

Charley wrinkled up her nose. 'I'm not sure I would. He's old enough to be one of our teachers.'

'Oh, I meant someone as old as say, twenty. With a car, preferably.'

'Someone that old would be far more mature than anyone from school anyway.'

'I can't believe you're getting grief again,' Sarah sympathised.

'Me neither,' she said sadly.

'Aren't you curious though? To know what it's like?'

Charley shrugged. 'I'd rather not get pregnant. I never want to end up like my mum.'

What she didn't voice is that if she did do it with anyone, she would want it be Alex.

Somerley Market hadn't just got the usual Monday-morning-blues feel to it. It had all-round-abysmal stamped over it. Sophie hadn't wanted to come into work that morning but being your own boss hardly gave her an excuse to wallow in her own emotions. Beth was in a strop because it was the beginning of the working week and Nicci was in a mood after suffering Jess whinging all weekend.

As if that wasn't bad enough, across the aisle Jess was getting down to some serious flirting with Ryan. Enough to put Matt in a bad mood and for Beth to notice too.

'What's with Jess hanging around the boys' stall?' she asked Nicci. 'She's been chatting to Ryan more than she's been working on her own stall. I thought she was supposed to be helping her dad so your future mother-in-law could take some time off.'

'She should be.'

'Well, she's spending more time across the way with our Ryan. If she doesn't watch what she's doing, I'm going to have words with her soon.'

As she served the waiting customers, Beth covertly watched Jess. She was really lapping up the attention from Ryan, leaning across the counter so that she could be nearer to him. She saw Matt's face once or twice. He was scowling and it didn't suit him. Matt was one of the most happy-go-lucky people she knew.

Once there was a lull in customers, she would go over, see if he knew why Ryan and Jess had become thick all of a sudden. She knew her brother had wandering eyes and hands after the last time two years ago, when he'd had an affair. She thought he'd really messed up but her sister-in-law Cassie took him back after a temporary split.

The next time she looked across, both Ryan and Jess had disappeared. She went to the edge of the stall and looked either way down the aisle but still she couldn't see them.

'Where's Ryan?' she shouted to Matt.

'Stock room.'

'What are him and Jess up to?'

Matt shrugged. 'Could you watch the stall for a moment?'

Beth nodded, then spotted Sophie behind her.

'You know I was ill last Saturday?' Sophie began. 'How about I make it up to you this weekend?'

Beth smiled. 'Only if you're up to it. You know I love to spend time with you. I've missed you.'

Before Sophie could reply, Beth spotted Damien walking towards them.

'The Lone Ranger returns,' she whispered.

Sophie cursed under her breath. 'Can you look after things for a moment? I need to speak to him.'

CHAPTER TWENTY-SIX

Sophie had texted Damien, asking if they could meet. It was only fair to explain things to him face to face rather than over the phone. She wasn't surprised when he didn't reply but she hadn't expected to see him at the market this morning.

They went to the back of the building, out into the staff car park. After the bright winter sun of yesterday, the sky was grey and it was drizzling slightly. Two smokers huddled together underneath the shelter.

'I'm sorry. I didn't know he was going to turn up like that,' Sophie said after it was obvious Damien wasn't going to speak first. 'In fairness, I didn't know you were coming either.'

Damien gave a half-smile. 'Trust me to be spontaneous. My mum liked her surprise bunch of flowers, though.'

Sophie smiled.

'It was so awkward. I had no idea what to do.' Damien reached for her hand.

'I don't suppose any of us did.' She left it in his for a moment. 'It felt like I was in a sitcom. I was half-expecting a studio audience to gasp.'

In silence, they pretended to watch a lorry that was

reversing in front of them.

'Do you still love him?' Damien asked afterwards.

'Yes.' Sophie wasn't going to lie any more.

Damien dropped her hand.

'I'll always love him,' she said. 'I've known him so long, since we were teenagers. It's hard not to remember a time when he wasn't around. But that's where the problem lies. We became too familiar.'

The reverse warning beeps stopped on the truck and the brakes hissed. The driver got out with a slam of his door.

'What do you want to do?' Damien asked.

Sophie looked away for a moment. She didn't have a clue how things would work out between her and Reece but she couldn't string Damien along. It wasn't fair.

'I have to let you go,' she told him. 'I can't play around with your feelings.'

'But can't you see what we'd started might be even better? I can give you as much as Reece, more in fact. I could be here for you every night and not just at the weekends.'

She shook her head. 'For all I know, I could be making the biggest mistake of my life, but I have to give my marriage the chance it deserves. I want to stay loyal to Reece. I tried not to get attached to you, and yet I knew I was developing strong feelings for you. But I owe it to my husband to try and make it work.'

Damien folded his arms and looked into the distance.

'I'm sorry if I hurt you,' she added.

Silence fell between them as men began to unload the lorry.

'Are you sure?' Damien asked eventually.

Sophie nodded slightly: she wasn't certain at all, really.

'I can't persuade you otherwise?'

With tears glistening in her eyes, Damien pulled her into his arms and hugged her tightly. Sophie inhaled the scent of him for one last time. As they drew apart, her body relaxed for the first time in a long while.

'I'll go then.' Damien kissed her lightly on her cheek.

She watched as he walked away, feeling deflated but okay with herself.

Damien stopped and turned back.

'Remember, you have my number.' He winked before continuing on his way again.

Sighing, she went back to the stall. She prayed she was doing the right thing. It felt like the way to go but only time would tell.

Jess and Ryan were in the stock room. It was the only place Jess could think of to get him on his own without Matt scowling at them or one of Ryan's sisters butting their noses in. Or being asked to come back to the stall because she'd been missing for the past half an hour.

She looked at the list her dad had given her. Cola cubes, Kopp Kops and sherbet lemons. She'd remembered them fondly before she'd come back to Somerley. Now after eating them whenever she'd weighed a bag out for a customer, she was sick of the sight – and the smell – of them all.

She reached up, trying to see the top of the shelving unit, knowing that a flash of her stomach would be on show. She glanced back at Ryan. Yes, he was looking. Good boy.

'Can I pass you these down, please?' she asked.

Ryan read the label on the plastic bottle. 'Sherbet lemons? I bet you'd like something more substantial on your tongue.'

Jess placed the tip of her index finger into her mouth suggestively. 'I don't know what you're insinuating. I like aniseed balls too. Something for me to roll around my tongue.'

'Do you have to be such a tease?' Ryan moved in closer

but the door opened behind them. Seeing that it was Matt, Jess stooped down quickly so that she was hidden behind a pile of boxes.

'Ryan, I need you on the stall, mate. What the hell are you doing in here?'

'I'm after some ... some clips.' Ryan pretended to search around, jumping slightly as her hand crept up the inside of his leg. 'I could have sworn we had some.'

'Where's Jess?'

'She slipped out for something, I think.'

The reply seemed to throw Matt a little. 'Hurry up then,' he snapped back.

The door closed behind him and Ryan breathed out a sigh of relief. He looked down at Jess, her hand up to his thigh by this time.

'What are you doing? I nearly had a heart –'

The door opened again and Matt was back. Ryan held his breath as the zip went down on his trousers.

'While you're there, mate, can you see if we have any cans of WD40?' Matt shouted.

'Will do.' Ryan's voice came out as a squeak as Jess slipped a hand inside his jeans. He cleared his throat. 'Be with you in a minute.'

The door closed again. Ryan sighed with relief. He pulled Jess to her feet, quickly fastening his zip.

'You can't do that when people are around!'

'No one will see us.' She moved towards him, stopping with her lips an inch from his. 'And we're going to get it on after hours this evening, aren't we? When everyone has gone.'

'Maybe.' Ryan's voice was thick with lust.

'So it won't hurt if I give you a little something to remember about me until then?'

She searched out his zip again. This time there was no hand to stop her.

CHAPTER TWENTY-SEVEN

Nicci had dragged herself into work again. Since Jay had found out about the wedding, he'd gone quiet on her. He'd been coming home later than usual and then going to bed soon after. He'd been civil but not his usual self. After a strained weekend, she'd had the silent treatment that morning as well. She wasn't sure what to do but she needed to talk to him.

Jess had come in late on the night Jay had found out about the wedding and gone straight to her room to avoid confrontation. Nicci had wanted to charge upstairs and have it out with her but she'd needed to speak to Jay first. Now none of them were barely speaking to each other and there was a terrible atmosphere in the house.

'Morning,' Beth greeted as she got to the stall. 'How's the bride to be?' she whispered as she took off her coat.

Nicci was barely able to hold back her tears as she finally told her sister what had happened.

'I don't know what to do,' she said. 'Why doesn't he want to marry me?'

'Maybe he needs to get used to the idea.'

'That's not very nice!'

'I meant it in a positive way. Life can't be romantic all the time.'

'What do you mean?' Nicci frowned.

Beth hauled a sack of carrots up and began loading them into the display rack. 'Jay's never really been that keen before.'

'You think I pressurised him into it?' Nicci accused.

'No, I didn't —'

'Yes, you did.'

Beth rummaged for the dregs in the bottom of the bag and then scrunched it up. She was about to say something else when Sophie shouted through from the back room.

'What are you two talking about?'

'We were discussing Wedding Belles,' she said when Sophie appeared in the doorway. 'Aren't we always? It's Nic's favourite show.'

'Ah, love's young dream,' Sophie teased. 'What it must be like to be young and in love.'

Nicci gave a weak smile.

'Are you okay? You look a little peaky.'

Nicci nodded. 'I'm fine but I've got a dodgy tummy. Might nip to the loo before we open.' She removed her overall and trotted off before either of them could ask any more questions.

Charley and Sarah were walking to school.

'What's Alex got to say today?' Sarah said as she hooked her arm through Charley's.

'He says he wishes he had the money to come to Somerley and hook up.' Charley's face lit up with a smile. 'I wish he had too. I'd love to meet him in person.'

'Let me see his profile pic again.'

Charley got out her phone and located it for her, checking her messages first to see if he had got in contact since the last time she checked. 'Hang on, he's left me a reply.'

'Ooh.' Sarah leaned forward. 'Let me see.'

Charley pulled back the phone. 'I want to see it first.'

'Since when has anything been private between me and you?' Sarah pouted.

Since I found someone I could talk to who didn't go to my school, she thought. Although the rumours that had been circulating about her had lessened, the name calling hadn't and she was sick of it. Alex knew what people were saying because he could read her Facebook feed. Still, it didn't seem to be bothering him at all.

She read his message:

'I love watching Strictly Come Dancing but don't tell anyone. Some of the dancers in it are quite fit. Not as fit as you are, though. That is you, isn't it? You haven't used someone else's photo, have you? Ha!'

Charley's grin widened.

'He likes the photo I emailed to him.' This time, she let Sarah take the phone from her.

'He is rather cute.' Sarah studied it before handing it back. 'When you finally get to meet, do you think he'll have any friends I can tag along with?'

'If only I *could* meet him.' Charley sighed. 'Wales is miles from here.'

'There must be trains that go from Manchester. That's not far from here to change over. Or you could get a coach.'

'They both cost money I haven't got.'

'Why not work on the market stall? Sophie's always after you to do a Saturday shift.'

'Hey, I might do that.' Charley beamed. Ever since she could remember, she'd always been against the idea. Saturdays were for going shopping and chilling with Sarah, not being with your mum, hurling potatoes and apples into pensioners' shopping trolleys. But she could ask Sophie again. Then she could go and see Alex.

Lost in a dreamy daze, Charley wondered what it would be like to kiss him. She sighed. It wasn't fair that he lived so far away.

Later, before lessons began, Charley took out her phone and ran a finger over the image of Alex, as she had on many occasions now. His hair was dark, black almost, and cut short. Teamed with a cheeky grin were the most amazing brown eyes, with a twinkle that made her stomach flip every time she saw them. He sat on a wooden bench with his dog beside him; a German Shepherd called Murphy.

She thought of something witty to say and sent him a message back.

'I'm assuming that is you with Murphy and you're not actually a dog! xx'

Once the message had been delivered, she thought about that kiss again. Charley tapped the phone lightly on her lips and grinned. Maybe things might start to look up if she could meet him soon. Then she could forget about the idiots who were making her life hell here.

CHAPTER TWENTY-EIGHT

Nicci took several unnecessary breaks to the bathroom that morning. In a stall, she sat down on the toilet lid, closing the door to the world.

What was she going to do? If she cancelled the bookings she'd already paid deposits for, she'd lose all that money. It seemed a ludicrous idea, and she really did want to get married.

She typed out a text message to Jay. Then she deleted it. Then she wrote another, this time adding kisses. Each time the words looked wrong, the tone too harsh. But she desperately needed to talk to him.

In the end she settled on something and pressed send.

Jay, please can we talk tonight? Nx

She washed her hands at the basin, the woman staring back at her looking frazzled and vulnerable. But then she pulled up her shoulders and took a deep breath. There was no point dragging this out. She would have it out with him tonight, as soon as she got home. Find out the real reason he didn't want to marry her. And if Jess was in, she could either go to her room or get out of the house until they'd sorted things. She had no time for her now anyway. This was her fault.

For the rest of the day, she clock-watched. She added up stock with Sophie, cleaned down shelving with Beth, finished serving the last few customers and was out of the door the minute it turned five thirty.

When she got home, Jess was nowhere to be seen but Jay was sitting at the kitchen table. His face looked as pale as when he'd seen her notebook. In front of him were a pile of envelopes.

'You need to see these.' He pushed them towards her, not meeting her eye.

Nicci slipped off her coat and sat down across from him. 'What are they?'

Jay didn't offer any explanation.

She took the first letter out of the envelope and read it. Then she took out the next, and the next. Her hand covered her mouth as she saw the sums detailed on the statements. £2,000 owed on one. £792 on another. £3,000. £800. Then the final one: £8,263.47.

Nicci glanced up at him for an explanation. 'You owe all this money?'

Jay nodded, still unable to look at her.

'How?'

'Sharon.'

Jay's ex-wife had met another man and left Jay suddenly, a couple of years before Nicci had started to date him.

He finally raised his eyes. 'When we split up, you know she took everything. She also left behind a mountain of debt that was in both our names. She wouldn't pay anything towards them and as the companies knew my address and not hers, they latched on to me for payment. And every few months they wanted more and more. When the house was finally repossessed, the building society wanted so much back per month that I couldn't afford to pay off these debts too.'

Nicci picked up the first bill – Kitchens Unlimited. 'You still owe money for a kitchen?'

'Ironic, isn't it?' I still have to pay for what I no longer have.' Jay sighed. 'Since I've met you, I've been able to keep up with the payments if I did a bit of overtime. But I can't afford to pay for a wedding too.' He reached across for her hand. 'That's why I've been struggling with what you've done. I want you to have the best of everything but I want to pay for it all.'

'That's a little sexist, don't you think?' Nicci remarked. 'I go to work too.'

A faint smile appeared on his face. 'That's not what I meant. How can I get married again when I haven't finished paying for mistakes from my first one?'

'I still can't see why you didn't tell me about it all.' She pointed to the pile of letters.

'I was embarrassed. It wasn't even my doing, it was hers. She always wanted the best of everything and I was a soft touch. I tried to get out of the mess but I got in deeper and deeper. I'm so sorry.'

Nicci smiled then. Here she was thinking that Jay didn't want to marry her and all the time it was because he had money problems. It wasn't anything to do with them as a couple. A flood of emotion rushed through her.

She leaned across the table and kissed him. 'You big dope. I've been worried that you were trying to get out of things.'

'No. I really do want to marry you.'

'None of it matters as long as we're together.' She kissed him again. 'Who needs a marriage certificate when they have what we have? I'm not giving that up for anything.'

Jay smiled then, and she could see that this time it was with relief.

'Jay, will you "unmarry me?"' she asked.

He laughed, only stopping to kiss her again.

When she got in, Jess couldn't believe she could hear laughter coming from the kitchen. Really, were Nicci and Jay so loved up that they couldn't stay angry with one another for more than a week? If so, she'd seriously underestimated Nicci.

She walked into the kitchen to find her brother and what still seemed to be her future sister-in-law holding hands across the table, heads close together.

'Oh, you're not at it again,' she said.

'We are indeed. Nothing – or no one,' Nicci looked pointedly at Jess, 'will stop true love.'

Jay sniggered. 'I think that's a bit too lovey-dovey for me.' He smiled at Jess who was scowling. 'But I am happy we got things sorted.'

'That's wonderful news.' *Not*. Jess forced out a smile before leaving the room. She made her way upstairs and pushed open the door to her room – the box room, that tiny room that most people saved for the first addition to their family. It was only big enough to fit in a single bed and wardrobe but how she wished she had a house and a box room right now.

Tears welled in her eyes. Why couldn't she be in love with someone who loved her back in the same quantities? What sort of future was she going to have now?

CHAPTER TWENTY-NINE

Saturday evening found Sophie and Beth in a popular wine bar in the centre of Hedworth. Even though Sophie didn't really want to be out on the town, she liked it in Atmosphere. It had the feel of a retro American bar, with embossed steel plates advertising things such as tea and peanut butter adorning the walls along with posters of Marilyn Monroe, James Dean and a young Elvis Presley. A replica pilot's uniform and memorabilia could be seen displayed behind a glass cabinet.

Sophie could enjoy herself here; hold a conversation because the music wasn't hurting her ears. She could actually see people who were older than her. In most of the places Beth usually dragged her to, she wouldn't have been surprised to see Charley and Sarah lurking in the background.

How had she become so old and feeling past it when it came to a Saturday night out?

'So, spill the beans,' Beth said, after they'd each got a drink. 'Are things okay between you and Reece now?'

Sophie froze. She still hadn't told anyone what had happened between them, hoping it would blow over. Reece was coming from Sheffield to see her tomorrow for a couple of hours and she was looking forward to it.

'The last time we went out you spent most of it moaning that you wished Reece would come home for good, so that you could feel like you were still a couple,' Beth went on. 'Then there was this thing with Damien and since then you've hardly mentioned either of them, come to think of it.'

'Reece and I are fine.' Sophie nodded, moving forward slightly as someone wanted to get past them. 'And you know I ended it with Damien.'

'I still think you should have —'

'Come on, Beth. It was wrong what I did with him and—'

'What do you mean, what you did with him?' Beth's eyes widened. 'Did you do more than snog Damien Wilshaw, you dirty cat?'

'No!'

'Then what?'

'I don't want to talk about it.'

'Okay, okay. Keep your hair on.'

They sat in silence for a while. When Beth knocked back her drink and went to the bar for another round, Sophie was left with her thoughts. If Beth got wind of what had happened, she'd be livid that she hadn't told her. Then she'd be worrying that her friend might slip up. It wasn't even that she didn't want to share things with her. Usually she would, but if she told Beth what she and Damien had done, and then that Reece had left, she'd put two and two together and make four which, unfortunately, would be the right answer. And Sophie didn't want anyone to know how disgusted she felt with herself, especially if Reece decided to come back.

Beth returned with their drinks and they clinked glasses together. Not wanting to be miserable on her night out, she caught Beth's eye and smiled. She was always good company:

it wasn't her fault that she didn't feel so good about things at the moment.

The wine flowed and before they knew, it was nearly midnight.

'I'm bushed,' Sophie said when they were re-applying lipstick in the bathroom. 'Shall we head off home?'

'It's too early.' Beth flung an arm around her neck. 'You and I are going clubbing.' She held up a hand when Sophie started to protest. 'I haven't been dancing with you in a long while. I fancy a good boogie. What do you say?'

Sophie paused. She couldn't recall the last time she'd had a dance. And if it meant getting Beth off her back for a while before she had to do it again, she might as well give it a shot.

She nodded. Beth squealed like a pig, much to the fright of some of the teenagers re-applying their lip gloss.

Twenty minutes later, they headed to Rembrandt's, the best in nightclubs that Hedworth had to offer. Once they were inside, Sophie decided to forget about everything and have a good time with her best friend.

Matt woke with a jolt to see it was nearly midnight. His arm was dead where he'd been leaning against it. He stretched, yawning noisily. The television was playing something he couldn't recall starting to watch. All he could remember was Charley going to bed shortly before midnight.

He really enjoyed watching over Charley. In her own sweet way, she reminded him of Beth when she was younger; sassy, cocky and full of life. Yet tonight he'd noticed she'd been a bit subdued.

He'd cracked a few jokes with her, which had raised the odd smile but that was all he'd got. Something was bugging her, but he'd have to find out when she was ready. She'd talk to him if she needed to.

He went through to the kitchen and made himself tea and toast before settling down in front of the television again. He could go to bed – there was one made up for him in the spare room. Beth would let herself in, albeit somewhat noisily. But he always stayed up until she got back, waiting for her to check in. He couldn't sleep until she was home so what was the point of lying awake tossing and turning anyway?

He watched an old movie for a while before his eyes shut again.

The next time Sophie glanced at her watch, it was nearing one a.m. Coming out of the loo for the umpteenth time since they'd arrived, she searched around for Beth, only to find her on the dance floor, arms wrapped around some man as they shared a slow dance. If Beth didn't want to feel bad about herself on a Sunday morning again, Sophie had better rescue her. She tapped her friend on the shoulder.

Turning towards her, Beth smiled and gave her a hug, forgetting all about the man she'd been dancing with. Sophie found her head being crushed into Beth's chest.

'I'm ready to go home,' she shouted in Beth's ear.

'I can't hear you,' Beth shouted back.

Sophie took her hand and pulled her towards the edge of the dance floor.

'Let's go home.'

'I don't want to go yet.' Beth pointed to the bar. 'Let's have another. It's my round.'

'I think you've had enough already.'

'Fine, you go and I'll stay.'

'I'm not leaving you behind. Look at the state of you.'

Beth's eyes nearly came out of their sockets. 'I'm not *that* drunk.' She tried to point a finger but swayed dangerously.

Sophie grabbed for her before she fell. Beth tried to pull

her arm away but Sophie held on to it. She didn't exactly drag her away kicking and screaming, but there was plenty of protesting as they left the nightclub.

'I can't believe you did that,' Beth continued to complain as they got into a taxi parked outside the entrance. 'I was having a good time.'

'I was saving you from yourself.'

Sophie pulled the car door shut behind them, giving the driver Beth's address. Although her house was the nearest, she needed to make sure Beth was home before she could relax. In her drunken state, she wouldn't put it past her to ask the driver to take her back to Rembrandts once Sophie had got out.

She turned her face and stared out of the window. But Beth wanted to argue.

'Why are you so uptight?' she slurred. 'Is it because you and Reece don't have sex anymore?'

'Beth!' Sophie remonstrated, appalled to see the taxi driver smirk through the rear-view mirror.

'It's true.' Beth sat forward, ending up with her face in Sophie's shoulder as the driver took a corner. 'You only see him for one night every week or two. What do you do for the rest of the time?'

Sophie shook her head. In this state, it was better for Beth to think she'd had the last word.

'And you must be frigid,' Beth added.

Despite herself, Sophie wouldn't let those be the last ones. 'That's enough. You don't know anything about it.'

'Whassup? Truth hurt?'

They sat in silence for the rest of the journey. Sophie was grateful to see Beth's road when it came up ahead. At least now she'd get some peace.

The taxi came to a halt and Beth handed the driver

money to cover the fare so far. But then she struggled to get out of the door. Cursing, Sophie tried to help her.

'Would you wait while I see her to the door please?' she asked the driver as they practically fell out onto the pavement. 'I've a feeling it'll be quicker than this one trying to find her keys.'

The light went on in the hallway as they walked up the path. Matt came to the door and stepped out towards them.

'Hello gorgeous,' Beth smiled at him, as Sophie transferred her into his arms. 'Ya missed me tonight?'

'Like a hole in the head,' Matt muttered. 'I can't believe you're in this state again. Come on. Let's get you into bed.'

'Ooh, I'll let you take advantage of me, ifyerlike.'

'I'll call you tomorrow,' Sophie cried to their disappearing forms. Turning back to the road, she had never been so glad to see the taxi waiting for her.

CHAPTER THIRTY

As Sophie left in the taxi, Matt helped Beth upstairs. She was all but a dead weight as they tried to negotiate each step. She banged her head on the wall several times, missed a step and almost collapsed on the landing carpet.

'I love you, Matt Ratcliffe,' Beth slurred as he finally got her into her room.

'I love you too, you drunken tart.'

Matt slipped off her shoes. As she dropped onto her bed, she was like one of the sacks of potatoes that she emptied day after day. Hearing her snort, her eyes already closed, he tucked her under the duvet and sat down on the bed beside her. He watched her for a while, tenderly brushing her hair away from her face. Her make-up was smudged everywhere but she was still beautiful to him. If only she could look at him as more than a friend, he'd take care of her. He'd provide for her and Charley.

Ever since he'd started to hang around with Ryan and Jay when they were teenagers some twenty years ago, Matt had always had feelings for Beth. He'd watched from the side lines as she'd turned from a girl into a woman – a kick-ass lady with a kick-ass attitude.

The pregnancy had shocked him at first but it hadn't dampened his feelings towards her; he still wanted to be with her. But even though Matt and Beth had been out on a few dates when they were younger, Beth hadn't really wanted things to become more permanent. Her mind seemed to be elsewhere, on someone else rather than him. In the end, he'd accepted that the only way he would get to be part of her life was to stay friends with her, to become the person that she could always turn to, rely on.

When she'd found Brian Thompson and ended up getting married, he'd wondered if it was too quick. They'd only been together a few months but they seemed to love each other nonetheless. And for a while, things changed between him and Beth. It meant he couldn't pop around for a chat or a takeaway. Matt had missed both Beth and Charley.

So when the marriage was over, he was there for her again – even if it was with a comforting arm around her shoulder rather than in her bed. In the back of his mind, he'd always hoped that Beth would be his eventually, especially as Charley saw him as a father figure.

But even then, Beth didn't notice him. She thought of him as a good friend. He'd been around for so long it was as if he was part of the paintwork, part of the family. Someone there for her and Charley, who could be relied on but not loved.

Over the years, Beth had often taken advantage of him. Now Charley was fifteen it wasn't so bad, but when she couldn't be left alone for any length of time, Matt had become an unpaid babysitter. Although Ryan and Jay had constantly told him that he was a mug, he didn't mind so much. Looking after Charley was something he loved to do.

He couldn't wait to find a woman of his own and settle down to start a family.

But as time went by, somehow he could never find the right one. His relationships would finish after a year or so – mainly because he spent so much time with Beth and Charley.

Still, at least he got to look out for her, even if it was in a tiny way. And no matter what, he knew he'd always be there for her.

Maybe one day she'd change her mind, see that he loved her. Maybe one day she would love him too.

Beth was snoring loudly now. Matt went to fetch a glass of water and a packet of paracetamol and placed them by the side of the bed. Then with a heavy heart, he left the room.

Arriving home after dropping Beth off, Sophie let herself in and stood in the hallway for a moment in the silence. Still a little tipsy, the emptiness distressed her and she burst into tears. She really didn't want to go clubbing every weekend to find someone to care for her. No wonder Beth acted as she did. If she had to come home to a house as empty as this one felt right now, she'd soon be getting her kicks drinking as much too.

In the space of one evening, she'd realised how lonely Beth must be after being on her own for so many years. Even though Reece hadn't been around as much as she would have liked, Sophie had always known she had him as her other half. The awareness was always there that he was only a drive down the motorway if she needed him.

Feeling the urge to talk to him, she kicked off her shoes and located her phone. Through watery eyes, she flicked through the contacts to find the one she wanted. Her fingers hovered over the button. It was nearly two a.m. now. Should she ring him? Of course she shouldn't. She would see him tomorrow.

Feeling alone and wondering how she had made such a mess of her life, Sophie dropped onto the settee and sobbed into the cushion.

CHAPTER THIRTY-ONE

The next morning, Jess didn't feel like getting up. What had she got to look forward to? A Sunday with the loved-ups cooing over the breakfast table, letting her know for certain she had overstayed her welcome. Both her brother and Nicci had been cold with her since she'd tried to sabotage the wedding, but at least they had said she could stay a little longer. It wasn't an ideal situation, but what else could she do? She had nowhere else to go.

The day was going to drag. Thinking of her predicament made her think of Laurie, wonder what he would be up to right now. No doubt, he'd be spending the day with his wife and children while she was alone again. Did he even think about her since she'd been gone? Remember the happy times they'd shared, the love-making as well as the sex?

If she was a real bitch, Jess would have made sure his wife knew about his extramarital bliss, plus the baby, and she would have gone after him for maintenance when the child was born. But even though she was needy, she didn't want to do that to him. Which is why she was making Ryan fall for her instead.

Desperate for the bathroom, she swung her legs up and out of the bed. As she stood up, nausea took over and she only just managed to get to the toilet in time to throw up. Morning sickness, ugh. She was nearly fourteen weeks gone: she couldn't wait for that to be over and done with.

She sat on the side of the bath. The tears pouring down her cheeks took a long time to stop.

Beth opened her eyes slowly, knowing full well that she already had the headache from hell, even if she hadn't woken up properly. She'd been dozing for a while, every now and then the voices of Charley and Matt floating up from down-stairs. She'd been wanting to join them for ages but equally didn't want to get out of bed for fear of feeling worse than she did.

In the end, she didn't have to. There was a knock on her door.

'I've a mug of coffee if you're awake and decent,' Matt spoke through the door.

'Come in,' Beth croaked. She coughed to clear her throat.

'Morning, drunkard.' Matt wafted a hand in front of his face. 'It smells like a brewery in here.'

'It's not that bad.' Beth attempted to rise on one elbow but her head began to pound so she lay back again.

'You were in a right state when you came in last night.' He sat on the bottom of the bed. 'I worry about you when you get like that.'

'I'm fine.' She took a sip of water, unable to look Matt in the eye. 'I didn't say anything I shouldn't, did I?'

Matt sniggered. 'The usual stuff – how much you love me and I'm such a good friend.'

'It's all true.' She still couldn't look at him, feeling her cheeks burning.

'You're flushed,' Matt noticed. 'Are you feeling ill or hungover?'

'Is there a difference?'

'I suppose not.' Matt clapped a hand on his thigh before standing up. 'If you're staying in bed, I'll head off home. But if you're thinking of getting up, I'll cook a fry up.'

Beth's body spasmed at the thought of anything greasy. 'Not unless you want the contents of my stomach on the plate too,' she replied.

'You are gross at times.' Matt stopped and turned back before he got to the door. 'I'll do me and Charley a breakfast anyway. If you want to join us come down.'

'Like this?' She pointed at her pale face.

'You're still gorgeous.'

'Stop teasing.'

He stared at her but she looked away.

'Okay, I'll see you tomorrow then,' he smiled. 'I'll text you later to see how you are.'

As soon as he was gone, Beth regretted not going downstairs with him. He could always make her smile, laugh too. He was an excellent tonic for mornings like this.

She knew she was in for a long recovery back to the land of the non-drunk. Still, she couldn't resist trying one more time to get out of bed. When the room began to spin, she lay down again promptly. She'd have to miss her time with Matt this morning.

Despite not having much sleep, Sophie had got up early to prepare for Reece's arrival. Every time she glanced at the clock, she had butterflies in her stomach. She cleaned the house from top to bottom as she did every Sunday morning, but this time it seemed different. This time she cleaned the windows – and the oven. It was as if everything had to be perfect.

Pull yourself together, it's only Reece, she chastised herself as she made sure there wasn't any litter on the driveway that had blown in with the wind last night. Then she paused.

It's only Reece.

Those words spoke volumes said in that context. Because it wasn't only Reece this time. It was Reece, her husband who wasn't sure if he wanted to be married to her anymore. And maybe the fact that she'd thought it's only Reece had been the problem all along – that she took him for granted.

The visit loomed as she put her make-up on. Despite the tears of the previous night, and the pallor of her skin due to excessive alcohol and a late night, she managed to look half-decent for his arrival.

He arrived promptly at one o'clock, his eyes focussing on anything but her. Already it was as if they didn't know how to act around each other.

She'd prepared a Sunday roast, really making an effort to cook it as he liked. It hadn't been a good idea because at first they'd sat in silence while they'd eaten. Then the small talk began.

'How's the stall?' he asked.

'Doing fine.' Sophie nodded, pleased to have something to talk about. 'That range of organic chopped mixed fruits that we sourced locally are doing well.'

'That's great. I did wonder if they might not take off. And how are the sisters? Is Beth being her obnoxious self?'

'As ever.' She smiled but it faltered. 'She's still drinking too much. I tried to keep her from its clutches by going out with her last night but it didn't stop her. Not sure I want to go clubbing again, though. It's not really my scene. Do you remember Jay's sister, Jess? She's back in Hedworth.'

'Oh?' He looked up at her.

'She's working on the sweet stall. I was surprised, to be honest. I mean, who would swap London for Somerley Market selling strawberry bonbons and liquorice allsorts? I couldn't begin to—'

'Sophie,' Reece interrupted, holding up a hand. 'How would you feel if I moved back in?' He glanced at her. 'Are you able to give us another try?'

'I thought you'd changed your mind,' she confessed.

'I needed time to think.' He paused. 'What about you?'

Sophie shook her head. 'We've always been good together. We just lost our way when—'

'When we couldn't conceive a child,' Reece broke in. 'We should have been more grown up about it, I suppose.'

'I'm not sure I realised anything was happening to us until it was too late,' she admitted.

'I think maybe it was easier for me to run away too, rather than face it at the time. But if I do come back home again, what happens if we still can't have children? How would you feel then?'

Sophie gnawed on her bottom lip before speaking. 'Is that what you thought? That I didn't want to be around you anymore because I couldn't get pregnant?'

Reece shrugged. 'I'm not sure. It might have been me that didn't want to be reminded. But even so, will it cause us problems?' The anguish was clear in his eyes.

'Neither of us know if we can have children with anyone else, though, do we?'

'Is that what you wanted to find out?'

'No!' Sophie recoiled slightly at his suggestion. 'I – I missed being a couple, I think.'

Reece went to speak but changed his mind. Sophie cringed, wondering if he was thinking that she'd slept with

Damien so she could be pregnant with his child. But his next question removed any doubts.

'So what do you think?' He smiled at her the way he used to, cheeky yet unsure, before reaching across the table for her hand.

Sophie nodded, relieved and hopeful. After all these years, how could they not try again?

CHAPTER THIRTY-TWO

The next morning at work, Sophie had a spring in her step. Reece had stayed the night and despite their nervousness, they'd made love and again that morning before he'd set off really early back to Sheffield. She couldn't believe that he'd be home for good when he came back next weekend. She made a mental note to get something nice in to eat, and some decent wine on her trip to the supermarket.

She added a reminder to her phone to make an appointment to see the doctor too. Having spoken about children again, they were going to look into fertility testing.

She went outside to the skip with a handful of cardboard boxes. As she stamped on them to crush them down, she noticed Jay dropping Nicci off and waved to them. Once she'd finished, she looked up again to see that Jay was still sitting in his car, staring ahead. She walked over to him.

'Hey.' She dipped her head to come level with his window. 'How're things with you?'

'So, so,' he replied, not even managing a smile.

'Oh, dear, sounds ominous. You and Nicci haven't fallen out, have you?'

'We had a row but everything is sorted now.' He paused. 'Actually, have you got a few minutes to spare?'

'Sure.' Sophie clambered in beside him. Suddenly Jay was telling her everything. About the proposal, finding the notebook, the secret wedding, the argument, the debt he had, the money Nicci had spent.

'Wow.' Sophie was a little dazed by how much she had to take in. 'I bet that was good to offload. So what happened next?'

'Since we made up we've sat down together and devised a new plan to pay off the money I owe, as well as put a little away each month towards a wedding in a couple of years.'

'And is Nicci happy with that?' Sophie knew how much she wanted to get married. It was all she ever talked about.

'She says she is.' Jay drummed his fingers on the steering wheel. 'But it didn't make me feel good to see her so hurt. And all that money she's wasted because of me. Most of the deposits she sent are non-returnable. Either the order goes ahead or the money is lost. I wish there was a way round it all.'

They sat in silence for a moment, each mulling on their thoughts.

'I don't know what to do.' Jay sighed out loud.

'Hey.' Sophie touched his forearm gently. 'It's not the end of the world. Nicci will understand. And having a roof over your head without any debt is always a top priority in my eyes. Plus, she did do it all without you knowing.'

'That's true, but she only wanted to do something nice to surprise me.'

'Even so ...'

'I really want to marry her.' Jay struggled to keep his emotions inside. 'I want to have children and I – I love Nicci so much that she deserves the best of everything. It killed me to keep the debt secret from her. Couples shouldn't have secrets. I'm actually glad it's out in the open now.'

Sophie's eyes brimmed with tears, touched that Jay would share that with her. He and Nicci always seemed so happy together. There must be something she could do. An idea began to form in her mind.

'Does anyone else know about this?'

Jay shook his head. 'I know it's underhand but I had to share it with someone. And I couldn't talk to Matt or Ryan.'

'Why don't you turn the surprise around?'

Jay looked puzzled.

'How about we do something, oh I don't know, in the market hall? Dress it up to look all romantic, get everyone around the stalls involved and keep it from her until the day.'

'It's a bit far from what she wanted, don't you think?'

'Not necessarily. If we make it romantic and special, people will be talking about it for years to come. Nicci would love that.'

Jay was silent for a moment. Then he smiled.

'She did say that the most important thing is that we get married.' He paused. 'Are you sure that would work?'

'It'll be tricky but yes, I'm certain.' Sophie nodded. 'Do you think you can keep it a secret from her?'

He nodded. 'And if she does find out, perhaps she'll be happy that we're getting married regardless. Win-win in my eyes.'

Sophie smiled. 'There are three things I need you to do. The first is to have another look at that list she wrote and see if there's anything there to suggest a dress and shoes. Arranging little details without Nicci knowing is one thing, but a bride has to have the final say on her dress and accessories. If the dress she likes is too expensive, maybe we can get Cynthia on the fabric stall to make up something comparable? And Riley might be able to order in some similar shoes at Chandler's Shoes.'

'I'm on it.' Jay nodded.

'Then I need you to find out which parts of the wedding she's already paid money towards and I'll chat to everyone, see if we can salvage anything. If I tell them what we're doing initially, you can go and speak to them afterwards.'

'Okay.'

'Finally, check what's the earliest date the registry office can do. Some are opening on Sundays now. Do you think you can manage that?'

'Yep.' Jay nodded again.

'Good.' Sophie got out of the car. 'Then I suggest you get yourself off to work and don't mention that you saw me today. This is going to be some secret to keep.'

Sophie walked back through the market, her eyes flicking onto every stall as she passed. Already, she was planning. Once Jay came back to her with exactly what she needed to do, then she'd get cracking with the arrangements and start roping people in to help. With glee, she realised she'd need to make a list.

A secret wedding, how romantic. It made her recall her own. Reece proposed to her about a month after her dad's funeral, although they didn't get married straight away. Since Martin wouldn't be there, Sophie didn't want a fuss. A small wedding in the local registry office had sufficed, so there was no need for anyone to walk her down an aisle. They'd gone out with a few close friends for a meal afterwards and then everyone had trooped back to their house for a knees-up where more people were invited.

As weddings went, for her and Reece it had been ideal. There was no falling out about colours and flowers, no bickering about who'd been invited and who hadn't and best of all, no terrible presents to laugh about, as everyone had given them holiday vouchers. They'd booked a week in the Canary Islands and set off the next month.

It wouldn't suit some but both she and Reece had enjoyed it that way, even though there had been tears when she'd wished her dad had been there to see how happy she was on the day.

And yet now, look at them. Almost on the brink of splitting up because they had grown apart. Well, she was going to try her hardest to make it work again.

Where was she? Ah, yes, the list. Melissa from the make-up counter could do Nicci's face and nails. She could ask Sally at Cupcake Delights to do the cake and Mr Adams to do the overall catering. It would seem fair for each stallholder to do a bit each. Everyone liked Nicci, she was always so upbeat and positive about everything. Most people knew Jay too.

The sweet stall – Jay had said he'd let his parents know of the plans, so there was no rush to tell Malcolm and Maureen. But he'd have to ensure they gave Jess the minimum of information. Sophie wouldn't put it past her to sabotage the wedding purposely. Then there was Matt and Ryan. Well, there was only one job for those two.

'She's back at last,' Beth cried when Sophie finally drew level with her own stall. 'I thought you'd driven to the incinerator to destroy the boxes, you've been that long. How did it go with Damien?'

'So, so.' Seeing Nicci close by, Sophie shrugged her shoulders but as she passed Beth, she leaned in close. 'Actually, I was chatting to Jay and he told me all about the wedding.'

Beth looked up quickly. 'I couldn't tell you. I was sworn to secrecy.'

'Oh, never mind that. Let's go to the café for a quick coffee. I have something to discuss.'

.   .   .

While Sophie and Beth discussed the wedding, in between serving customers Matt had his head in the morning's newspaper. Behind him, Ryan was drinking a coffee.

'Hey,' Ryan nudged him. 'Will you do me a favour, buddy?'

'That depends on what it is and if it involves me being out of pocket.'

'I need you to cover for me while I attend to a little business.'

Matt looked up at Ryan. He could see his friend was watching the sweet stall – or rather, he was watching Jess. Suddenly, it all clicked into place.

'You've got to be kidding,' he replied. 'That's why you want me to cover for you?'

When Ryan grinned, Matt shook his head.

'No way. I told you after the last piece of skirt that I wasn't comfortable lying to Cassie. I sure as hell won't do it again.'

'Go on, mate,' Ryan pleaded. 'It's only this once. No one will know.'

'*I'll* know.'

'But it wouldn't be—'

'I said no!' Matt slapped his hand on the boxes piled up in front of him, causing a few people walking past to look around.

'I was only going to take her out for a drink after work one night, that's all.'

'Right. So you wouldn't want to see her again? And you wouldn't want me to cover for you then too? And again and again?' Matt prodded him sharply in the chest. 'I know you of old, *buddy*. You've done this on me before and I won't be dragged into it again. The answer is no.'

'Fine. But it doesn't mean that I won't see her. I'll have to think of another excuse.'

'Yeah, you do that. You selfish piece of shit.'

Matt pushed past him and out into the aisle. He glared at Jess as he stormed past. Fury almost blinded him. Why would Ryan want to risk everything for a fumble with a woman who was only after a bit of fun? Surely he could see what he had – a wife, children and a lovely home.

All that Matt had ever wanted, yet Ryan was willing to chuck it all away.

CHAPTER THIRTY-THREE

Sophie was late in to work after calling into the GP's surgery to see the nurse. She'd wanted to discuss a few options with her before booking an appointment to see the doctor about her inability to conceive. On the stall, she spotted a card shoved down by the side of the till.

'Happy Valentine's Day, ladies.' She looked at Beth and pointed at the card. 'Yours, I presume?'

'It is.'

Sophie grinned. Even though it wouldn't be signed, they knew it would be from Matt. He always sent her a card. She wondered if Beth ever wished it was sent with feeling rather than in humour. Or maybe it was. She reached for it and put it on display.

'Hey!' Beth tried to take it down but her fingers were slapped away gently.

'True love needs to be acknowledged,' Sophie teased.

'It would be, if it was love.' Beth pointed at Nicci who was smiling brightly. Behind her was a single red rose in a cellophane box and a red heart-shaped helium balloon. 'That's real love.'

Sophie smiled, thinking about the secret wedding they were organising. She really hoped it all went to plan. And at least it stopped her thinking of Damien, who had started to invade her thoughts over the past few days because of Valentine's Day. Was it really a month since he'd come to find her in the stock room? She wondered what lucky woman would be the recipient of flowers from him this year.

'You had anything from Reece?' Beth asked.

Sophie shook her head, blushing slightly for thinking of someone else. 'Just a card. We're far too married for that.'

Sophie had deliberated about it for a while and then wondered why. Even though a card seemed false and a little over the top at the moment, it was a token gesture she was happy to go along with.

So when a bouquet of flowers was delivered to the stall an hour later, she was left a little shamefaced. She smiled, feeling her skin flushing as customers cooed at her.

But then goosebumps broke out over her skin as she wondered who they were from. Get a grip, she chastised herself. She opened the accompanying envelope and sighed with relief, thankful that Reece had put his name to them rather than leave it a mystery.

'Aw, flowers for you, too,' Nicci said. 'Aren't we the Valentine honeys.'

'Speak for yourself,' Beth said. 'I might have a card but it doesn't mean anything.'

Sophie raised her eyebrows at Nicci as Beth stared over at Matt.

Charley was in a great mood. That morning, she'd opened an email from Alex to find a Valentine e-card and a message that she'd memorised since reading it again and again. "I wish I could kiss my Valentine. One day I hope you will be mine."

Even the boys at school continually provoking her couldn't dampen her spirit. She was still thinking about it at lunchtime.

'I really wish I could meet him,' she told Sarah again as they sat on the steps eating their sandwiches at lunchtime. 'It was such a lovely card – with music and hearts and flowers.'

'*I* wish you'd stop talking about it. I'm getting a bit sick of hearing about him, Charl.'

Charley frowned. 'That's not a nice thing to say.'

'All I hear is Alex this and Alex that.' Sarah picked at the corner of her bread. 'Alex has done this and Alex has done that.'

'But I listen to you,' Charley protested, stung by her friend's words.

'I'm surprised you want to know me at all.'

'Oh, don't be stupid.' Charley brushed crumbs from her shirt. 'I talk to him because he doesn't know anything about me.'

'I thought he knew *everything* about you. You've told him so much.'

'I mean—'

'I know what you mean.' Sarah raised her voice slightly as a lorry went rumbling past on the main road. 'But don't you think you ought to be more careful? He's someone you met online.'

'So?'

'So he isn't really a friend. He's someone you can talk to. I thought I was your best friend.'

'You are.' Charley paused. How could she explain to anyone how Alex made her feel? Just one look at his photograph made her go all squishy inside. She watched a group of boys from her year walk past. None of them were a patch on Alex, she mused, especially when they started pointing at her and laughing.

'He's so ... lovely,' she continued. 'He's always there for me—'

'No, he's not. He's on Facebook every now and then at the same time as you.'

Charley raised her eyebrows. 'We arrange times to be online, if you must know.'

'Like we used to,' Sarah said pointedly.

'Like we still do.'

'Whenever you aren't talking to him.'

Charley sighed. 'I like him. He never judges me, and he makes me—'

'What's that supposed to mean?'

'You don't understand what it's like being me. People at school don't call you names.'

'You should ignore them.'

'That's easy for you to say. Who called me Charley Cock-head this morning? I heard someone shout it when we went to double maths.'

Sarah laughed.

But Charley didn't find it funny. She screwed up her silver foil and shoved it into the bin.

'For your information, I'm sick of you laughing at me too.' She glared at her friend.

'I'm not laughing *at* you,' Sarah insisted.

'Yes, you are. And a true friend wouldn't do that. A true friend would support me. That's why I like talking to Alex.'

Sarah huffed. 'You really need to chill out. Stop getting your knickers in a twist. Not everyone is out to get you.'

'You're as bad as the rest of them.' Charley stood up. 'I can't believe you'd turn on me too.' She began to walk away, shouting over her shoulder. 'Alex doesn't judge me.'

'Charley,' Sarah shouted. 'Charley, wait up.'

Charley didn't stop. No wonder she was always thinking

about Alex. She had no one else to talk to. He was the only person who completely understood her.

After work, Jess had arranged to meet Ryan in the stock room. She'd bought him some aftershave for Valentine's Day. She knew he wouldn't be able to take it home, but that hadn't been her intention anyway. Instead, she planned to keep the aftershave in the stock room and bring it out whenever they met up illicitly there. It would be their secret – their code, in fact. She'd purposely bought him Armani Code as a joke between the two of them.

Ryan arrived in the stock room some ten minutes after her. It was nearly six as they'd had to wait until everyone had gone home. Even though there was a caretaker to lock up every night, all stallholders had front entrance keys. Ryan had told Mike he would set the alarms on the main doors once he'd finished stocktaking. Now, they were all alone.

'Hey.' Ryan walked towards her, carrying a red gift bag.

'Hey, yourself,' she replied.

They kissed passionately. Jess pressed her body close to his and ran her hands over his back. They pulled apart and he thrust the gift bag into her hands.

'For you, my Valentine,' he smiled, raining kisses over her face. 'Sorry I don't have much time.'

Jess pulled out a box of perfume. She unwrapped it and sprayed it around liberally.

'It's gorgeous,' she smiled and kissed him again. As the scent of water lilies and white birch enveloped them, they slipped to the floor.

Nicci couldn't wait to get home that evening after the text message she'd received from Jay earlier in the day.

'I have something waiting for you on the table.'

All the way home, she wondered what it could be. By the time she opened the front door, she was bursting with anticipation. She could smell something cooking. She sniffed. Ooh, curry. She hoped it was one of Jay's specials.

She took off her coat and almost ran through to the kitchen. But it was no different to how she'd left it this morning. The table wasn't set for a romantic meal for two.

Confused, Nicci went through to the living room, then smiled as she stood in the doorway. Jay was sitting on the floor, his back to the settee. His chest was bare, his legs covered with the duvet from upstairs. Next to him, the coffee table was piled high with food, a candle lit either end. There was wine chilling in an ice bucket, chocolates waiting to be opened.

Nicci giggled. 'You meant coffee table, didn't you?'

'Actually, I didn't,' Jay said. He stood up, the duvet dropping to reveal his nakedness. 'I intend to ravish you over the kitchen table.'

'What about Jess?'

'She's not coming home until ten. I bribed her.'

Nicci beamed. Despite what she'd done behind Jay's back, at least he wanted to make her happy. And he clearly still loved her – as she did of him.

Who cared if she had to wait a couple of years to marry him? It would be worth it to become his wife.

CHAPTER THIRTY-FOUR

Over the next fortnight, Sophie was kept so busy arranging the details for Nicci's secret wedding that she didn't have time to think about herself. There was a lot to organise before the date, set for the second Sunday in April, but at least now she had a list of definite things to show Beth and Jay, who were the only two people who knew for now.

They'd met up to discuss things, Jay pretending he was working overtime. So far the hotel Nicci had booked the reception at had emailed back and offered a reduced rate as an incentive to rebook, but wouldn't do anything about giving a refund for the deposit she had paid. After discussing finances with Jay, she'd managed to negotiate a luxury room for the wedding night instead.

Sophie had decided to call everyone together at the end of the week and announce it in one go. It would be far easier that way, and time was short with only a few weeks to go. They needed to keep it quiet, so thought it was best to spring it on people as late as possible. She studied her list again:

Dress – Jay had given her details of a particular one that Nicci had left notes about in her notebook. Nicci had also cut out a picture from a magazine, so Sophie was going to see about getting it sewn up at a fraction of the cost.

Shoes – she'd spoken to Riley at Chandler's Shoes and was due to go back to see if she had found anything suitable.

Melissa had said she'd do the make-up for all of the women in the bridal party. Charley, Beth and Ryan's twin girls were going to be bridesmaids, as per Nicci's notebook.

Mr Adams was making a cake like the one in the clipping Jay had brought for him from the wedding planning book.

All that was left to organise was the flowers. Sophie had given the florist notice of the wedding, and the colour scheme. All she needed to do was ask Jay if he knew Nicci's favourite flower.

Sophie put the list away in her pocket. All in all, planning a wedding without letting the bride know was still possible but it would take a lot of organisation and co-ordination. Still, as queen-of-the-list-makers, she couldn't wait to get started. And at least it kept her mind from her own worries.

At five o'clock, Jay came to the market on the pretence that he'd knocked off work early after dropping off a delivery for his boss. Sophie suggested that Nicci might as well finish now that he was here, rather than hang around for another half hour. Once they'd gone and the doors to the general public had been closed, everyone gathered around her stall. Sophie stood at the front, Beth by her side.

'I won't keep you back for long,' she shouted, looking around at a sea of puzzled faces, 'but we have something we need your help with.'

She told everyone about Nicci and Jay's story. Not about the debt and the on-off wedding proposal, but about a hard-working couple who were struggling to plan their big day. She then asked for offers of help to make the day perfect for them.

Everyone began to pipe up with ideas. Sophie held up a hand as they all spoke at once.

'I have to explain first that there isn't much money so I'll need you to offer your services for as cheap as possible. Maybe even,' she paused, 'for free?'

'I wouldn't want paying,' Mr Adams said. 'Nicci's like one of our own.'

'And Jay too,' added Nigel Beaconsfield, from the butcher's counter.

'I love picking out wedding colours,' Melissa cried out in an excited pitch. 'I already have some in mind that I've seen. I know Nicci will love them, depending on the dress, of course.'

Beth's eyes teared up. 'Thanks, you guys,' she spoke quietly.

Sophie glanced around at everyone, still not quite believing what she'd heard. She caught Jess's eye, her face like thunder, but decided to ignore her. She wouldn't sabotage this wedding.

'Are you all sure you're happy to do this?' she asked again, to clarify.

'Of course we are.'

'Yes, absolutely.'

'She's a good girl, is Nicci.'

'And Jay's a great guy too.'

'Well, it looks like we have a secret wedding to plan,' Sophie shouted, amidst a few whoops and cheers.

Beth smiled at them. 'I can't thank you all enough. Nicci will be thrilled.'

Sophie nodded, along with a few other people. Weddings were so good for the soul. Then she remembered something else.

'Before we all disappear. Matt, Ryan?' she shouted. 'Are you still here?'

Ryan was back on his stall. 'Yep, still here.'

'Me too.' Matt appeared beside him.

'Jay wants you to be his best men. What do you say?'

Matt grinned and shook hands with Ryan. 'Looks like we'll have to do a joint speech.'

'Yeah, we can be double funny,' Ryan replied.

'Or double naff,' Malcolm shouted.

Everyone laughed and headed back to pack up their stalls for the evening.

Sophie high-fived Beth before hugging her. It looked like things might work out for Nicci after all.

'I know which one I'd say is the best out of the two of you,' Jess said to Ryan. 'I'd say that's definitely the right name for you. The best man,' she purred.

A couple of heads turned abruptly and Ryan caught a few frowns and strange looks. He seemed to pretend he hadn't heard anything and continued to banter with Matt.

But Beth and Sophie had clearly caught what Jess had said.

'What did she mean by that?' Beth asked.

'I'm not sure,' Sophie replied, not wanting to start an argument as they were all on a high after soliciting help for the wedding.

Ryan watched as everyone around him dispersed, hoping he'd got away with it being no more than a throwaway remark. He'd scowled at Jess to let her know that he was mad at her, and she'd sidled off back to the sweet stall with a dramatic sigh.

But Matt didn't let it go unnoticed. 'Did you meet up with her?' he wanted to know.

'A few times. I –'

'And have you screwed her?'

Ryan didn't speak but his silence gave Matt his reply.

'You ... you ...' Matt pointed his finger in Ryan's face. 'You lowlife piece of shit. You said you'd never—'

'It was only the once!' he lied. 'I admit that batting too close to home wasn't such a clever idea but I haven't seen her since.'

'And you expect me to believe that?' Matt grabbed his coat. 'You can lock up tonight. I need some fresh air before I punch you.'

'Mate, it's not what you—'

But Matt was already gone.

CHAPTER THIRTY-FIVE

At home, Jess thought about what she had done. Stupidly, she'd made some brash comment and now Ryan was angry with her. Things had been going so well after they'd met up in the store room on Valentine's Day, too.

Once most people had left the market that night, they'd had words about what she had said. He'd told her Matt had sussed what was going on. Jess had apologised but Ryan had stormed off regardless. Maybe she had pushed her luck a little too much.

She decided to bring her plan of action forward. She took a shower and sprayed herself liberally with the perfume Ryan had bought her. Sleeping with him again twice last week would have worked out in her favour too. It would make everything seem more believable. He'd fall for it, she was certain.

A few days later, Jess executed her fainting fit with precision. She knew that Matt and Ryan moved a lot of their electrical stock and locked it away in the stock room every evening in case anyone broke into the market. At the end of the day, while the traders were packing away, she watched the two of them leave their stall and followed behind carrying a plastic jar of sweets in the crook of each arm. She pushed open the door, saw them in front of her and suddenly dropped to the floor, letting the jars clatter to the ground.

Matt got to her first. 'Are you okay?' he asked, bending down to see.

Jess screwed up her eyes and frowned, as if she was trying to focus on them.

Ryan waved a hand in front of her eyes. 'What happened?' he asked. 'Did you slip?'

'I'm not sure,' Jess lied. She tried to get up, pretending that she was dizzy.

'Whoa.' Ryan steadied her by the arm. 'Are you sure you're okay?'

'Here.' Matt pulled a plastic chair from a stack at the side of the room. 'Sit down here a minute and get your colour back.'

Once Jess had their undivided attention, she decided it was now or never. 'I'm fine,' she said. 'I've just found out that I'm pregnant and—'

Ryan's hand moved from her arm. 'What?'

'I only found out yesterday. I was going to tell you.' Jess looked up at him, this time with tears in her eyes, hoping he didn't know too much about pregnancy.

'What's going on?' Matt glanced from one to the other. 'Tell me you're not responsible!'

'I can't be.' Ryan coughed after his voice came out as a squeak.

'You are,' Jess said quietly. 'I haven't been with anyone else.'

'But it's too soon.'

Matt glanced at Jess with disgust. 'You planned this, didn't you?'

'No!' Jess lied again. 'I would never trap anyone.'

'In that case, get rid of it.'

'You can't tell me what to do!'

'Too right, I can't.' He poked Ryan's chest. 'But he can. And he'd better do it soon. You prick.'

'What am I going to do?' Ryan paced the stock room. 'Cassie will kill me.'

'What do you mean, what are *you* going to do?' Jess challenged, suddenly forgetting all her earlier fainting antics. 'This is *our* baby. We're in this together.'

'In what together, exactly? I only slept with you because you threw yourself at me. What man in their right mind could refuse that?'

'I did,' Matt remarked.

'Shut up,' Ryan told him. 'I'm in enough trouble without you going on at me.'

Jess rested her hand on Ryan's arm. 'We're in this mess together. But it'll be okay, you'll see.'

'A mess, that's right,' Matt said before walking away. 'You two deserve each other.'

'Wait,' Ryan shouted after him.

But Matt didn't stop. The door back into the public area slammed shut behind him. Jess stood silently, wondering if her plan had worked or not.

Ryan began to pace again.

'I'm still here, you know,' Jess said, annoyed at being ignored. 'Maybe we should meet somewhere to discuss things?'

'Yeah, I think we should,' Ryan agreed. 'I'll meet you after we finish tonight and we—'

'I have a doctor's appointment.' It was a lie but Jess wanted to keep him keen.

'Tomorrow night, then.'

Ryan had at least stopped pacing but the look of fear on

his face made Jess feel secure. She had the upper hand for now. And once he'd got used to the idea, they could talk.

Charley wished she'd never come to meet her mum from work. While she'd waited for her to finish, Sophie had asked her to fetch some paper bags from the stock room. She'd opened the door to the sound of raised voices and saw Matt, Ryan and Jess up ahead. She should have walked away but natural curiosity got the better of her. Closing the door quietly, she'd sneaked across the room and hid at the side of a shelving unit in the distance.

From where she stood, she could hear some of the conversation. She held her breath as she watched first Matt, then her Uncle Ryan storm out of the stock room. A moment later, Jess followed and Charley was alone with her thoughts.

Her heart beating wildly, she stood for a while trying to put together the different snippets she'd heard.

Jess was pregnant and Matt was going to become a father. Charley's eyes brimmed with tears. She thought he cared about her mum, and if she was honest, she thought he cared about her as well. What would happen if there was a baby too, and with Jess? How was that going to work out? She and her mum would be out of the loop.

She shook her head, this wasn't happening. It couldn't happen. It would ruin everything.

CHAPTER THIRTY-SIX

The disagreement between Matt and Ryan continued when they were back on their stall.

'Is it yours?' Matt wanted to know. 'She's only been back since New Year. Have you been seeing her since then?'

Ryan wouldn't look him in the eye. 'She got under my skin, okay! I couldn't get enough of her. But I was about to knock it on the head because Cassie started to get suspicious.' He gulped. 'I told Cassie I was with you a couple of times.'

'I said I wouldn't cover for you,' Matt seethed, clenching and unclenching his fist.

'I'm sorry. She collared me about being home late again and I – I said the first thing that came into my head. That I was with you. I told her we'd started running to lose a bit of weight in time for the wedding. Best men, and all that.'

'But can't you see how awkward that is for me? I've known you both for years. I'm not going to lie to her. It makes me as devious as you.'

'Anyone would think I'd murdered someone and was asking you for an alibi. It's not such a big deal.'

'She's pregnant,' Matt cried, then lowered his voice, aware again of his surroundings. 'And you're not married to Jess.'

'Okay, okay. Keep your hair on!' Across the aisle, Ryan could see Sophie glancing over. He could tell she was wondering what was going on. 'How about if I talk to her, finish things and –'

'You can't hide a baby, you stupid –'

'I can deny being the father, though.'

'What?'

'Everyone knows Jess is a dick tease. Of course she could make out it was mine, but she could just as easily have come back from London pregnant. She's so thin she might not show for ages. And even I know it's a bit early. I reckon she's trying to trap me.'

Matt was astounded at his friend's nerve.

'Sometimes I don't understand how we've stayed mates for so long.' He shook his head. 'You make me sick at times. It's all about how Ryan can get away with it, isn't it? And this time it's come back to haunt you.' He pointed at Jess who was also watching them carefully. 'If you think you can walk away from her, then you're stupid.'

'She won't say anything.' Ryan shook his head as if to make himself believe that. 'And I'm going to finish it anyway.'

'She's got you over a barrel.' Matt glared at him before he really did punch him.

But Ryan was watching Jess.

'Look at her anymore and everyone will know what you're up to,' he snapped. 'especially after that best man comment the other day.'

This time, Ryan looked away swiftly.

Sophie had watched Matt tear into Ryan across on their stall. 'What's going on over there?' she asked Beth.

Beth stopped what she was doing and turned to look.

'Beats me,' she said. 'But Matt looks fit to burst. Oi, you two,' she shouted across to them. 'You sound like a pair of girls in a catfight. What's up?'

But the men ignored her. They were too busy arguing to respond.

'Charming.' Beth spotted Charley coming back. 'Did you see anything going on with those two while you were in the stock room?'

'No.' Charley shook her head. 'I didn't see them.'

Charley rushed through to the back room, for fear her reddening cheeks would give her away. What was she going to do?

She wished she had someone to confide in. She couldn't tell her mum – she wouldn't be able to keep it a secret. And if she hadn't fallen out with Sarah, she could have rung her. Sophie would be an obvious choice but it would be hard to get her alone. Or maybe she should ask Matt? Or even have it out with Jess?

Charley couldn't decide. In the meantime, she'd have to act like nothing had happened.

'Good day at school, Charl?' Beth called out to her.

'Glad it's over,' came her reply.

'Sounds about right. I hated it too.' Beth removed her apron and washed her hands.

'Beth?' Matt appeared suddenly. 'Do you want a lift home? I'm heading off soon. Hey, Charl, how goes it?'

Charley stiffened. Matt smiled, but she couldn't look at him. Pushing past him, she walked away.

'Don't you want a lift home with us?' Matt shouted after her.

'What does it look like?'

'Charley?' She heard her mum shout but she ignored her. There was no way she was getting into Matt's car until she got to the bottom of this mess. She would email Alex. He would tell her what to do.

'What's up with her?' Matt looked puzzled. What was it with people today?

'Beats me.' Beth grabbed her coat. 'Too many hormones, I reckon. She's been a right moody sod lately.'

'Takes after her mother,' Sophie said from behind them. Matt sniggered.

'Ha, ha.' Beth's voice was thick with sarcasm. 'Anyway, Matt – care to tell us what you and my brother were falling out about?'

'It's nothing.' Matt's shoulders drooped. 'Just boys' stuff.'

'That's worse than womens' problems,' Sophie giggled.

'If it weren't for you women, we men wouldn't be falling out in the first place.'

'Why, you cheeky—'

'You little—'

Even though they were joking around, Matt turned abruptly and went back to the stall. He opened his mouth to speak to Ryan but decided better of it. Instead, he grabbed his coat and stormed off down the aisle.

He couldn't stand to be in the fool's company a minute longer.

CHAPTER THIRTY-SEVEN

The following day, Matt was buying lunch for him and Ryan from the high street. He'd come out of Somerley Stores with two pies when someone tapped him on the shoulder.

'That's far too fattening for a best man to eat,' a voice rang out.

Matt turned to see Cassie smiling at him.

'Not that there's an ounce of fat on you anyway,' she continued.

'Hi Cassie.' Matt returned her smile, but inside he was dying. She was the last person he wanted to bump into. 'Haven't seen you in a while. How are you?'

Cassie sighed. 'Busy as usual. What with the wedding coming up and the girls so excited about being bridesmaids, I don't have time to think.'

Matt nodded. 'I'm really looking forward to it.'

Cassie laughed. 'But you're a man. You're supposed to hate that type of thing.'

Matt shrugged. 'I suppose I'm not your stereotypical man.'

Cassie sighed. 'I wish Ryan was the romantic kind. He hasn't got an ounce of it in him.'

At the mention of Ryan's name, Matt's guilt surfaced. Despite the goings on, it looked like Cassie hadn't got a clue about Jess, nor the baby. As a friend, he desperately wanted to tell her, but knew it wasn't his place. He changed the subject quickly.

'I hope we can keep everything secret.'

They walked side by side through the shoppers, chatting amicably. Soon they were at the entrance to the market.

'Are you coming in?' Matt asked as he held open the door, already dreading the scene if Jess caught sight of Cassie.

But Cassie shook her head. 'Tell Ryan he'd better be on time tonight, though. I'm tired of him coming home late.' She smiled. 'It's no wonder there isn't any excess weight on you, with all those miles you clocked up last week.'

The smile slipped from Matt's face before he checked himself. But his silence spoke volumes, along with the blush creeping across his face. As the shoppers of Somerley went about their daily business around them, Cassie stared at him.

Shit, thought Matt. *Think of something to say ...*

'I think he's taking this best man thing a little too seriously.'

Cassie's eyes dropped to the floor for a moment and when she lifted them again, they were watery.

'I've known you long enough now to know when you're lying,' she said. 'You're covering up for Ryan. What's going on?'

'I'd better get back.' Matt jerked a thumb over his shoulder. 'He'll be wondering where I've got to.'

Cassie held on to his arm with a firm grip. 'Is he playing around again?'

Matt gulped. 'I– I don't know what you mean.'

She continued to stare at him, making him feel uncomfortable, as if she was trying to read his mind. All of a sudden, she let go of his arm.

'Sorry,' she said quietly. 'I shouldn't hassle you. It isn't you at fault. I've had my suspicions.' Her eyes dropped to the floor for a moment. 'One more thing. Exactly how many times did you not go running with him?'

'I ... I ...'

'It's okay.' She nodded. 'I get the picture.'

The wedding chatter was going on behind the scenes now. Everything seemed to be fitting into place nicely. Beth was pleased that it would all work out well for her sister, but she couldn't help feeling envious. She knew she was a strong woman and didn't need a man to validate herself, but she missed being in a secure and loving relationship; the feel of an arm around you as you slept.

While there was a lull in customers, Ryan came over. He noticed her mood straightaway.

'What's up with you?' he asked as she gave out yet another heavy sigh.

'I don't know,' she replied. 'I'm sick of everything at the moment. I feel like my life is so boring.'

'Tell me about it,' Ryan agreed.

'Don't you sometimes wish you could up sticks and move away, where no one knows you? Maybe start again?'

'Yep, but it isn't that easy.'

'You two are always the same,' Nicci shouted as she reached over for a bunch of bananas. 'It's enough to make me get out my violin. I wish you'd both cheer up.'

'We can't all be sunny and positive like you,' Beth retorted.

'Yeah, shut up Little Miss Sunshine.' Ryan nudged her arm, making her drop one of the potatoes she was now packing into a bag.

'You never change.' Nicci retrieved it as it rolled away. 'Even when we were younger, you were always moaning about something or other. You should be thankful for what you've got.'

'And you're our younger sister, so we should be lecturing you,' Beth said. 'Although I do agree with you, for once. I don't know what's wrong with me half of the time. I think I need a man.'

'I thought you said you were through with men,' Nicci retorted.

'There's only so much time I can spend in my own company without going loopy.'

'Maybe Sophie will start coming out with you again now Reece is home permanently,' Ryan said.

'Permanently?' Beth frowned. 'I don't know what you mean.'

'He's got work in Hedworth for the next twelve months.' Ryan paused. 'She never told you they fell out?'

'No, she didn't.'

'Me neither,' added Nicci.

'He came home one Friday night and some fella turned up on the doorstep with flowers and that was that,' Ryan explained. 'He stayed in Sheffield for a while but now they've decided to give it another go. He moved back a couple of weeks ago. I can't believe she hasn't said anything.'

'No, neither can I.' Beth couldn't hide her discomfort.

'Ah.'

She turned to look at the back room where Sophie was. Upset, she wondered why she hadn't told her what had happened. And who had turned up with flowers – it must have been Damien. She'd wondered why his name had become off limits so quickly.

But what hurt the most was why hadn't Sophie confided in her? They were supposed to be good friends.

CHAPTER THIRTY-EIGHT

In the staff room, Sophie had heard all of Ryan's conversation. In fact, she'd cringed through every word of it. While she waited for Beth to come and speak to her, she rubbed at her neck.

'Why didn't you tell me you and Reece had fallen out?' Beth demanded as she barged in.

Sophie closed her eyes momentarily and pinched the bridge of her nose. 'Because I didn't know if it was permanent. As it turned out, it wasn't.'

'So I'm not good enough to confide in now, is that it?'

'Don't be silly. I was so ashamed over what happened with Damien and I didn't want to talk about it.'

Beth looked like she was going to burst. 'You fall out with Reece but you don't want to talk to me?'

'Don't make a big deal out of it,' Sophie pleaded. 'It's a little raw right now, okay?'

Beth folded her arms. 'Were you ever going to tell me at some point?'

'Of course.'

'Before or after you'd shacked up with Damien?'

Sophie shut the laptop lid. It was clear Beth wasn't going to let things drop.

'I keep telling you, nothing happened between us.'

'Did Reece find you with him?'

'No!' Sophie pushed the door closed with a kick. 'And do you mind not airing all my dirty laundry in public?'

Beth lowered her voice. 'So what happened?'

'Reece came home unannounced one Friday evening. The weekend before he'd told me he was planning on going to Germany for two or three months.'

'Germany?'

'Yes, but he wasn't going really. He was testing me to see if I would make a fuss about it.'

'And you didn't?'

Sophie shook her head. 'Because I was all messed up about Damien.'

'And how did he come to be there?'

'Reece turned up unexpectedly. We were chatting, trying to work things out when Damien knocked on the door. I had no idea he was coming either.'

'No way.' Beth covered her mouth with her hand.

Sophie nodded. 'When Reece saw him, and the flowers, he flipped. I can't say I blame him. He's back now, and we're going to make a go of it, so I was hoping not to have this conversation.'

'Why not? I'm your friend. We usually share everything. A problem shared is a problem halved, you know that.'

'Of course I do. But you're also friends with Reece.'

'I have more loyalty to you!'

'I didn't want to talk about how awful I felt, knowing I'd hurt him. I didn't want to explain how I thought I'd effectively thrown my marriage down the drain, even though I hadn't slept with Damien.'

Beth looked confused. 'You didn't sleep with Damien?'

'No.'

Beth was shamefaced. 'I thought—'

'You see?' Sophie shook her head in disdain. She'd had enough of Beth's insinuations. 'Ask yourself the real reason I didn't tell you about Reece leaving. It's because you don't care about anyone but yourself. You're so wrapped up in Beth's little world that you haven't noticed how upset your best friend's been.'

'I—'

'You're so wrapped up in Beth's little world that you also don't see that something is eating at Charley and needs to be sorted.'

'But—'

'And the worst of it all?' Sophie found she couldn't stop now that she'd started. 'You're so wrapped up in Beth's little world that you wouldn't even care if anyone else had a problem that they might want to talk about. All you want to do is talk about yourself.'

Beth stood still for a moment after Sophie had finished. Then she grabbed her coat and handbag.

'I don't have to listen to this,' she said. 'I'm going home. Tell the boss I have a headache.'

'Yes, run away rather than face the music,' Sophie snapped.

Beth stormed out of the room.

Nicci, who was on her way in after hearing raised voices, looked up as she flew past her.

'Beth, what's wrong?'

'Everything!' Beth turned back to her sister. 'There seems to be an awful lot of secrets around here at the moment and that's without this bloody wedding!'

'What wedding?' Nicci frowned. 'Who's getting married?'

CHAPTER THIRTY-NINE

It was Saturday evening, and Beth and Charley were having a standoff in Beth's bedroom. At that particular moment, it wasn't clear who had the upper hand.

'I don't want to be looked after by Matt,' Charley snapped at her mum. 'I'm old enough to look after myself.'

'I know that.' Beth ran a comb through her wet hair, 'but I might be really late. Besides, the law says that—'

'You just want to go out. You're so selfish, thinking of yourself all the time.'

What was it with everyone, just lately? That was the second person who had called her selfish that week. Beth and Sophie weren't exactly on speaking terms after their earlier bust up.

'Oi.' Beth prodded Charley in the arm. 'Less of the cheek or else you're grounded.'

'You won't do that because you'd have to stay in then.'

'No, Matt would still be available to look after you. Anyway, there was a time a few weeks ago when you couldn't wait for me to go out.'

'I'll only be in my room or in front of the telly,' Charley tried to reason with her mum again. 'I don't need him here.'

'Maybe not, but he's coming round nonetheless.'

'Oh, whatever.' Charley flung her legs off the bed and flounced out of the room and into her own.

Beth wondered if she should stay in with the girls. But she wanted a break from normality and this was the only way she could get it. Besides, she had all day Sunday to share with Charley.

She'd make it up to her tomorrow.

Jay and Nicci had gone out for a meal so Jess had the house to herself. Yet she was hiding away in her room curled up on her bed, squeezing her eyes tightly to stop tears from falling.

With silence all around her, the house seemed as empty as she felt. Her mind wouldn't let go of the conversation she'd overheard between Ryan and Matt. They'd thought they'd lowered their voices enough for no one to hear, but she had caught every word.

Ryan was going to deny the baby was his. He'd also denied having any feelings for her. He'd called her a slapper. Said she'd been gagging for it. Matt had surprised her by saying that Ryan was the bigger slapper of the two. He'd walked off then, and she had pretended to be busy when Ryan had looked in her direction.

Jess knew she might be able to win Ryan over. He needed attention as much as she did. But she realised now that getting involved with him had been a stupid thing to do, a gut reaction on the rebound because Laurie hadn't wanted to know. She didn't want to be anyone's bit on the side anymore. And, let's face it, did she really think after they'd slept together a few times he would fall in love with her and leave his wife and children to be with her?

More to the point, had she been thinking at all? She knew as soon as she'd told them she was pregnant that it was a selfish and childish thing she'd done. She could barely look at herself in a mirror.

She turned over onto her back and ran a hand over her stomach. She had two people to think about now. This little thing inside her deserved more from its mother.

'I won't let you down, bump,' she whispered.

As Jess contemplated her future that night, so too did Sophie. She sat on the settee in her living room looking at, but not watching, some drivel on the television. Reece was on the other settee, legs stretched out. It was Saturday evening. He'd been asleep for over half an hour and it was only just gone eight o'clock.

It was strange to think that they'd only been living together again for two weeks. When he'd first come home, they'd been spending time together and chatting over nice meals. But already they were sitting at either ends of the living room, with hardly a bit of conversation between them.

She wondered how long it would take to adjust to having Reece home full time. It certainly wasn't coming naturally. Did they both want this to work but it was too damaged to fix – or perhaps things would settle down in time? It was bound to be awkward at first, but they could get through it, couldn't they?

Reece gave a loud snore, waking himself up momentarily. He opened his eyes, caught her looking at him and winked before closing them again.

Sophie sighed. She was as lonely now as she had been before Reece moved back. Except now she felt crowded too. Fighting for space to call her own. It seemed so strange having him home again.

If this was what being part of Reece and Sophie was, she wasn't sure if she'd ever get used to it again. Or if she even wanted to.

As soon as he got to Beth's house that evening, Matt wanted to know what was wrong with Charley. He'd noticed she'd been cold with him for a few days but he hadn't got a clue what he'd done to upset her. Usually when he came to look after her, she would run to him, arms thrown around his neck in greeting and he would tease her affectionately. But tonight she was in her room and even when he shouted up to her, she didn't reply.

'What's wrong with Charley?' he asked Beth while he made himself a coffee.

Beth, who was busy finishing off her make-up at the kitchen table, shrugged. 'I don't know, but she's really annoying me lately. It's as if she doesn't want me to go out and enjoy myself.'

'Have you ever thought she might want to spend some time in with you?'

Beth stopped applying her mascara and glared at him through the enhanced eyelashes on one eye. 'I only go out at the weekends, and I deserve it. I work all week.'

'So do I but I don't feel the need to get off my trolley drunk every Saturday.'

'That's because you're a bore.'

'Thanks for that.'

'Well, I don't know another man who stays in as much as you, despite doing a favour for me. And what about Lorraine? What does she say about it?'

'About me being at your beck and call all the time? Or about me not wanting to get bladdered every Saturday night?'

'You know what I meant.' Beth pumped the mascara wand in and out of the container.

'If I did go out every weekend, then you wouldn't be able to, so I'd quit while you're ahead.' Matt stirred his drink and then took it into the living room.

Beth followed him.

'What's wrong with *you*?' she asked. 'You're not usually this grumpy. Have you fallen out with Lorraine?'

Matt sat down and grabbed the television remote control. 'If you must know, we've split up.'

'Oh, no.' Beth sat down next to him. 'When did this happen?'

'Last night.'

'Any particular reason why?' she pressed.

Matt shrugged. 'It wasn't really working.'

'Well, you know you can spend as much time around here as you like, and that doesn't mean babysitting all the time.' Beth paused. 'It's not anything to do with me and Charl, is it?'

'No. I won't let any woman dictate to me who I can and can't see.'

'That's good to hear. I mean, for Charley. She really enjoys having you around.'

'Apart from this last week.'

'Yes, I've seen the way she's been acting around you. Have you said something to upset her?'

'I don't think so but she's been really funny since I saw her in the market. I can't think—'

'What's the matter?' Beth prompted when Matt stopped.

'Nothing.' Matt frowned, remembering the last time he'd seen Charley. It was after he'd been in the stock room with Ryan and Jess. Had she overheard them talking? He changed the subject. 'Has Sophie forgiven you yet?'

When Beth had blurted out about the secret wedding, Sophie had been furious. But Nicci had been delighted and hadn't stopped talking about it since. She'd rung Jay immediately and cooed down the phone at him. At least for now, she had no idea where the reception was being held. They had managed to keep that secret. And Nicci seemed pleased she had time to enjoy it too.

'I'm not getting the silent treatment anymore,' Beth said. 'Me and my big mouth. At least Nicci doesn't know everything that's happening on the day.'

A horn peeped outside. Beth jumped to her feet, checked her appearance in the mirror above the fireplace and pouted. She turned back to Matt and planted a kiss on his cheek.

'Thanks for this. I won't be too late. Are you stopping over or going home?'

'That depends on how late you are.'

But Beth was already gone.

CHAPTER FORTY

Matt went to the window and once the taxi was out of view, he went upstairs. From the landing, he could see Charley through the half open door. She was lying on her bed, watching television. He knocked and she glanced at him before returning her eyes to the screen.

'Can I come in?' Matt stood on the threshold.

Charley shrugged.

He stepped inside the room, then stood in silence, unsure what to say. When it was clear she wasn't going to say anything to him, he sat next to her on the bed.

'What's wrong? It's not like you to ignore me.'

'It's because you hurt me.' Charley drew her knees up to her chest and hugged herself.

'I *hurt* you?' Matt raised his eyebrows. 'Have you heard something that's worrying you?'

'If it was a good thing to hear, you wouldn't be asking me that.'

'I don't follow.' Actually he did, but Matt needed to be sure.

'I always thought having no dad around was good because

I got to spend time with you. You've always been like a dad to me, someone who I could have a laugh with.'

Matt noticed the subtle change from present to past tense. 'What is it, Charl?'

Charley had tears in her eyes, obviously struggling to keep in her emotions. 'I thought you cared for Lorraine. And my mum. I thought you cared for her too.'

'I did care for Lorraine but that's over between us now.'

That threw Charley for a moment. 'Oh.'

'And I do care for your mum. You too.' Matt leaned forward to tilt up her chin. 'I hate to see you upset.'

'You won't have time for me, or Mum now, will you?' Charley pulled her head back. 'Not now that you've got Jess pregnant.'

Matt closed his eyes for a moment. He knew it. Bloody Ryan Pellington!

'I didn't get Jess pregnant.'

'Yes, you did. I heard you talking about it. You, Uncle Ryan and that – that bitch.'

Matt bit on his bottom lip as he wondered how to get out of this one. If he lied to Charley, he'd run the risk of losing her respect forever. But if he told her the truth, not only would he land Ryan in it, but he'd then be in trouble with Beth for covering up for him – and not telling her that her own brother had cheated on his wife again.

And if any of this got back to Cassie, then all hell would break loose and she might even take the twins away from their father. He couldn't have it on his conscience. There was too much at stake.

'If it wasn't you, who was it then?' Charley asked.

'I – I can't tell you.'

'It was you. You're trying to deny it!'

'No, it wasn't me. It's ...' Matt couldn't say Ryan's name. 'Complicated.'

But Charley had worked it out. 'Uncle Ryan?' she gasped. '*He* got Jess pregnant.'

Matt was still at a loss as to what to say. 'You need to let the grown-ups sort this out.'

'How could he do that? And ... oh, no. He was the one denying everything, wasn't he?'

Matt didn't answer that. 'Think how your auntie Cassie would feel if you went over there blurting all this out? She won't want to believe you.'

'You're wrong. I'm her niece. And I know he's done it before. I might not be *grown up* but I do know these things.'

Matt stayed quiet then. He could only dream of the pain this would cause Cassie after the last time.

'I think you should talk to your mum about this in the morning,' he said. 'Someone will tell Cassie, when they think the time is right.'

'But you were covering for him.'

'No, I wasn't really. I didn't want Cassie to get hurt.'

'He met Jess anyway, didn't he?' When Matt said nothing, Charley shouted, 'The sneaky bastard.'

Although Matt agreed, he tried to reason with her. 'I'll speak to your mum first and see what she wants to do. Maybe it'll sort itself out but we mustn't make things worse for Cassie, okay?'

Charley nodded.

'I'm sorry,' she told him, shamefaced. 'I guess I didn't want to lose you either. I like that you come around all the time and I was scared that you wouldn't.'

'Does that mean I have to suffer some dross on the television downstairs then?'

Charley grinned.

'It does, doesn't it?' Matt clicked his fingers with the wave of a hand. 'Damn. We should have had this conversation later on.'

'Shall I run to the shop and get us some goodies?' she suggested.

Matt nodded. 'It's a deal.' He held out his hand and she shook it. Then he gave her a hug. 'I'd never do anything to hurt you. I love you like you were my own daughter.'

'I'm sorry,' Charley said. 'One day I hope to find someone as lovely as you.'

'I doubt there's anyone else out there as good as me,' he chuckled. Although, he wished Beth could see that she had someone special right underneath her nose.

Beth had been out for two hours, yet she was still sober. She'd gone into Hedworth to meet up with Melissa from work but couldn't relax into the night.

For the first time in ages, she wanted to be at home. She wished she was sitting on the settee with Charley and Matt eating pizza and sharing a bottle of something chilled. She glanced at her watch. Was it too early to admit defeat?

Melissa had spotted someone she knew and had been off once they'd bought drinks. It was someone Beth vaguely recognised but couldn't be bothered to go and chat to. She glanced around the bar, its clientele of mixed ages. In front of her were three women and three men out together as couples. To her right, two teenagers getting to know each other a bit too much, considering they were out in public. To her left were a couple in their mid-forties laughing about something or other.

Everyone seemed to be with someone.

For as long as she'd been going out in the pubs and clubs around Hedworth, Saturday nights had been known as couples' night. Friday nights were nights out with friends, so it never seemed as obvious that she was lonely. But Saturdays, when she thought it was imperative to have a man or risk feeling out of place, was when Beth felt her loneliest.

Tears welled in her eyes as she caught a glimpse of Melissa. It looked like she was exchanging phone numbers with the guy now. And what did she have to look forward to? It would be another boring week, working on the market stall and going home to sit on her own while Charley stayed in her room and chatted to her friends online.

Beth would love to have someone show a bit of interest in her. She wasn't bad looking for her age. She didn't dress slutty – well, not too obviously anyway. She was clean and tidy, and so was the house. She worked hard for what she had and had a good sense of humour.

She laughed inwardly at her thoughts. It sounded as if she was reading a profile on a dating site.

Melissa re-joined her after a few more minutes, a huge grin plastered on her face. 'That was Simon,' she shouted above the background noise. 'He's going to call me in the week and arrange a night we can meet.'

'How flipping marvellous,' Beth shouted back, her voice dripping with sarcasm.

'What? I can't hear you.'

'I said, that's great.'

As Melissa was pacified with this answer, Beth decided she'd had enough and called it a night. Charley was asleep on the sofa when she arrived home just before eleven. Matt was watching a football match. He indicated his surprise with raised eyebrows.

'I know, I know.' Beth sighed. 'I must be getting old. I wanted to come home.'

'Do you have a thermometer?' Matt gasped comically. 'I think you must be coming down with something.'

Beth grinned. 'I'm making a cuppa. Want one?'

'Sure. Although I think you might need something stronger … I have something to tell you.'

'That doesn't sound good.'

Matt followed Beth into the kitchen and closed the door so as not to wake Charley.

'Let me guess.' She grinned. 'You've had a call from Lorraine and she's pregnant so you're stuck with her.' But then she turned away abruptly. Although she made a joke of it, inside she prayed it wouldn't be true. She didn't know what she'd do without Matt popping in as much as he did, plus helping her out with Charley, being there whenever she needed him.

'It isn't me who got someone pregnant,' said Matt. 'It's Ryan.'

Beth turned back quickly.

'I shouldn't be telling you but Charley overheard us talking. It's why she's been funny with me.' He paused. 'It's Jess who Ryan has knocked up.'

Beth covered her mouth with her hand. Oh, no, this was awful.

'That's not the worst of it. Cassie knows about the affair too.'

CHAPTER FORTY-ONE

'You will never guess what happened yesterday,' Beth said to
Sophie the minute she got into work the next morning. 'I was
going to text you, then I thought I'd ring you, but it's not my
secret to tell and—'

'You mean you've actually kept something to yourself for
twenty-four hours?' Sophie sniggered.

'Yes. Don't sound so surprised.'

'Well, you certainly didn't keep the one about the wedding
to yourself.'

'I didn't blurt that out on purpose.' Beth leaned in close to
Sophie, ignoring her tone. She was dying to talk to someone.
'If you must know, our Ryan has been sleeping with Jess and
now she's pregnant.'

'No! I mean, are you sure?'

'Matt told me. Jess told him and Ryan.'

'Wow, I'm surprised you kept it to yourself at all, the way
you revel in watching other people's downfalls.'

'That's really mean, Soph.' Beth looked hurt.

'It was a joke.'

'I didn't have a go at you when you were having a fling with Damien.'

'That's not the same.'

'It's *exactly* the same. You were messing around with him—'

'I was not messing around with him!'

'—just like Ryan was having an affair with Jess. It *is* exactly the same. You were both cheating on other people. You're as bad as each other.'

'It's not ...'

A rush of customers came to the stall. But even after they had gone, Beth was still stung by Sophie's words. She appreciated she was out of order too; she shouldn't have said what she did about Damien. What was happening to them lately? They used to be such good friends. Now they were all falling out. Ryan and Matt, Charley and Sarah, her and Sophie. Thank goodness she and Sophie never let an argument fester.

That Jess had a lot to answer for.

And after seeing how upset Sophie was, Beth couldn't risk Cassie getting hurt too. She would bide her time, but she would tackle Jess and tell her to back off her brother. And then decide when she would tell Cassie.

On the other side of the stall, Nicci was a happy girl. She couldn't believe everyone around her would do all that for her and Jay. And although she loved the idea of a secret wedding – once Sophie had got over the fact that Beth had let slip their plans – she also cherished the fact that she could now join in with the excitement.

'I'm getting married in three weeks, can you believe that?' she said. 'I never thought it would happen. Oh, it's going to be magical. I'm so glad that Hedworth Registry Office opens seven days a week now.'

Sophie smiled. Last night, they'd had a get together and discussed where they were at with the arrangements. Nicci was blown away with the organising. So too with the generosity of the stallholders, most of whom she'd grown up beside.

'Everyone loves a wedding, don't they?' Nicci sighed with content.

Sophie rolled her eyes at Beth. Even though she was looking forward to Nicci and Jay's, weddings were the furthest thing from her mind at the moment.

Having now had time to think things through, Jess had made her mind up about what to do next. Tears welled in her eyes as she pressed a hand to her stomach, feeling the delicate bulge, knowing that it would soon be visible to everyone else, wondering what people would say when she was the talk of the market. Apart from Ryan and Matt, she hadn't told anyone about the baby.

At lunchtime while she was in the stock room, she texted Ryan to let him know where she was. When he didn't appear after five minutes, she rang him.

'I'm waiting for you in—'

'Yeah, I know. I'll be there.' The phone went dead.

Jess hugged herself against the cold of the room. It was mid-March and although it was fairly mild outside, sometimes the stock room could be as cold as the middle of winter. She sat down on a pile of boxes and waited.

A few minutes passed before the door opened. She looked up to see Ryan approaching.

'What do you want?' His tone was sharp.

'You,' Jess said quietly. 'It wasn't long ago that I gave you a blow job behind these boxes.'

'I haven't forgotten.' Ryan was silenced for now.

Jess took a step towards him and pushed him out of sight behind the boxes. 'Good. Because I didn't want you to come to the stock room to talk.' She pushed him back some more. 'I wanted to be somewhere that no one can see us. Somewhere we can be private. Do things in private, if you catch my meaning.'

Ryan's back was against the wall now. Jess placed a hand on his crotch and leaned forward to kiss him. He groaned as her tongue searched the inside of his mouth, his hand moving to clasp her breast. She left it there for a moment, then pushed him away roughly.

'Just as I'd suspected.' She wiped her mouth in disgust.

Ryan looked baffled.

'You are *more* of a slapper than me.' Jess prodded him in the chest sharply. 'You only think of yourself. I heard you the other night, talking to Matt. "Everyone knows Jess is a dick tease," you said. "I reckon she's trying to trap me," you said.'

Ryan stood motionless. 'I was ... I didn't ...'

She held up a hand. 'But you were right about one thing.' Jess paused and with a sigh continued. 'The baby isn't yours.'

'If you'd only listen to me ... I— what?'

'This little squirt.' Jess placed her hand protectively over her stomach. 'This is my mistake.'

'But why did you tell me it was mine?'

'Because I wasn't thinking straight, and I was lonely and I could see you were easy to manipulate.'

'You – you –'

'Lost for words? I thought you wanted to finish things with me. That's what you told Matt. That I was a sleep around.'

For a moment, Ryan was quiet. Then he glared at Jess with such venom that tears pricked her eyes.

'As much as I'm glad to be out of this situation and as

much as I am equally to blame,' he said, 'that is still some fucking low trick to play.'

'I know.' Jess fought to hold in the tears as she nodded slightly. 'That's why I have to tell you. I want to finish this mess and walk away with my head held high. What I did was wrong but what we did was wrong too. You're so lucky to have what you have. Go back to your wife,' she pointed to his crotch, 'keep that in your pants and – be grateful for what you have before you screw it up completely.'

'I wish I'd never met you.' Ryan pushed past her and out of the stock room.

Jess covered her hand with her mouth and squeezed shut her eyes. But it didn't stop the tears from falling. What was it with her? It was one thing for her to choose the wrong men but to pull a trick like that, when there was no purpose except to make trouble for Ryan? Could she really blame that on hormones?

One thing was certain. Jess needed to sort herself out. She owed her baby that much.

CHAPTER FORTY-TWO

At the end of the day, Beth watched as Jess closed up the sweet stall. Since she'd started to work there, Jess always stayed behind for the last couple of hours of the day, allowing Malcolm to finish early or catch up on his paperwork in the café. Or so they'd all thought. It was obvious now that she'd been hanging around waiting for Ryan so they could sneak off for a secret rendezvous.

She couldn't contain herself a minute longer. 'Oi!' she shouted to Jess as she was putting on her coat. 'I want a word with you, miss can't-keep-her-knickers-on.'

'Leave me alone,' Jess said, keeping her back to her. 'It's nothing to do with you.'

Beth grabbed her shoulder and twirled her around. 'It has everything to do with me. I know you're pregnant and I know that you're trying to pass it off as Ryan's, but it can't be.'

'And why's that?'

'I've always been good at maths, funnily enough. That bump.' She pointed to Jess's stomach. 'That bump seems more like four months gone than a few weeks.'

'How would you know?'

'Dur – I have a daughter, remember?'

'Oh, I do. But no one knows who her father is, right?'

'That's none of your business!'

'And this is none of yours. So keep your nose out.'

'Why, you little—'

'That's enough, you two.' Sophie, who had followed Beth over when she heard raised voices, interrupted. 'You're not children anymore.'

'She acts like one,' Beth muttered.

'You also need to get your facts right,' Jess countered. 'I am pregnant but it has nothing to do with your brother, so back off.'

'I said that's enough!' Sophie turned to Jess. 'You. Go home and think yourself lucky that you're not having this conversation with me. Because if you were, baby or no baby, I'd be telling Ryan's wife what was going on. I wouldn't be keeping any of this to myself.'

'It's all secrets on this market, isn't it?' Jess raised her voice purposely. She pointed at Beth. 'With your reputation, I wouldn't be surprised if her husband,' she gestured to Sophie, 'was Charley's father. I wouldn't put it past you not to screw your best friend's husband, the rumours I've heard about you.'

'Why, you nasty little bitch!'

'Leave her, it's not worth it.' Sophie pulled Beth away. As they went past Matt's stall, she spotted Ryan trying to blend in with the shelves at the back. 'This is your fault.'

'Yes,' agreed Beth. 'You and Jess, it stops right now or I'll spread some rumours of my own. Do you hear?'

'I hear you. And it's over.' Ryan nodded curtly.

'Men!' Beth shrugged on her coat, ready to declare the day well and truly done with. 'All they do is make you argue. Are you sure you want to get married, Nic? It could all go wrong once that ring is on your finger.'

'You won't put me off, big sis,' Nicci shook her head. 'I'm going to be so happy.'

Beth couldn't help but smile, wishing the same of herself. Why couldn't she find someone who wanted to marry her and for keeps this time, not like stupid Brian Thompson? Idiot that he was, she had loved being married. Belonging to someone, going home to someone, not having to do everything on her own, make her own decisions, good or bad.

And anyone that could help with Charley and her teenage strops and tantrums would be extremely welcome right now.

When she got home from work that evening, Beth found a letter in the post from Charley's school. She ripped it open. Charley's form teacher was asking to see her. What a perfect ending to a crappy day.

She shouted to Charley to let her know she was home, but ten minutes later, her daughter hadn't surfaced. She went upstairs to see why, Matt's words ringing in her ears. The door was ajar. Charley was sitting at her desk on her laptop.

Beth tapped on the door and went in. 'Hey, Charl,' she smiled. 'Good day at school?'

Charley closed the lid. 'The usual stuff,' she replied.

'Have you made up with Sarah yet?'

Charley shook her head.

'Bit strange for you two not to be speaking for this long.' Beth paused. 'Want to talk about it?'

Charley shook her head again.

'Look, if there's anything that –'

'Mum, I'm fine!'

'Okay, okay.' Beth turned to go but stopped. 'It's just, if you ever want someone to talk to, I'm here for you. You do know that?'

'Okay, I got it.'

Beth sighed and left the room. She wasn't sure she would ever understand Charley. One minute she was complaining to Matt that she wasn't there for her; the next when she tried to speak to her, she didn't want to know. Sometimes she had total sympathy for her own mum trying to get through to her teenage self. But parenting was so hard when there was only one of you.

Not wanting to say anything about the letter until she knew the reason why she'd been called into the school, she let the matter drop for now.

Once her mum had gone, Charley grabbed her phone and sent a message to Alex. There were still certain things that she couldn't talk to her mum about.

CP: Are you there?

She waited for a moment, hoping he would be around to reply. His response came back in seconds:

AL: Yeah, here. What's up?

CP: I really hate going to school right now.

AL: Still bad?

CP: Yeah. If it wasn't for that stupid rumour that started it all off, me and Sarah would still be friends. Now she's gone off with Angela Wilson, I have no one to talk to except you ...

Charley paused. She was going to type and you're not always there when I need you, but realised that wasn't his fault.

CP: I haven't been going to school. I don't feel like I belong there anymore.

AL: Don't say that.

CP: It's true. I don't feel like I belong anywhere really. Mum doesn't care about me. Everyone at school wants to spread rumours about me or laugh at me and call me names. It's horrible being on my own. At least when Sarah was around, I had someone to stick up for me. Now I have no one.

AL: You have me to talk to. I know it's not the same but I thought we were friends.

CP: We are!

AL: I have to go. Mum is calling me. Speak later, yeah? And remember, Charl, I like you. I like you a lot.

Charley's smile was faint as she typed goodbye. At least someone cared about her.

CHAPTER FORTY-THREE

Beth got the letter out that morning at work. She wasn't partial to both Sophie and Nicci seeing it.

'I've had a letter from the school,' she said. 'I have to go and see Charley's form teacher. I've rung and he can see me this afternoon. Is it okay if I finish early tonight?'

Sophie nodded. 'Any idea what it's about?'

'Apparently she hasn't turned up for a full week since January. Honestly, it's like looking after a mini-me. How can I tell her off for something I used to do all the time?'

'I remember it well,' Nicci said. 'I was jealous because you hardly ever went to school during your last year.'

Beth grinned as she remembered too. 'Mum was always having a go at me.'

'But she only did it because she cared. Don't you want Charley to get on in life and have a good education?' Sophie asked.

'I suppose so. She's clever enough to go to university if she put her mind to it. Not that I'd ever be able to afford the fees.'

'She's working here, though,' Sophie replied. Charley had

done a shift on the stall for the past few Saturdays. 'That shows initiative, so I reckon she'll provide for herself. I've enjoyed having her here, too. She's quite the little worker.'

'Then why isn't she going to school?' Beth said.

'Have you asked her?'

'I tried speaking to her last night but she said she was okay. And I didn't want to push it until I'd spoken to her teacher.'

'I bet she misses Sarah.' Nicci was putting together an order for a woman who had left her a list while she did her shopping. 'It seems strange not to see them together anymore. Charley looks lost without her. Did you find out what they'd fallen out over?'

'No.'

'Do you ever talk to Charley and ask her stuff?' Sophie held a bag open for Nicci as she weighed out potatoes and slid them in. 'You sound as if you don't really know each other.'

'We don't.' Beth sat down on a stool. 'I can't seem to get through to her anymore. One minute, she was a sweet kid; the next a stroppy teenager. And now I have to go into school and face the teachers. Just the thought of that makes me feel like I'm the one in trouble.' She shuddered. 'Brings back bad memories.'

'It'll be something and nothing, you'll see.' Sophie tried to soothe her fears. 'There might be a valid explanation once you get there. If it helps, I can call in on my way home from work. Give you a bit of moral support if you need it?'

'Would you?' Beth nodded. 'Thanks. It annoys me to say but she always listens to you.'

'That's because I'm not her mum.'

Beth pouted. 'I think it's because she can't stand me.'

'Well, there is that.' Sophie grinned.

Beth threw a satsuma at her.

. . .

At the end of the day, Sophie locked up the stall and made her way over to Beth's house. After all the recent fallings out, she was looking forward to a couple of hours with her friend. They hadn't had a good chat in ages, despite seeing each other every day on the stall. Maybe if Charley wasn't sulking too much after Beth had spoken to her, they could all sit down together and have a laugh. And if it meant a couple of hours away from Reece and the tension in their home, she was all for it.

'How did it go at the school?' Sophie asked as she shrugged off her coat in Beth's hallway.

'Flipping awful,' Beth replied.

'Oh dear. Where is she?'

'In her room.' Beth pointed to the ceiling. 'And she can stay there as far as I'm concerned. I've had enough of her lip.'

Sophie sat down at the kitchen table as Beth banged crockery around while she made coffee. Then she turned back to her, fury etched across her face.

'That teacher of hers has accused me of neglecting her, can you believe that?'

Sophie could actually, but didn't want to inflame Beth any further by saying so. 'Did he give any reason why she was skipping days?'

'He reckons she's been unhappy for a couple of months now; says that if I spent more time talking to her, and encouraging her to talk to me, then we might be able to get to the bottom of things. Patronising git.' Beth added sugar to one mug and slammed down the lid of the container.

'Did you tell him that she'd fallen out with Sarah?'

'I didn't get the chance. *He* told me. He said Charley has become withdrawn, not wanting to join in with any discussions, sitting in the class on her own – when she can be bothered to turn up.'

'That doesn't sound like her,' Sophie commented as a mug of coffee was put down in front of her with another bang.

'He reckons she's been the victim of a smear campaign. You know, a little ribbing and something called cyber bullying.'

'You mean on Facebook and such?'

Beth nodded. 'And children sending texts and these Snapchat things.' She sat down opposite Sophie with a scrape of her chair across the flooring.

'That sounds terrible,' Sophie balked. 'Do you know what it's all about?'

Beth shuffled in her seat. 'He thinks it something to do with the boys teasing her about being a sleep around.'

'But that's absurd.' Sophie frowned.

'He thinks everyone is teasing her because – because of me.'

'He said that?' Sophie was outraged for her friend. 'I'd complain about it if I were you. He shouldn't –'

'Okay, he didn't exactly say that but that's what he was getting at.'

Sophie raised her eyebrows. 'What did you say in response?'

'I told him that children can be nasty when they want to be. And latching onto a clever girl at school is what they do. They try to bring them down to their level.'

'What did Charley say when you spoke to her?'

'She told me to mind my own business. Said that I didn't care about her.'

'And what did you say to that?'

'I grounded her.'

'You never addressed the fact that she was getting bullied at school?' Sophie shook her head.

'She didn't give me the chance.'

'She won't confide in you if you lash out every time she gets upset.'

'She shouldn't have said that to me.'

'What kind of mother doesn't have sympathy for a child who's getting bullied?'

'She should have some respect.'

'Like you did for your mum, no doubt. She's fifteen, not twenty-five.'

'I knew you'd side with her.' Beth put down her mug and folded her arms. 'You always think you know better than me.'

'Don't be ridiculous. I just see things from a different perspective. You and Charley are so alike, you're bound to argue. But,' Sophie shrugged a shoulder, 'she's your daughter.'

'Yes, she's MY daughter. Nothing at all to do with you.'

Sophie recoiled from the bitter edge of Beth's voice. How had they come to be arguing already?

'You're as bad as that teacher, practically accusing me of neglecting Charley and—'

'I've done nothing of the sort. I merely said I think you should try and talk to her, get her to tell you what's wrong and if you can't get through to her, then I'll try. She's crying out for help by not going to school.'

'She won't get anything at all if she gets me into trouble.'

'Oh, Beth.' Sophie pinched her nose. 'I know that you're being defensive because you're upset but why is everything about you?'

'If you think you'd be so good at parenting, why don't you take Charley for a couple of months and see how you get on with her? See how cheeky she is, how rude she is.'

'It's part of being a teenager.'

'Some of it is,' Beth agreed. 'But some of it is downright stubbornness. If I ask her to wear a blue T-shirt, she'll wear a red one. If I ask her to come downstairs, she'll sit in her room. If I ask her to run the hoover round or peg the washing out, she's having a go before I've even finished the sentence. It's not—'

'You're back to feeling sorry for yourself again,' Sophie interrupted. 'Why can't you admit for once that you think you've failed Charley?'

'What?'

'Firstly, you never told her who her father was.' Sophie looked directly at Beth. 'Then when you married Brian, she looked on him as a father figure but you couldn't keep him. And now there's Matt looking out for you, but you don't appreciate him either.'

Beth stood up, her face contorted with rage. 'You're no better than me,' she sneered. 'Reece left because he caught you with Damien.'

'He didn't leave. And he's back now so I don't see your point.'

'You must have slept with Damien. Reece would never leave you unless it was true; he worshipped the ground you walked on.' She paused. 'Lucky bitch.'

Sophie stood up too and they faced each other over the table.

'*I'm* a lucky bitch? You have the only thing I've ever wanted, a child of my own. It literally tore us apart because I couldn't get pregnant.'

Beth sat open-mouthed while Sophie continued.

'You had your chance at happiness but you blew it.'

'I didn't ask to get pregnant with Charley,' Beth complained. 'I was only seventeen when I got caught. I had my whole life ahead of me until she came along and spoilt everything.'

'I doubt that very much. You were quite capable of making a hash of it before you became pregnant. And I still can't believe you wouldn't tell me who her father is.'

'You really want to know who it was?' Beth opened a drawer, rummaging round in it until her hand clasped onto a small mirror. She thrust it into Sophie's hands.

'Look at it!'

'Why?'

'Look at it and tell me what you see.'

'Nothing but my own reflection.'

'Which is what I see every time I look at Charley.'

Sophie frowned. Why would Beth see her face whenever she looked at her daughter?

Realisation dawned on her. Her hand covered her mouth and her eyes widened in disbelief.

'My dad was Charley's father?'

CHAPTER FORTY-FOUR

Sophie didn't know what to say. Could it be true that Charley was in fact her half-sister? She did the sums. Charley was sixteen soon and Beth had her when she was eighteen. Beth was thirty-four, which meant that her dad would have been thirty-four too when they had slept together. It would have been a couple of months before he died.

'You slept with my dad?' Sophie whispered.

Beth nodded slightly. 'I've never told you before because I knew it would hurt you too much to find out the truth. Let me explain. I –'

A cry came from the hall.

'I HATE YOU!'

'Charley.' Beth and Sophie spoke in unison, rushing out of the kitchen.

When they reached the hall, they found Charley sitting at the top of the stairs, clutching her knees.

'I heard you,' she yelled. 'I heard every word.'

Beth rushed up the stairs towards her but Charley ran to her room and slammed the door shut.

'Please, let me explain.' Beth went straight in.

'You should have told me.' Charley threw herself on the bed.

'You should have told me, too.'

Beth turned around to see Sophie standing in the doorway.

'I couldn't.' Beth looked from one to the other. 'I thought I was doing the right thing – by both of you. I thought I was protecting you.'

'You were protecting yourself.'

'I wasn't!'

'By not telling me, you've played on our friendship for years. You thought if I ever found out I wouldn't want to know you anymore. You had no right to deceive me like that.' She turned to leave.

'I didn't deceive you.' Beth followed her downstairs.

Sophie pointed up. 'No wonder that poor girl feels like she's not wanted. You've never got close to her because you've always blamed her for your mistake. She's there as a constant reminder of what you did.'

'It *was* a mistake. I didn't mean for it to happen.'

'Like I believe that.' Sophie glared at her. 'Charley will never forgive you for this, and neither will I.'

At the bottom of the stairs, Beth sat down. 'I was seventeen,' she sobbed.

Sophie retrieved her bag from the kitchen, swiped her coat from the banister and left the house with the slam of a door.

In her room, Charley had her hands over her ears. It couldn't be true, could it? That her mum had slept with Sophie's dad. He would have been so much older than her.

She wished she had Sarah to talk to now. She would have been shocked too but she would have comforted her. Instead, she logged into Facebook to see if Alex was online to chat. Luckily, he was.

CP: I hate her. She says I was a mistake. How can she say that? So hurtful.

AL: She doesn't deserve you. I think you should teach her a lesson.

CP: How?'

AL: Maybe you should go somewhere for the night, not tell her and let her worry.'

CP: I'm not sure what good that would do.

AL: If she really cared about you, she would be concerned.

CP: Maybe. But I don't have anywhere to go.

AL: My mum and dad have a mobile home near to the sea at Rhyl.

Ugh, a caravan. Charley paused. That was her worst nightmare.

AL: Think about it. Just for one night.

CP: I don't know how to get to Rhyl. I don't even know where it is.

AL: I could show you. I could stay with you too, if you like.

Charley stopped typing. What Alex really meant was that they could sleep together in the caravan. A little tingle ran through her. She was ready, wasn't she? This is what she wanted, wasn't it? To show how grown up she was. To show her mum that she was a woman and not a child?

CP: Do you think we could do it?

AL: Yes. Make her worry about you for a change. See how she likes it.'

Even though Alex couldn't see her, Charley nodded through her tears. Oh, how she wanted to make her mum worry. She wanted to make her hurt, like she was hurting. Someone had to pay for all those lies.

But more importantly, she wanted to be held by Alex.

Comforted in his arms. Be loved by him, feel wanted by him. Alex would make everything better.

She pulled out a shoe box from the bottom of her wardrobe. Inside it was the money she'd saved from her Saturday job. There was thirty pounds there now, plus twenty pounds of her own she'd saved from birthday money. Was it enough? She decided to chance it.

CP: When?

AL: Tomorrow?

CP: Okay.

AL: Really?

CP: Yes, really.

AL: Cool!

The screen went blank as they each gathered their thoughts. Then the cursor flashed so that she knew Alex was writing something.

AL: I can't wait to meet you properly.

Charley gave an excited squeal.

CP: I can't wait to meet you too.

AL: I'll check train times and figure out somewhere we can meet and then I'll email you. Laters. x

Beth sat in the living room, a wet tissue screwed up in her hand. The television was on but all she could see were Sophie's angry eyes and Charley's face screwed up with pain. Two of the people she cared most about and she'd hurt them both in a matter of minutes.

She shouldn't have taken her anger out on Sophie. It wasn't her fault that Charley's teacher had wanted to see her. And why had she let things escalate so that she hadn't kept her mouth shut about Martin? More to the point – why hadn't she come clean to Sophie all those years ago? If she'd said something to her straight away, none of this would be happening. She'd wanted to, ever since she'd first found out she was pregnant, but in the end it had gone on too long.

You silly cow, Beth chastised herself.

She couldn't have told either of them. Not even if Martin was still alive. It would have been spiteful and no matter what Sophie thought, she hadn't kept the secret to save her own skin. She'd done it because she cared. She knew how much losing Martin had devastated Sophie and she didn't want to do anything that would taint him in her eyes.

No wonder she had never found the right words. There had never been any.

Sophie sat under the oak tree in the middle of Somerley Square. She'd often go there in her teens to either wait for Beth or to drown her sorrows and do some thinking. It was a beautiful place to sit in the peace and quiet of the evening. Almost like a comfort blanket as she watched the world go by around her.

She thought back to her last words with Beth. She'd always known the truth would come out eventually but she hadn't realised it would have something to do with her. Tears filled her eyes. She longed to let them out but had to keep them hidden for now.

She tried to put herself in her friend's position. Had Beth been wrong to sleep with her dad, way back then? Beth had been wild as a teenager. That's what she'd loved about her. Opinionated, daring, extrovert and quite the opposite of her. She'd enjoyed hanging around with Beth because of it. Would that have changed if she knew she was after her dad?

She wondered how long it had been going on, and how hadn't she noticed that Beth had fallen for him? She tried to think back but it was too far. There were no memories she could recall that would make her think about anything in particular. Beth always seemed to be round at her house because her own was too noisy. She had to share a room with Nicci so being there with Sophie was more private.

Why hadn't Beth told her? Was it because she'd known that she'd lose her? After Martin's death, would Sophie have been excited about a baby he'd fathered? She very much doubted that.

She held in a sob. Beth could have chosen her as a godmother to Charley because of their father. She could have stayed friendly with Sophie all that time because of the connection between them. She had to admit she'd always thought of them as true friends.

Eventually, it was too dark to see so she headed home.

'Did you have a good evening?' Reece shouted as Sophie came through the door.

'Not really, I don't feel well,' she replied.

'What's wrong?'

'Just a headache.' Sophie flopped into the armchair. She wasn't quite sure why, but she didn't want to tell Reece what she'd found out.

He stood up. 'I'll make us a drink.'

He ruffled her hair as he walked past and Sophie smiled faintly. A few minutes later, he handed her a glass of water and two painkillers, then brought in their drinks before lounging out on the settee. With a quick smile in her direction, he went back to watching the television.

Sophie sipped her drink and excused herself as quickly as she could. At least in the shower, she could cry in solitude. Once under the water, she let the tears fall. For her; for Charley; and most of all, for her dad.

Bringing this up now made her wonder what it would have been like if Martin was still alive. Sadly, she would never find out.

And that's what hurt the most.

CHAPTER FORTY-FIVE

The next morning, Charley had been awake since five a.m. She'd stayed upstairs the evening before, gathering together the things she needed.

She glanced around the room she'd always loved so much. She and Sarah had hung around in it, had a laugh together so many times over the years. Yet lately, it had become her prison as well as her sanctuary.

She still couldn't believe what she'd learned last night. Ever since she could remember, she'd dreamed of meeting her dad one day. She'd dreamed about him holding her in his arms, saying he'd never stopped thinking of her. She'd daydreamed about him saying he was sorry and that it was her mum who'd told him not to stay in touch; to stay away. And now she would never get to meet him. Charley would never forgive her for keeping this secret.

Tears glistened in her eyes as she thought of the last time she'd seen her best friend. Sarah had been with Angela Wilson again. She couldn't understand why she didn't want to hang around with her anymore. They'd been friends for years.

She thought they'd be friends for life. She thought Sarah would stick with her through thick and thin.

All of a sudden, she realised she had no one to depend on but Alex. He would look after her. Yes, a night away would be enough to teach her mum a lesson. Then maybe she could come back and move in with Sophie – or even Matt.

She logged onto her laptop and checked her emails. There was one from him, giving details of the train times and where he'd meet her at the station. She pressed print. Then she logged onto Facebook to see if he was around. When there was no reply, she remembered what time it was; Alex would still be asleep.

Instead, she sent him a quick text message to say she'd received his email. She'd try again later if she had time before she left for the train.

It was nearing seven fifteen when he replied:

'Really can't wait to see you. x'

She typed back a reply:

'Me too. Am excited. x'

Her bag packed, she lay underneath her duvet, fully clothed, in case her mum tried to talk to her before she left for work and spotted she was dressed.

A knock on her door at half past seven made her jump.

'Charley?' Beth said.

'Leave me alone,' Charley shouted, glad that her mum hadn't barged in like she normally did.

'I'm not coming in and I'm not going to try and talk to you right now. And even though I really shouldn't do this, I'm going to ring the school and tell them you're sick and won't be coming in today. Okay?'

'Thanks,' she replied.

'Okay. Call me if you need anything ... or, you know, if you want to talk.' A pause. 'I'll see you later then, yeah?'

No, you won't. Charley said nothing, knowing that she'd

given herself a bit of time to get away. If her mum thought she was at home, she could travel to see Alex, safe in the knowledge that no one would find her until she was ready to come home.

She smiled. See how her mum coped with worrying about someone other than herself for a change.

While Charley made her way to the train station that morning, things were decidedly icy on the fruit stall. Although they kept up a front, Sophie and Beth were pussy-footing round each other. Nicci was the first to comment about it.

'What is it with you two?' she asked. 'You've obviously fallen out over something.'

'No, we haven't,' Sophie said.

'It's nothing,' Beth said. 'Tell me about the flowers you've chosen.'

Pleased to discuss the wedding and throw themselves into something that didn't involve much personal conversation, Beth and Sophie went over some of the finer details with her between serving customers.

'Jay needs to collect the suits for the boys and I have my last dress fitting this weekend,' Nicci said finally. 'And you two need to come as well.'

'You know they've forecast snow for that week,' Beth teased.

'In April?'

'It's been known to happen before.'

Nicci slapped her arm playfully. 'There will be no snow on my wedding day, thank you very much.'

'But think how magical it would make it.'

'Think how cold my feet would be.'

'We could get you some wedding wellies,' Sophie laughed.

Beth picked up her phone and rang Charley but there was no answer.

'Did you speak to Charley last night?' Sophie gave her a warning look that she took to mean not to say too much in front of Nicci.

Beth shook her head. 'I tried again this morning. Said I'd ring the school and tell them she was ill.'

'What's up?' Nicci asked.

Beth filled her in on some of the happenings of the previous night. She watched as Sophie squirmed, wondering how much she would tell. But she wasn't going to let on about their row. She'd never told anyone about Martin until last night and she certainly wasn't going to announce it to the world now.

'What do you think I should do?' She rubbed her hand across her chin.

'How would I know? She's your daughter,' Sophie said pointedly. Then she seemed to relent. 'Charley's a bright girl. She'll work it out for herself.'

'She will,' Nicci added. 'Give her some time to calm down. Right who's for coffee? I think it's my turn to make it.'

As Nicci collected their mugs, Beth gave Sophie a half smile. One less than that was returned. She really hoped in time Sophie would come to understand that she'd been young and stupid. Then again, she was *still* stupid. Not even getting older had made her wiser. Or wise up to herself.

Beth sighed again. What was she going to do about Charley? Like every parent, she wanted the best for her child. She didn't want her making the same mistakes she had. Shame rushed through her as she thought how much her life had impacted on Charley. Beth had mostly put herself first, never her child. Charley was living with a mother who had no ambition, with no father figure to look up to. Apart from

Matt, she supposed. Matt doted on Charley. Something else she was jealous of.

She tried Charley's phone to see if she would answer. When there was no reply, she left a voicemail.

'Hi, Charl, it's only me. When you get this message, give me a quick call, yeah? Speak soon. Love you. Bye.'

'Any luck?' Sophie asked, passing her a mug of coffee over.

Beth shook her head. 'The stubborn little minx isn't answering.'

Nicci laughed. 'Like mother, like daughter.'

Neither Beth nor Sophie joined in.

CHAPTER FORTY-SIX

Although she was nervous about catching – or rather missing – two trains to Rhyl, excitement bubbled up inside Charley. She gazed through the window at the passing scenery, wondering if Alex would be as nice in real life as he was online. Despite him suggesting it, they still hadn't spoken on Skype.

Was his profile picture really him, all sexy eyes and dark, spiky hair and sleek like a racehorse or would he be a spotty boy with greasy hair and a weedy frame? She smiled to herself. Soon she would find out. And at least she'd bought a return ticket home. She wasn't that stupid.

Twenty minutes later, the train pulled into the station. Charley reached for her holdall from the luggage rail above her head and stepped down onto the platform. Her eyes searched through the people milling about but she couldn't see anyone that resembled Alex.

Unsure what to do, she moved to the side by the coffee stall where she'd arranged to meet him.

No one came towards her. She checked her watch: the train was on time. Where was he?

Fear gripped her as she wondered if it had all been a big joke. That Alex wasn't really going to turn up. Had it been someone from school winding her up, pretending to be her friend? Tears brimmed in her eyes.

Then she noticed someone waving. She looked across the platform. An old man in his fifties, with greasy grey hair and a scruffy jacket over disgusting looking corduroy trousers walked towards her.

He was smiling at her.

Oh no, she didn't know what to do. She'd heard stuff about men who lured young women away, pretending to be someone younger than they were. Please, no.

She turned towards the coffee stall, getting ready to scream as he came closer, anxiety starting to flood through her. Then she let out a sigh of relief when the man moved past and said hello to a lady behind her.

'Charley.' A hand rested on her shoulder.

She turned and this time she knew it was Alex.

'I'm sorry.' He struggled to get his breath. 'I missed the bus and had to wait an age for another one. I see you got here on time.'

She was sure her heart stopped beating for a moment as she stared at him. Close up, he really was all sexy eyes and dark, spiky hair. He wore a thick fleece jacket over a jumper that was zipped up at the neck, dark jeans and Converse boots. And that smile. There was no mistaking him.

'Hi,' she said shyly.

'Hi yourself,' Alex replied.

They stood for a moment in the chaos around them and then they laughed.

'This is weird,' he said eventually.

And then he kissed her. Right there at the side of the platform, right next to the coffee stall. It wasn't a long kiss, but it was a good kiss. A warm welcoming and tender first kiss; she hoped it would be the first of many.

He reached for her hand and they walked away, suddenly unable to stop talking.

Charley brimmed with happiness. She was actually here with Alex.

'What am I going to do with her?' Beth asked Matt as they shared a quick break in the café. 'I can't seem to get through to her, no matter what I say.'

'I'm not sure.' He added sugar to his coffee. 'Ordinarily I'd tell you to wait until she's calmed down, and then try to talk to her again. But she's skipping school. You have to do something or you'll both be in trouble.'

Beth glanced out into the aisle, watching the passing shoppers. Matt was right but he hadn't come up with any practical advice. What she wanted to know was how to handle the situation. How to get Charley to go to school. Or more to the point, find out the exact reason why she wasn't going.

What she couldn't tell Matt was the reason Charley hadn't gone to school today was not why he thought it was. She frowned, annoyed with herself. Even now, after all that had gone on, she was still keeping secrets.

'Penny for them,' Matt interrupted her thoughts.

'Hmm?' She glanced back at him. 'Sorry, I was just thinking.'

'How about I have a word with her?' he suggested. 'Maybe she might tell me something that she wouldn't talk to you about.'

'You mean you want to be a negotiator?' Beth teased. 'You've been watching too much TV. Charley's fifteen, remember. She won't spill anything, unless it's to Sarah.' Beth sighed then. 'I wish those two would hurry up and get together again. I miss the laughter they bring to the house. It's like a morgue in there at the moment.'

'The offer is on the table.' Matt squeezed her hand before knocking back the dregs of his drink and standing up. 'A man's perception might do the trick.'

'Ha, ha. Any idea where I might find one?' Beth planted a smile on her face.

Joking aside, she was worried that she'd messed everything up with Matt. Because that wasn't the only offer she was interested in.

CHAPTER FORTY-SEVEN

Charley and Alex were getting off the bus they'd caught outside the railway station when Charley's phone rang again. She pulled it from her pocket to see who it was.

'Is it your mum?' Alex looked at her.

Charley nodded.

'Are you going to answer it?'

'Nope.'

'Nice one.'

Alex grabbed her hand again and they walked together along the pavement.

A long, straight main road stretched out in front of them. On one side, there was a row of guest houses and hotels for as far as the eye could see and on the other, a three-foot hop over the wall led to the beach. The sea was choppy, sand flailing about with the wind, but Charley didn't mind. She caught the smell of fish and chips wafting in front of her nose and checked her watch to see it was lunchtime.

'I'm starving,' she said. Apart from a piece of toast this morning, she hadn't eaten anything substantial since yesterday lunch. 'Fancy some chips?'

They each had a cone and walked on for a good twenty minutes before Alex pointed to his right.

Charley saw a gate and a sign announcing Sun Valley Caravan Park.

'That's the entrance.' He pulled a key from his pocket. 'We should be okay here tonight.'

'Aren't your parents going to worry about you?' Charley asked as he let them in.

'I told them I was stopping at my friend's house. They won't be looking for me any time soon.' Alex took out his phone and waggled it about. 'Aren't these things amazing? I can speak to them or text them from anywhere and they wouldn't have a clue if I was in the next room or had caught a plane to America. Unless they wanted to check up, of course.'

Charley giggled. 'I've never been to America. We could go there tomorrow.'

'Or maybe Australia.'

'Or to the moon.'

Alex laughed too, as he closed the gate behind them.

'You're so cool.'

Charley's cheeks heated up as he kissed her again. This time there was no one around to bother them. She wanted to stay there forever but soon after, Alex grabbed her hand and they ran to the caravan.

From first impressions, it seemed okay. It wasn't one of those tiny four berth nightmares that she remembered loving when she was younger but didn't want to go near now she was older. This caravan was more like a small flat; she reckoned it could sleep about eight people. It had two separate bedrooms, one with a fixed double bed. The living area had a table with four chairs, a settee and armchair, a small flat-screen television and a gas fire, which they were going to need as it was freezing.

Alex pointed to the large bedroom with the double bed.

'Put your bag down in there and we can go for a walk and get some food. There's plenty of stuff like soup and pasta in the cupboards. And there's always coffee and teabags so all we need is bread and milk and something to drink.'

Charley could hardly contain herself. Alex was so grown up compared to most of her friends, as well as being gorgeous. If only Sarah could see her now, she would be green with envy.

As soon as she got home that evening, Beth shouted out to Charley. When there was no reply, she listened for music but couldn't hear that either. She stomped up the stairs, expecting to find Charley with her earphones in, but the room was empty.

She glanced around the teenage detritus on the floor before going back downstairs and trying Charley's phone again. Still no answer and there were no missed calls from her. Unsure what to do, she started to prepare something to eat. Charley would turn up soon, no doubt.

But when it came to half past seven and several phone calls were still unanswered, Beth decided she'd clock-watched enough and rang Sophie in a panic.

'I'm sorry,' she said quickly. 'I realise we're hardly on the best of terms but Charley hasn't come home yet and I don't know want to do.' She swallowed down the lump in her throat. 'I don't know where she is.'

'It's probably something and nothing. Maybe she's still annoyed about what happened yesterday. Have you contacted Sarah?'

'No, they're not speaking, remember?'

'But all the same, she might be able to tell you what's been going on with Charley lately. Do you have her number?'

'Yes, it's stored on my phone.'

'Is Charley's phone switched off?'

'No, but it's been ringing out for hours.'

'I'm on my way over. You try to reach Sarah and see if she can shed any light on it.'

'What if something has happened to her?' Beth began to cry. 'She's all I've got.'

'I'll ring Matt. Don't worry. We'll find her.'

Sophie was round at Beth's house within fifteen minutes. Reece had joined her too. Neither of them was surprised when Matt answered the door.

'She's in pieces,' he told them. 'Reckons it's all her fault for being a bad mother. I can't get any sense out of her.'

Sophie went through to find Beth sunk in the settee, clutching her phone. Forgetting their recent argument, she rushed across to sit next to her.

'She's run away with a boy!' Beth cried.

'How do you know?'

'Sarah told me. His name is Alex.'

Sophie wrapped her arms around her. 'Is he someone from school?'

'It's much worse than that. She met him on Facebook. Sarah said Charley is obsessed with him. She was always emailing, texting him, messaging him through Facebook and that thing called WhatsApp, and that's what they'd fallen out about. Why didn't I know?'

'And she's sure she's with him?'

Beth shook her head. 'She says they haven't spoken to each other in a while. They used to be such good friends. But she says Charley might have gone to meet him.'

'Do you think we should call the police?' Matt suggested.

Sophie didn't know what to advise. On the one hand, no one had seen or spoken to Charley since this morning – she could be anywhere by now. But she was a fifteen-year-old girl; she could easily be sulking, trying to teach Beth a lesson. They'd all look silly if she came rolling in as they were reporting her missing.

It was hard to know where to draw the line. And more so now that there was a boy involved. For all they knew, he could be someone older than he was making out to be. He could be a paedophile.

What would she do if it was her child that was missing?

'Maybe we should leave it for another hour or so?' Reece proposed. 'I know it isn't ideal but I think you can trust Charley. If she's safe, she'll let you know.'

'But what if she isn't?' Beth said. 'She could have been kidnapped and tortured. She could be in danger right now. I'd be responsible for that.'

'I know it's a risk but Reece is right, Beth.' Sophie got out her phone. 'And I bet if the police knew you'd been arguing yesterday, they'd tell you to wait a while longer too.'

'You had a row?' Matt said.

Beth said nothing.

Sophie began to type out a message. 'Let's see if she'll contact me, to let us know she's okay. Hopefully, she'll text me back. At least if she does that, we'll know she's all right.'

'But I need to know where she is *now* so that I can go and fetch her.' Beth started to cry again. 'I want her home with me, where I can see her.'

Sophie held her while she wept. 'She'll be okay, she said, stroking her hair. 'She'll be okay.'

She looked up to see both Matt and Reece staring back at her. They wore the same worried expression that she did.

CHAPTER FORTY-EIGHT

It was evening when Charley and Alex arrived back at the caravan, each carrying a shopping bag. After hanging around the centre of town for most of the afternoon, drinking coffee and window shopping, they'd bought a pizza to share and a bag of salad. Charley had added sweets and chocolate into their basket: Alex, a bottle of coke and a few cans of lager.

But Charley was getting increasingly worried every time she looked at her phone. There were more phone calls.

Alex put the bags down on the table and, seeing her apprehension as she checked it once more, he stopped to give her a hug.

'It'll be okay,' he reassured her. 'You can go home tomorrow but you must make her worry about you. Do you want to check out what's in the cupboards while I switch on the gas? It's just outside.'

Charley watched him disappear out of the door. She could have made a run for it quite a few times during the day. Even now, she'd only have to go back to the main road and flag down a taxi or something.

But she didn't want to. She felt safe with Alex. She had

nothing to prove to him: he liked her for who she was. It was what she needed right now.

She opened kitchen cupboards and put away their little bit of shopping. Then she emptied her bag, placing things down on top of the fitted dressing table. Glancing at the double bed, she worried about what would happen later.

She picked up her phone. There were lots of missed calls from her mum – voice messages too. And text messages – including one from Sophie.

'Hi Charl. Wherever you are and whatever you are doing, it's okay. But you need to let your mum know you're safe. Text me back. S x'

Charley typed a reply. She supposed she was okay with letting her mum know she was all right.

When she heard the caravan door open and Alex bounding up the steps, she pressed send, switched off the phone and shoved it back inside her bag.

Sophie wasn't sure what to think when she read the text message. Nor what she should tell Beth, who was standing in front of her.

'What does it say?' Beth asked, apprehension clear in her voice.

'Charley's okay, for starters.' she decided to tell her the good news first.

Beth cried with relief. 'Oh, thank goodness.' But then she panicked. 'That text might have been sent by anyone. Someone could have her phone. Let me read it. What exactly does it say?' Before Sophie could stop her, she snatched the phone from her hand. The message from Charley read:

'Tell Mum I'm ok and I'm not coming home tonight. Cx'.

Beth frowned as she looked up at everyone. 'Do you think she's with that Alex? Alex might not even be Alex, for all we know. He could be some sex fiend acting as a boy called Alex. I can't stand around anymore. I'm calling the police.'

Sophie shivered, her eyes filling with tears as she listened to Beth reporting Charley as a missing person. She was right: that text could have come from anyone.

Although Charley and Alex chatted quite amicably for most of the evening, by half past nine their conversation had more or less dried up. They'd enjoyed the pizza and Charley had had a can of lager but she didn't want to get drunk. She needed to keep her head clear for what was about to happen.

If they had been on a first date, she'd be dying to go home now so that she could recall their first kiss in detail, think about what had happened, analyse everything Alex had said to her. She'd go to bed with a big grin as she looked forward to their next date. Now she was so nervous that her left leg kept shaking involuntarily.

She was worried about the night to come, even more than she wished she'd never run away. The caravan was cold, despite the gas fire being on full so Alex fetched the double duvet from the bedroom. She made coffee and they settled down underneath it and watched television. It would have been great if there wasn't an atmosphere of dread.

She wondered if Alex was nervous. He was only sixteen. Was this the first time he'd slept with anyone? She wanted to ask him but didn't dare. What if he'd been with lots of girls and she wasn't good enough? She glanced over at him. He was checking his phone again. He'd been doing that regularly for the past couple of hours. Was he regretting letting things go so far, too?

She drifted off to sleep for a while and when she woke up, she and Alex began to fool around. She tried to enjoy it, hoping it would be over soon. There had been a bit of kissing and fumbling earlier but neither of them seemed to want more. And now Alex had stopped again.

'I'm tired.' He pulled back the duvet. 'I'm going to brush my teeth and call it a night.'

Charley fought back tears. What was wrong with her? Didn't he want to sleep with her? Was she – what was the word they used at school – frigid? Did she give off 'keep away' signals?

Then she gasped, all of a sudden understanding that he wanted to get into bed with her. Maybe he thought it would be more comfortable, or more romantic? Either way, it sent her into a complete panic. How would she take off her clothes?

Charley cleaned her teeth after Alex. With dread, she came out of the bathroom. Alex stood in the kitchen area waiting for her.

'I don't know about you,' he said, hardly able to look at her, 'but I think it's too cold to get undressed. I'm going to sleep in my clothes.'

The relief must have shown on Charley's face, because Alex grinned.

'You obviously don't mind then?'

'I – I'm not sure. Don't you want to sleep with me?'

'Of course I do!' Alex looked sheepish. 'I mean – well, I think you're gorgeous but it's ... I've never done it before.' He smiled awkwardly. 'I think I'm more scared than you are.'

'I'm not scared,' retorted Charley.

'It was your leg that shook every time I came near you.'

There really was no point in getting mad at Alex. She didn't want to sleep with him either.

'You can take the double bed,' he said.

They stood there awkwardly.

'I'll have one of the smaller beds,' he added.

A few minutes later, Charley lay in the dark, fully clothed

underneath the double duvet. Even though Alex was only a few feet away, part of her wished he was here with her. He could warm her up and cuddle into her, even if they didn't want to do anything else. She pulled the duvet closer around her neck and tried to get to sleep. The sooner she did, the quicker the morning would arrive and she could go home.

Alex knocked on the bedroom door a minute later. He got into the bed beside her.

'Don't panic,' he said. 'I'm not going to do anything. It's just warmer under the duvet.'

It was so quiet that Charley could hear the silence ringing in her ears. She could feel her heart beating wildly inside her chest. She didn't dare move a muscle and knew she wouldn't be able to sleep.

Again, she wished she was at home. How had she thought that staying away overnight was a good idea? Despite the danger she could have been in, things had turned out all right with Alex. But she missed her mum. And she didn't feel right punishing her for something that happened so long ago. Maybe she *had* been trying to protect her and Sophie.

Perhaps she should try to be a better daughter when she got home; not stay in her room so much, join in with things. Help more around the house.

But right now she needed to get some sleep. If that was at all possible.

CHAPTER FORTY-NINE

Beth never went to bed that night. Reece went home about ten and, despite Matt sleeping over in the spare room, Sophie had insisted on staying downstairs with her – a fact that she was grateful for.

It was five a.m. While Sophie dozed, Beth thought about Charley. She prayed she'd be okay and that this was some kind of schoolgirl prank that she'd thought up to wound her. If it was, it had definitely done the trick. Beth was hurting so much there were no words to describe her pain.

She thought back to the first time she'd seen her daughter. She'd been at the hospital with her mum and Sophie, trying to make out that she was brave at eighteen when really she didn't have a clue what to do. The nurse had put Charley into her arms and she'd fallen in love with her, forgetting all the pain of the birth. A few days later, she'd taken her home with her parents as a six-pound bundle of screams and baby powder. If it wasn't for her mum and dad helping out, she wouldn't have coped as well as she did. But despite her downfalls, Beth always did the best she could for her daughter.

She remembered when Charley learned how to walk, her

first day at school. When she learned how to tell the time. The first width she swam in the pool, after she'd seemed to swim but get nowhere for ages. The time she'd dressed up as a rat in the school play, The Pied Piper of Hamlyn. When she won a prize from the school for the best written essay.

She recalled how stubborn she'd always been but what a lovely warm character she was too. And over the years she'd turned into a beautiful young lady, one Beth was proud to call her daughter. She was so ashamed that she hadn't let Charley know that, because she'd been too wrapped up in herself.

If she came home – no, when she came home, Beth was going to put that right. She'd start by telling her all the things she should have said. She'd stop messing around and act like a parent should. And she would make it known that she had the best daughter in the world.

She started to cry again.

Please don't let memories be all that I have left of her. Please let her be okay.

Despite her anxiety Charley managed to get a little sleep, but she still woke up early. In the dark, she could just about make out the shape of Alex sleeping next to her. He had his back towards her. She turned on her side and squeezed her eyes shut to stem the tears threatening to fall.

Last night had been one of the worst nights of her life. She'd tossed and turned, thinking about how mad her mum would be when she finally got home. She remembered scooting across to the other side of the bed when Alex turned over. More than anything, she wished she was back in her own bed the whole night through.

'Morning,' Alex said, making her jump. She hadn't realised he was awake.

'Morning.'

'What time is it?'

She reached over for her phone and illuminated the screen.

'It's quarter past six.' Charley saw an icon indicating a voice message. She went through to the kitchen and called it up.

'Charley, it's mum. I know you might not be able to hear this message or even respond to it in any way but I want you to know that I've called the police and they'll find you soon. And if it isn't Charley answering this phone ... if this is Alex, I'm talking to and you hurt my little girl, I ... I ... I'll fucking kill you!'

'Oh, no.' Her mum must have contacted Sarah. She was the only one who Charley had spoken to about Alex.

'What's up?' he asked.

Charley turned to see a light on in the room. Alex was sitting up now, his spiky hair in a definite bed-head style. Somehow his good looks of yesterday had gone and she saw him for what he was. A sixteen-year-old boy who'd befriended a fifteen-year-old girl. And now both of them were in big trouble.

'It's all gone wrong.' Charley burst into tears. 'My mum's rung the police and reported me missing. She'll—'

'Whoa,' Alex interrupted. 'She's contacted the police?'

'Yes. She rang them last night.'

'And are they looking for you?' Alex was pulling on his shoes.

'They must be. What am I going to do? I can't go home now. She'll kill me.'

'They'll kill us both if they find us here.' Alex was up now and running a hand through his hair. 'I'm in so much trouble.'

No, you're not.' Charley was going to learn by her mum's mistakes and admit the truth. 'This is my fault.'

'But, can't you see? I'm sixteen and I – I suppose I'm

responsible for you. If I get caught with you and they think we – we've – you know, then I could be in trouble.'

'But we didn't – you know.'

'You have to ring her. Tell her you're okay. It might not be too late.'

'I can't.'

'But you could get away with it if you talk to her.' He came to her then. 'Think about it. She'll be so pleased to hear from you, the police will stop looking for you and we can grab a coffee before you catch a train back.'

Charley paused. Was it really that easy? Alex went outside the caravan to switch off the gas. She flew down the steps beside him, the chilly sea air catching her breath. 'Alex!'

'Ring her,' he shouted above the noise of the wind. 'We have to go. Get your things.'

Charley didn't understand. What was all the big rush?

'What's going on?' she asked him once they were back inside. 'Why are you so afraid of the police?'

'I'm not.'

'It should be me who's scared. I have to go back and face the music. You can disappear into thin air, can't you?'

'Do you want me to do that?'

'No.'

Alex paused for a moment. 'My old man's a copper,' he admitted. 'He'll go mad if he finds out what I've done.'

She gasped. 'You dweeb.'

Alex grinned. 'I know.'

Charley realised if they weren't going to get into more trouble, there was nothing for it but to ring home.

CHAPTER FIFTY

It was half past six. Beth was now in the kitchen with Sophie. They were both sitting in silence when they heard Matt rushing down the stairs.

Beth's heart lurched when she saw him barefoot in hastily pulled on clothes. Because he was smiling.

'Guess who I've been woken up by?' Matt waggled his mobile phone in the air. 'I got a call from Charley. She's okay.'

'Oh, thank goodness.' Beth stood up and hugged him. 'Where is she?'

'She's safe and she's sorry and I'm going to pick her up.'

'Yes, but where is she?'

'She's in Rhyl.'

'Rhyl?' Beth and Sophie said in unison.

'What the hell is she doing there?' Beth added.

'Apparently she got a train,' Matt explained, 'went to the seaside, hung around a bit and then was scared to come home.'

'And what about this Alex? Was he with her?'

'I didn't ask. I thought it best not to. She's probably scared enough about what you're going to say anyway.'

'I'll try not to throttle her.' Beth laughed with relief. 'How long will it take to get there?'

'About three hours I reckon. I'll have a quick cuppa and then I'll go to fetch her.'

'Are you sure? I could get the train and then travel back with her?'

Matt shook his head. 'It's fine. I'd rather have her in my car safe and sound as soon as I can.'

Beth's heart went out to him. 'I'll get my coat.'

Matt touched her forearm. 'Do you think that's wise?'

'Of course I do.'

'But what happens if she's frightened and she—'

'Frightened of me?' Beth's brow furrowed. 'That's ridiculous.'

'Matt's right,' Sophie said. 'Charley was upset enough to stay out overnight. Shall I go instead? Maybe the reason she ran away could have been sparked by me as much as you, so she might want to chat it through first.'

'What reason's this?' Matt said.

'Women's talk,' Beth replied.

'We can be home in a few hours.' Sophie touched Beth's forearm. 'Why not go and do some shopping and treat her? Buy her something nice to eat for later, the two of you. Get her that chocolate cake she likes and stay in with her. Talk to her. Try to find out what's wrong rather than ...'

'Storm in and have a full-blown row before she's even got her feet through the front door,' Beth finished off for her.

Sophie said nothing.

Matt jangled his car keys in the air. 'I can't wait around all day. Which one of you is coming or am I going alone?'

'Sophie's right,' Beth said with a sigh. 'The last person Charley will want to see is me. You two go and bring her home and I'll have a chat to her afterwards.'

'And you'd better ring the police. Let them know she's safe.'

Beth baulked. 'How silly am I going to look?'

'You did what any responsible parent would do,' Matt said. 'They're probably used to this kind of thing resolving itself overnight anyway. They'll be pleased to hear she's okay.'

Once they were ready, Beth followed them to the front door. 'Ring me when you have her, won't you?' she asked.

Sophie gave Beth a hug. 'This will sort itself out, you'll see.'

Beth watched them drive off in Matt's car before closing the door. It was only then that she sunk to the floor, collapsed in a heap and sobbed.

Her little girl was safe.

Charley and Alex headed out into the cold and dark morning and off the campsite. Twenty minutes later, they were walking along the sea front when Alex pointed to a café that was opening its doors.

'Let's go in there,' he said.

'Good morning,' a loud voice boomed out as they entered the building. A man with a face as round as his stomach smiled at them from behind the counter. 'You're my first early birds today. What can I get you?'

They ordered tea and toast with scrambled eggs and Charley went to sit down as Alex waited for their drinks. The café was a typical seaside establishment. Plastic gingham tablecloths on square tables, hard-backed chairs with seats made of raffia. Charley sat down at a table and ran a hand across the steam on the window so she could see outside. The day was just beginning but already she could sigh with relief.

Lucky. That's what she'd been, Charley realised. Lucky to find someone as kind as Alex to look after her when she'd been so stupid. He could have turned out to be anyone. And even if he wasn't some weirdo in real life, he could have forced himself on her last night – but instead, he'd been as scared as she was. Neither of them was grown up enough to deal with the situation, despite both of them thinking they were.

What a fool she'd been, over-reacting like that. Fortunately she'd be home soon, once Matt arrived. She was pleased he was coming to fetch her with Sophie, although she'd yet to talk to her mum. But deep down, she knew she'd be able to sort things out eventually.

Would she ever have told her who her real dad was, she wondered? It still hurt that she'd been so secretive about it, but it wasn't as if she had stopped her from seeing him. He hadn't been alive. And she'd realised that Sophie was actually her half-sister. Now, that definitely wasn't a bad thing.

She'd been surprised to get a couple of text messages from Sarah too, asking if she was okay. Quickly, she sent a reply while she waited for Alex to join her.

'Hey. Just letting you know that I did stay out all night but I'll be home soon. Matt's coming to pick me up. Cx.'

A message came back almost immediately.

'So glad you're safe. Do you fancy hooking up in the market café later? Can't really stand Angela Wilson. You can tell me all about Alex. Sx.'

Charley grinned.

'Sure. Catch you later. Cx.'

She gazed out at nothing in particular. When Alex sat down opposite her, she grinned at him. He waited for her to share the joke.

'What?' he asked when she didn't come forward with an explanation.

'Your dad is a police officer?' she giggled.

Alex laughed then. 'I can't get away with anything.'

'No, you're too sweet to get into trouble. You're a decent boy. There's not many like you.'

Alex leaned forward and kissed her lightly on the lips. 'Will I get to see you again or is this it?'

Shy again now, Charley shrugged. 'I'm not sure. What do you think?'

'I think we should stay in touch online and see what happens.'

'Cool.'

The man from behind the counter whistled a tune as he popped down their breakfast. 'There you are, love's young dream,' he beamed. 'Enjoy.'

'Anyone would think we're having smoked salmon with these eggs,' Alex said.

Charley tucked into her breakfast.

'There is something you need to do for me,' she said after she'd eaten some of it.

Alex looked up with a forkful of egg in mid-air.

'Leave before Matt gets here. I don't want to scrape you off the floor.'

'Don't worry,' Alex said, 'I shall be *eggstra* careful and go soon.'

Charley laughed. Yes, she really had been lucky.

As soon as they were away from Beth's driveway, Sophie turned to Matt.

'Tell me what Charley really told you,' she said.

'She spent the night in a caravan with Alex.' Matt was deadpan. 'Then she found out that Beth had called the police and decided to ring me. She and Alex should now be having breakfast somewhere on the seafront.'

'Do you know if they – if he touched her?'

'No, but I hope he kept it curled up in his pants or else I'll search him down. He had no fucking right to do that.'

'We don't know he did do anything yet, so let's keep calm.' Sophie spotted his watery eyes. 'She means so much to all of us, doesn't she?'

Matt nodded, swiping away rogue tears that had fallen.

'And what about Beth? When are you two ever going to get together?'

'What?'

'We all know you love her.' Sophie glanced out of the window at the passing scenery.

Matt coughed.

'Why don't you tell her?' She turned back to him.

'Because she doesn't love me.'

'Yes, she does. She's mad about you.'

'No, she isn't.'

'I think you'll find that she is.'

Matt grinned. 'You're going to make me crash the car.'

Sophie smiled. At last the penny had dropped for one of them.

'Has she said something to you?' Matt enquired after a moment.

'She doesn't have to. I can see it when you're together.'

'When we're together, she treats me like her best friend.'

'Oi, I'm her best friend.' But even though Sophie made a joke about it, she didn't feel like laughing. Best friends didn't keep secrets from each other, and they'd both been guilty of that.

'I know.' Matt sighed. 'I think she sees me as someone to look out for her and Charley.'

'And you do it so well that she takes you for granted,' Sophie pointed out. 'Have you ever tried telling her how you feel?'

'No way.'

'Why not?'

'Because I'm a man, and most men don't do things like that.'

The satnav informed him that he needed to come off at the next junction.

'Do you want me to ask her if she'll have a date with you?' Sophie laughed. 'Like we did when we were at school?'

Matt laughed too. He checked in his mirror before indicating to change lanes.

Sophie read the sign to see they were three miles from Rhyl and would soon be with Charley.

'*Do* you love Beth?' she probed.

'What's love got to do with it?' Matt teased, channelling Tina Turner.

'Seriously, tell her before it's too late.' Sophie reached for phone. 'I'll text Charley to let her know we're nearly there.'

CHAPTER FIFTY-ONE

Charley and Alex had stayed in the café for as long as they could without overstaying their welcome. Now they were sitting in a shelter on the sea front while they waited for Matt to arrive.

When a text message beeped, Charley opened it eagerly.

'They're here, aren't they?' Alex said.

Charley nodded.

'How long have I got?'

'About ten minutes, I reckon.'

'Do I have to go?'

'If you value your life.' Charley grinned. They'd already decided to arrange to meet up again, once they'd got to know each other a bit better first.

'I wish you didn't have to go.'

'Me too.'

Now that the problem of them sleeping together had been lifted, Charley found they'd both relaxed enough to enjoy each other's company again. She'd been so grateful that Alex had waited with her. Sitting alone, she would have worried herself silly about the trouble she was in and would, without a doubt, have been crying by now. Being with Alex had made it bearable.

'You will keep in touch?' she asked, almost timidly.

He put his arm round her. 'Of course.'

Then he kissed her. Charley didn't want it to end. It was the last kiss they'd be able to share.

'Bye, Charl.' With a wave, he walked off. 'See you online.'

Charley watched until he was out of sight. She was still thinking about him when her phone rang a few minutes later.

Then panic began to set in.

'Whereabouts are you? Yes, come out near to the kerbside. What's near you? Look out for the clock tower,' Sophie told Matt. 'No, don't cry. Everything's fine. Look, she's there! Pull in, here.'

Matt did as he was told. As Sophie got out of the car, she could see Charley running towards her. The young girl rushed into her arms.

'I'm sorry.' Charley started to cry. 'I'm so sorry.'

'It's okay.' Sophie hugged her fiercely. 'You're safe, that's the main thing.'

Matt beeped his horn behind them. 'Stay here while I find somewhere to park.'

Sophie took Charley back to the shelter and they sat down together. Tiny bits of rubbish swirled around as a gust of wind took hold. The seagulls looked on eagerly, waiting for scraps of anything to eat.

Sophie passed Charley a tissue. 'Want to tell me about it?'

'I was – I was so mad with Mum when I found out about . . .'

'So was I.' Sophie put an arm round Charley's shoulder and drew her near again. 'I can't believe she kept it from both of us for so long.'

'Were you really upset?'

'Yes.' Sophie recalled how she'd cried the night she'd found out. 'But I suppose I can't blame your mum. She was only young. I think my dad should have known better though.'

'Did he know about me?'

'No. Beth didn't want to tell him but a few weeks later he died anyway. I don't know what she thought I would have said about it. I think that's what hurt the most. That she kept it from me. But I can see why, I suppose.'

'She really is a silly cow, isn't she?'

'That's your mum you're talking about.' Sophie could hear the affection in Charley's tone.

'She's still silly.'

'Yes, she is. But her heart's in the right place.'

'I don't think she has a heart.'

'Of course she does.'

Charley's face creased up again. 'Then why does she drink so much and shut everyone out?'

'She's afraid of getting hurt again. Sometimes it's easier to deny yourself happiness than dare to have another go at things.'

'You mean with Matt, don't you?'

Sophie grinned. 'It's clear to you, too?'

'I think it's obvious to everyone but Mum and Matt. I wish he was my dad.' Charley pulled away from her. 'Oh, I didn't mean –'

Sophie smiled. 'I know what you meant.'

They sat in silence for a moment. In front of them, the seagulls fought over the remains of someone's takeaway from the night before. The noise became deafening.

Sophie spotted Matt walking towards them, carrying three cartons of coffee. A small bag hung down; the handle wrapped around two of the fingers on his left hand.

She turned to Charley. 'I think you should text your mum to say that we'll be on our way home soon.'

Charley took out her phone. 'She's going to be so mad, isn't she?'

'Yes, but only because she cares about you.'

'She has a funny way of showing it sometimes.'

They smiled at each other.

Before Matt reached them, Sophie leaned in close to Charley again. 'Hey,' she whispered. 'It's great to have a little sister.'

It was so good to see Charley's face light up.

While Matt and Sophie went to fetch Charley, Beth did indeed go shopping. She came back with a bag full of Charley's favourite things to eat, trying to convince herself that she hadn't bought them to assuage her guilt. She also treated her to some clothes. They were all she could afford but Charley would like them – a pair of skinny jeans, a short jumper and a longer cardigan to wear with leggings.

She'd decided not to ring Charley, knowing it would put added pressure on her. She wanted to chat to her face to face. Instead she asked Sophie to send texts every now and then, updating her of their progress.

As soon as she saw Matt's car pull up outside her home, she opened the front door, flew out of the house and ran towards them.

Charley got out of the rear seats and fell straight into her mum's arms. 'I'm sorry,' she cried, holding onto her. 'I didn't mean to hurt you.'

Beth was crying too. 'I'm just glad you're back and in one piece. We were all so upset. But why did you leave?'

'I — I wanted to see if you cared enough to be worried.'

Beth pulled away. 'Of course I would.'

Charley smiled shyly. 'I know that now. I heard your phone message to Alex.'

They laughed together, relief amid the humour.

'Come on.' Beth took her by the hand. 'Let's go inside and have a catch up over a cuppa.'

Through her tears, she mouthed a thank you to Sophie and Matt before tightly holding onto Charley as she ushered her into the house.

'Should we go in or leave them to it?' Matt asked Sophie.

'I think we should let them sort it out together.'

'I'm glad it's a happy ending.'

'Me too.'

'I suppose we'd better check out what's happened at the market without us there.' Matt started the engine up again. 'I bet all hell's let loose without us.'

'Speak for yourself. I have Nicci manning my stall. She might be rushed off her feet but she's capable. Whereas you have Ryan.' Sophie smirked. 'I know who my money is on.'

'Yeah, you win.' He smiled. 'It's a good job all this happened when it did. It's going to be manic setting every-thing up for the wedding.'

'Maybe, but it might be good practice for someone sitting not so far away from me.'

'Oh, I reckon there'll be at least one more family fall out before the big day. It's part of the fun, isn't it?'

'You know that's not what I meant.'

'Sorry.' Matt turned up the radio. 'I can't hear you. La, la, la, LA!'

Sophie grinned back at him but the smile swiftly dropped from her face. If only the wedding was all she had to concen-trate on right now.

CHAPTER FIFTY-TWO

It was a week to go before the wedding. Sophie was curled up on the settee with a glass of wine. Thankfully, Reece had gone to have a couple of pints with Ryan and Matt so she had the house to herself. It was something that she'd already been missing.

All this wedding talk was making her think of her own marriage. How on earth was she going to tell Reece that things weren't working between them anymore? She couldn't stay with someone that she loved like a brother. Yes, the sex was still there but even that was beginning to get complacent again. A case of "if we must" rather than "I'd love to, darling".

Jay and Nicci's wedding was going to be fun but she'd be surprised if she got through the day without bursting into tears. Despite what had happened over the past few days, she missed Beth. She needed her support now more than ever but since Charley had come home, Beth was spending more time with her. Rightly so, in Sophie's opinion, but it left her with no one to confide in. Not that she was sure she would be able to talk to her right now. Her trust had been damaged severely.

So she was surprised to open the door shortly after seven o'clock and find an embarrassed looking Beth on the doorstep.

'I was thinking about you,' Sophie said once they'd gone through to the living room.

'Oh?' Beth sat down, sounding a little shocked.

'I was wondering how Charley was doing.'

'She's great, thanks. We've had a few long chats now.'

Beth had told Sophie briefly about the extent of the bullying. No wonder Charley wanted friends away from school. Beth had also been in to see Charley's form teacher again and they were keeping an eye on her, and the troublemakers. She hoped things would settle down for them both now.

'Good. I'm pleased.'

'Me too. Which is why I came round to see you.' Beth paused for a second. 'I'd like to talk to you, see if we can smooth things out now.'

'And what makes you think you can make peace with me that easily?'

Sophie left the room, leaving Beth to stew until she returned with another wine glass and poured her a drink.

'Well, go on then,' she said after she'd sat down.

'When I was seventeen, you know that I was round at your house so much because mine was always so noisy.' Beth smiled shyly at the memories. 'I used to love nothing more than spending time with you here because your dad was out at work a lot and we had the house to ourselves. It was like having our own pad.' She laughed, a little awkwardly.

Sophie remained straight-faced.

'I – I never told you, but I always had a crush on Martin. He was so good-looking and obviously mature compared to the boys we knew. There wasn't any flirting on his side. In fact, he never took any notice of me in that way at all, if I'm honest, because I remember feeling upset about it. But then I caught him on a rare occasion when he'd had too much to drink.

'I'd come over to see you one Sunday afternoon after I'd had a row with my mum and dad but you weren't in. Martin had been to the pub and was a little worse for wear. He said I should come in and wait for you. He offered me a glass of wine and for every sip I had, he took in more of the whiskey he'd poured himself.

'He suggested putting on a video and picked out Dirty Dancing. And after the I-carried-a-watermelon scene came on, he pulled me to my feet and we had a laugh trying to dance. He was so drunk he kept falling over and well, you can imagine the rest.'

Beth paused to catch her breath. Sophie was staring at the floor.

'Afterwards I was so embarrassed,' Beth continued. 'I went upstairs to your bathroom and sat for a while to gather my thoughts. It seemed so wrong – yet so right at the same time. But when I finally went back downstairs, Martin was fast asleep on the settee.' She looked at Sophie. 'After about ten minutes I went home. When I next saw him, either he remembered and didn't want to admit it or he didn't remember a thing, because he never mentioned it to me. There weren't any awkward moments either as he wondered if I'd bring it up. I don't think he even registered what had gone on.

'I was upset but relieved at the same time. I can remember imagining what would have happened if he really did have feelings for me. How terrible would that be – the old cliché, my best friend's father? And despite what you think of me now, I would never want to hurt you, so I never told you. And I never told him.

'Two months later he died, and a week later I found out I

was pregnant.' Beth paused to see if Sophie would speak. When she didn't, she carried on.

'I'm not proud of what I did but you must see that I did it to protect you too. Martin was your rock. You'd always looked up to him and I didn't want to change that over one stupid, childish moment of mine. He was drunk and I took advantage of him. I'm sorry.'

Sophie still didn't speak but there were tears pouring down her face. Beth started to cry too.

'I know I'm selfish but I only did what I thought was best. Maybe if Martin had been alive, I might have told him. Maybe I would always have kept it secret ... I don't know.'

'And my dad was definitely Charley's father?'

'Yes. I wasn't sleeping with anyone else then.'

'I ...' Sophie struggled to speak. 'I think you should leave.'

Beth shook her head. 'Not until this is sorted. You're my best friend and I want—'

'But don't you see? You've ruined everything. Every good memory I had has been tarnished.'

'No, I —'

'You took advantage of him and betrayed me because you were jealous of the relationship I had with Reece.'

'You're wrong. I was seventeen, unlucky in love and wanted a bit of fun. Unfortunately for me, I got a reminder of it for the rest of my life.' Beth swallowed. 'Still, I have Charley and despite our ups and downs, I love her so much.'

When it was clear that Sophie wasn't going to say anything else, Beth stood up. 'I'll see you tomorrow then. That is, if I still have a job?'

'Of course you have.' Sophie raised her voice. 'What do you take me for?'

'I wouldn't blame you if you never wanted to see me again, so...'

'I'll see you in the morning.' Sophie needed to be by herself to take everything in.

CHAPTER FIFTY-THREE

Sophie burst into tears again as soon as Beth left. For years, she had thought Charley was the mistake of a drunken one-night stand. She'd thought the father would be someone that Beth couldn't remember. Even when she'd caught Charley smiling, or laughing in a way that seemed familiar, never once had she imagined they would share the same father – and that her face resembled Sophie's own.

After so many years, the news was bound to come as a shock. But deep down, she realised why Beth had never told her; why she'd never said anything to Charley either. It was to protect them all. Beth didn't want Sophie to bear any malice towards Martin. She didn't want Charley to know because it would have made things awkward. And she didn't want Martin to be ostracised by people – even though, drunk or not drunk, at thirty-four he should have known better than to take advantage of a seventeen- year-old girl.

Some of the things she'd talked over with Charley the other day came back to her. People make mistakes, she'd told her. And maybe it wasn't fair for anyone to judge someone who was so young and found herself pregnant by her best friend's father who died shortly afterwards.

How would she have felt if Beth had told her back then? Would she have accused her of vying for attention, like Beth was always prone to doing? Either way, she knew their friendship would probably have been over. She wouldn't have wanted to see Charley growing up as her father's child. Now, knowing Charley for so long, she realised she was glad of that.

She also wondered if Beth would ever have told them the truth if she hadn't blurted it out that evening. Maybe – maybe not. But it was out now and they'd have to make the best of it.

Beth got home to find a note from Charley to say she'd slipped over to Sarah's house and would be home for half past eight. Her heart lurched as she thought back to the night her daughter had spent away from her. But since she'd been home, Charley and Sarah had become thick as thieves again and for the past two days, it was as if they'd never fallen out. It was great to hear their laughter around the house once more and it eased the tension as she and Charley both learned to forget what had happened and move forward. At least that way Beth could settle, knowing that giving her daughter the freedom to grow, despite wanting to have her close all the time, was good for both of them.

She flopped into the settee. Tears poured from her eyes but she wiped angrily at them. There was no time for self-pity. She had known for a long time that she needed to change. It was just so hard to do anything about it. But she'd appreciated lately there was more to life than putting herself first. She cared for Charley. She cared for Sophie. And she cared for Matt. Three important people in her life – and she had walked all over them to get her own way. Well, not anymore.

She might not ever be the best mother and she would never make the greatest best-friend-forever but she could improve on what she was and try to make amends.

After all, it was her mistake that had caused the heartache. She hoped that Sophie would forgive her eventually. Because although she had her daughter back, she might have lost her friend now. And that hurt more than she'd ever thought possible.

Two nights before the wedding, most of the women involved in the big day were round at Sophie's house for a girls' night in. Nicci didn't want a hen party; she hadn't fancied trawling around the pubs of Hedworth or going out for a meal. Beth hadn't even been able to persuade her to have a night out at the Hope and Anchor.

But she'd finally succumbed to pressure when Sophie suggested getting together at her house. She'd asked everyone to bring a plate of food and a bottle of something to drink, and the table in the kitchen looked fit to collapse under the weight of cupcakes, sandwiches, mini quiches and pizzas, and numerous nibbles, as well as every type of drink concoction possible.

Despite it being laid out in the kitchen, most of the women were in the living room. Reece, Matt and Ryan had gone into town to meet Jay and his friends for a low-key stag do. Charley had brought along a dance game. She'd been teaching her nan to Zumba for the past half hour.

'My back is going to be killing me in the morning,' Sandra said, 'and I'm mother of the bride ... I'm supposed to be sophisticated. At this rate, I'll be walking like John Wayne on Sunday.'

'Me too.' Beth's auntie Marilyn held onto her stomach as she laughed again. 'I haven't had so much fun in ages. I've got a stitch.'

As the games were swapped over, Nicci decided to join in. She grabbed Beth's hand and pulled her up too.

'Come on,' she said, a little unsteady on her feet. 'Let's show the young ones how to do it. You too, Sophie.'

'I'll join in later.' Sophie waved her away.

They stood behind Charley and Sarah, poised and ready to start. The music kicked in and they were off. Beth laughed as Charley and Sarah did a perfect routine to one of the songs while she, Cassie and Nicci bumbled along in hysterics, thrusting hips and waving arms around.

A few minutes later, Beth noticed Sophie sidling out of the room. They still weren't speaking properly and despite her intentions to change, Beth didn't really know what to do to make things better.

When Sophie had been gone for a while, she went to find her. She wasn't anywhere downstairs so she had a look upstairs. From the landing, she noticed Sophie's bedroom door slightly ajar. Beth peeped around it.

Sophie was sitting on the corner of the bed. There were photos spread over the duvet cover. She guessed they must be of Martin. Beth ached to go to her, to put her arms round her and hug her tightly, but she didn't feel able to intrude. She heard Sophie sniff and realised she was crying as she held one of the photos to her chest.

Beth turned to go back downstairs quietly, but a squeaky floorboard gave her away.

Sophie looked up, quickly wiping at her eyes.

'I came to see where you were,' Beth said. 'Are you okay?'

Sophie gathered the photos together and put them away in a drawer.

'I was just coming,' she said, waltzing past Beth and down the stairs without another word.

It was Beth's turn to wipe away tears. After keeping her secret for so long, she realised that she might have blown it altogether now it was out in the open.

And it made her feel desperately sad.

While the women enjoyed themselves over at Sophie's house, Jess sat curled up on the settee. With both Nicci and Jay out, it gave her time to sit and think without anyone interrupting her – or making her feel like she was in the way.

But she didn't really want time to herself because that made her realise how much she was dreading the wedding that weekend. She'd give anything not to be a part of it but it was too late to back out. And it was her brother getting married, not someone who she could lie to by faking illness.

She couldn't believe how nasty she had been to Nicci a few weeks ago. It had been pure spite, jealousy erupting because Nicci was happy and she was miserable. Jess hoped now that one day they could become friends. Nicci seemed quite nice once she'd got to see more of her, although she hadn't told her that yet.

She wasn't sure how she was going to get through the day seeing Ryan playing happy families with his wife and daughters. If only she hadn't been asked to be part of the wedding party. It was another adage that the bridesmaid got off with the best man but this time it would be true.

How could she have started an affair with Ryan? Talk about bringing it to your own doorstep. She was so ashamed of herself. She'd been looking for someone to blame her predicament on. What a terrible thing to do.

Crying now, Jess hugged a cushion to her chest and tried not to think about it anymore. Instead, she looked forward to when she would get married and have her own big day like Jay and Nicci, surrounded by family and friends. One day, she would find a man who would love her bump as much as her, maybe even have more children.

More importantly, she needed to ensure that she found her own man this time rather than think it was okay to use someone else's. And somewhere to live – she didn't want to be here when the married couple got home from their honeymoon if she could help it. There was a terraced house for rent in Hope Street. It was close to all her family, if they would let her back into their fold.

CHAPTER FIFTY-FOUR

'Oh, no,' Beth groaned as she opened the curtains the next morning. 'It's pouring down with rain. We're going to get soaked and–'

'It can't be – not today.' Nicci jumped out of bed and joined her sister at the window.

'Fooled you.'

Nicci thumped her arm, hard. 'You nearly gave me a heart attack.'

'I have to get my own back on you for last night. You snored like a pig.'

Nicci grinned. They stood silent for a moment and then she threw herself back on the bed, laughing.

'I'm getting married today. Can you believe it?'

'Believe it? I can't forget it. It's the only thing I've heard about in weeks since I let it slip.'

Beth sat on the edge of the bed as Nicci unzipped the cover of her dress; smiled as she watched her sister run a hand down the material afterwards. 'I'm so proud of you. I hope you have a fantastic day.'

Nicci shuffled back across the bed and gave her a hug.

'Don't worry, big sis,' she soothed. 'You'll find your Prince Charming one day.'

'Yeah, right. Who's going to have me?'

Nicci winked. 'You never know.'

Beth sniffed long and hard, her eyes lighting up with anticipation. 'Can you smell that?'

Nicci sniffed too. 'Bacon!'

'Race you for the first sarnie.'

As if they were teenagers again, they flew down the stairs and into the kitchen. Their dad Terry was the one frying the bacon; while their mum was busy buttering toast and making tea.

'Just in time, girls.' Sandra turned to them. 'Nicci, you can set the table and—'

Nicci looked puzzled. 'Since when have we set the table for breakfast?'

'Since my youngest daughter decided to get married.' With a warm smile, Sandra slapped Nicci's hand away as she tried to grab a piece of toast. 'Do as you're told, missy, or else … Beth, go and see where Charley is.'

'It's seven thirty, mum. She'll still be asleep.'

'Well, get her up then. We have a busy day ahead.'

'Yes, because,' Terry broke out into song, 'you're getting married in five ho-urs. Ding dong, the bells are going to CHIME.'

Nicci laughed and then her face was etched in worry. 'I hope it all goes right today. I've waited so long for this moment.'

'Everything will be fine.' Sandra placed a pot of tea on the table. 'And besides, something has to go wrong on the day – it's tradition.'

'It's also a tradition that the bride eats a lovely big fry up.' Terry slid bacon and eggs on to plates and handed one to Nicci. 'Get that down you, my lovely.'

. . .

Later that morning over at the market, Sophie stood mentally ticking off her list, scrutinising everything to make sure nothing was out of place or hadn't been done. She removed a rogue piece of cotton from the tablecloth at the wedding table and smiled. The wedding party wouldn't know but they would be sitting at several trestle tables covered in cream material, gold tassels hanging from a runner that ran the whole length and down the sides, almost touching the floor. Two chairs at its middle had been covered too, for the bride and groom.

She sat down on Nicci's seat and surveyed what everyone had worked hard to create. Gone was the market hall and in its place was a spectacular wedding room. All the junk had been moved to the stock room, leaving them ample space for eight circular tables set out for guests. Each table had mini chocolate wedding fancies for the women and miniature bottles of whiskey for the men. Gold and cream helium balloon decorations graced the centres.

The places were set and ready for Mr Adams who was bringing in the food. The wine glasses shined and awaited the drink. There was a space left in the middle of the floor which would do as a makeshift dance floor and DJ Dave had set up in readiness at the far end of the room. The only noise at the moment was coming from the clink of glassware as the bar was set up to her right.

Sophie prayed it would all go well for Nicci and Jay. It was lovely to see a couple dote on each other. She realised she and Reece must have been the same all those years ago, imagining they'd be together forever. She wished she knew the secret to keeping it that way. But for her, there was no going back.

'It really does look amazing.'

Sophie turned to see Beth walking towards her and smiled.

'It does, doesn't it? I've been worried that we wouldn't be able to pull it off, but it's actually quite perfect.'

Beth's eyes filled with tears and she laughed. 'Look at me, the wedding hasn't even started and I'm already getting emotional.'

Sophie's smile dropped too and she started to cry. But it wasn't about the wedding. 'Oh, Beth. I – I don't think it's working out with Reece in the way I wanted it to.'

Beth pulled Sophie into her arms while she cried. Everything came tumbling out, about how she really felt when Reece had left and then come home again. About how trapped she felt in her marriage.

She spoke about how much she loved Reece but more as a brother, and that she would never want to hurt him. About how she couldn't help thinking she had missed her chance with Damien, and how much she had really liked him. That she hadn't wanted to have a fling, but try at a proper relationship.

'Have you spoken to Reece about it?'

Sophie shook her head. 'It's complicated. He's only been home a few weeks.'

'But you've sensed he isn't happy?' Beth asked,

'Not as such but it's ...'

'More that it's over but none of you dare say for upsetting the other?'

Sophie nodded. 'He was so good to me when Martin died.'

'That's still not a reason to spend the rest of your life together. Relationships need passion.'

'I guess so. It's more like we want to be friends. We care about each other but we're not good together as a couple anymore. We've grown apart.'

'A bit like us?'

'What?' Sophie shook her head. 'No, not at all.'

'But we're not exactly best friends forever at the moment.' Beth pulled out a chair and sat down. 'I wish I hadn't messed up our friendship and that I could be there for you. I know I'm selfish but I miss you.'

Sophie sat down next to her. 'I miss you too.'

'Do you? Really?'

'Of course I do.'

'But I screwed everything up. I know I'm a bolshie cow. It's definitely where Charley gets her stubborn streak from.'

'I don't know so much. I think she takes after her father for that.'

Beth wiped away tears of her own now. 'You wouldn't have brought Martin into the conversation unless you're willing to forgive me.'

'We all make mistakes, Beth. I can't hold something against you that happened so long ago. And besides, I have the coolest goddaughter-come-half-sister ever.'

They hugged again.

'We'd better get going before we're missed too much,' Beth said eventually.

Sophie nodded. Taking one last look around, with great satisfaction and anticipation of what was to come, she left to get changed for the wedding ceremony. Things might not have gone to plan for Nicci but everyone had certainly done her proud today.

She couldn't wait to see her face.

CHAPTER FIFTY-FIVE

It was half an hour before midday. Upstairs in Nicci's old bedroom, the chatter was loud and the champagne was flowing. The women were adding the final preparations to ensure everything was perfect for the big day.

Beth and Sophie helped Nicci step into her wedding dress and then fasten it up. The off-white dress was understated perfection; long and sleeveless satin with a V-neck pleated bodice. The skirt was A-line and cut on the bias.

'At least you don't have to breathe in,' Beth sighed, zipping it up easily and fastening the hook and eye. 'It's so snug.'

'That's because I've been on the wedding nerves diet,' Nicci laughed.

'Don't worry.' Cassie ran a brush through daughter Abigail's hair as Amelia, her other daughter, tried to do her own. 'Besides, you've got the traditional good luck charms, haven't you? Something old, something new, something borrowed and something blue?'

'Have I?' Nicci turned around with a worried look on her face.

'Sure you have,' Beth said. 'Something old is Jay.'

Nicci slapped at Beth's hand playfully.

'Something new is your dress.' Sophie ran a hand down the front of it to smooth it out.

'Something borrowed is your necklace,' Sandra added, doing the same to the back. 'Borrowed from me, your old mum.'

Nicci fingered the thin gold chain with its diamond pendant.

'And something blue is this.' Beth lifted up the skirt of Nicci's dress, much to the annoyance of Sophie and Sandra, and snapped the elastic on her lacy garter. 'Perfect.'

Beth glanced at Charley. Her hair was piled up in a bun, tendrils hanging down by her ears to frame her face; tiny white flowers weaved in here and there. In her pale pink dress, she looked angelic.

'You're a princess.' Beth beamed with pride.

'I look more like a fairy.' Charley rolled her eyes. 'I can't wait to wear the new dress you bought me this evening.'

Cassie was helping the twins into their clothes, tying ballet shoe ribbons round two pairs of fidgety legs. They each wore halos of flowers matching their three-quarter length dresses with a huge bow at the centre of the back.

'Now, that's what fairies look like,' muttered Charley.

Beth tried and failed not to giggle.

Over in the corner of the room, Jess stood quietly, trying to get ready alone. She didn't want to join in even if they had let her; she wanted to blend into the background.

She stepped into a simple pink dress that stopped at her ankles. A month ago, it would have fitted perfectly but due to the baby bump she was now showing, the dress had to be let out at the last minute and was stretched to its maximum. Still, it was only for one day.

Jess put her hand around her back to pull up the zip. But it was a struggle to do it by herself.

'Here, let me help,' Cassie offered, coming over to her.

Oh no, not her of all people.

'It's fine.' Immediately, she sensed her skin flushing.

'It won't take me a minute.' Cassie pulled up the zip and turned Jess round to face her. She stared at her for a moment, eyes brimming with tears. Then she smiled. 'You look gorgeous,' she said.

'I look fat and pregnant,' Jess said.

'No. You look radiant because you're pregnant.' Cassie paused for a moment and then spoke quietly. 'Was it you?'

Jess decided she didn't want to lie again. She'd been deceitful and Cassie deserved to know the truth.

She nodded.

Cassie's eyes dropped and then met Jess's again. 'Is it his baby?'

'No.' Jess shook her head this time. 'It was only the once or twice.'

'Was it once or twice?'

'Well, I—'

'What does it matter anyway? It's another once or twice too much again as far as I'm concerned. Ryan is good-looking and he has the gift of the gab. You weren't the first woman to fall for his charms.'

The two women looked at each other. There was no need for any more words, even though Jess knew that Ryan wasn't the only one to blame.

'Mummy, Abby needs a wee and my ribbon has come undone,' Amelia shouted from the other side of the room.

Cassie took a deep breath and held her head high. With

one last look at Jess, she gave her a faint smile before reaching down for her daughter's hands.

'Come on then, poppet,' she said. 'Let's get you sorted. We can't have any mishaps, today of all days.'

Before she moved away, Jess reached for Cassie's arm. 'I'm so sorry,' she said. 'And for what's it worth, I've learned my lesson. I can't even say it was hormones but I don't know what came over me. It was stupid and selfish. I just never saw what this would do to you, and your family.'

'I don't blame you,' Cassie replied. 'I blame Ryan.' She paused. 'Still, that won't be my problem soon. Okay, okay, girls. I'm coming!'

As Cassie was dragged away by an impatient Amelia, Jess stood alone again. She wanted to cry but knew she needed to stay strong. This wasn't the time or the place for self-pity. Besides, she didn't want to stress herself out. She knew it wouldn't be good for the baby.

She cradled her bump and looked around the room – grandmother, mother, sister, niece, auntie, all intent on making this day special. And she would be Nicci's sister-in-law soon, despite trying to scupper the wedding when she'd come back to Somerley.

If she changed, she had a loving family to bring her baby into. And she needed them. Bringing up a child on her own would be hard enough. She could do far worse than settle in Somerley again, surrounded by family – and maybe even make some friends. She could make a fresh start.

She glanced at her own mother, Maureen, who was laughing at something Sandra had said to her. Maureen caught her eye, smiled and beckoned her over.

Jess paused for a moment. She had two choices. Either she joined in and enjoyed the day or she sat back and sulked, causing an atmosphere.

She chose the former.

CHAPTER FIFTY-SIX

With minutes to spare, the cars arrived to take them to the wedding. Amid lots of chatter and laughter, they all took their places and set off. At the registry office, Nicci waited for Jay to arrive, nervously playing with the pendant on the chain around her neck. But he was early, much to her surprise.

Terry Pellington walked his youngest daughter through the gathering of friends and family to where Jay was waiting. Matt and Ryan stood by Jay's side, Ryan keeping his eyes ahead but Matt kept glancing over at Beth. Sophie smiled when he caught her eye and he grinned back at her.

Neither Nicci nor Jay fluffed their lines, Beth and Sophie failed to keep their tears in, laughing at each other when they spotted they were crying. Both sets of parents did the same.

In what seemed to be no longer than a blink of an eye, Nicci became Mrs Worthington. Photo after photo was taken – Jay joked that his jaw was aching from posing for pictures. Then with the formalities over, the bride and groom climbed into their wedding car and headed off to the reception.

'Can't you tell me where we're going, Jay?' she pleaded as they sat in the back of the car, sharing a bottle of champagne.

She giggled as the bubbles went up her nose. 'I promise I won't tell anyone and I can act surprised.'

'Certainly not,' he admonished, sliding a hand up her leg. 'I hear brides wear garters, let me see.'

'Stop changing the subject.' Nicci slapped his hand away playfully.

Jay grinned. Leaning in close to her, he kissed her on the nose. 'I don't know where we're going either. All I know is that it will be very special. But first, we have to call in at the market. Sophie has something for you but she doesn't want everyone at the reception to see.'

Nicci nodded and then her hand moved to cover her mouth. 'I think I'm going to be sick.'

'Charming.'

'It's the build-up of the day.'

'You're not actually going to be sick, are you?' Jay looked a little concerned. 'Because if you are, you'll start me off too.'

'I'm fine, really.'

'At least you don't have to do a speech. What if I have a fit of giggles or some squeaky voice comes out? Or worse than that, what if I faint like they do on those clips on You've Been Framed.'

'That reminds me, I need to make sure I video you on my phone, just in case,' Nicci teased. 'I can't miss an opportunity to make £250.'

Jay's eyes twinkled. 'I love you, Mrs Worthington.'

Nicci gave him a kiss this time. 'I love you too, Mr Worthington.'

'They're here,' Ryan cried as he ran into the hall where everyone had rushed to after the service. 'Take your places, and, remember children, be quiet!'

'You need to pipe down,' Beth whispered loudly as she punched him in his arm. 'She'll be able to hear you shouting.'

'Sorry.'

Beth turned to Sophie and rolled her eyes. Then she frowned when she saw her friend's worried face. 'What's wrong?'

'What if Nicci hates it?'

Beth shook her head. 'How could she? You have the place looking beautiful. No one would recognise it.'

Sophie turned back to see that it was indeed a sight to behold. All in all, everyone had made a tremendous effort. And now they were lined up either side of the doors. Family and friends from the market stalls, who had given their time and their wares for free to make Nicci and Jay's big day perfect.

As the door handle went down, everyone in the room froze. Then there was a mighty roar as congratulations rang out around the room.

Nicci squealed and turned to Jay wide-eyed. When she saw him grinning, she clicked in. 'You knew, didn't you?'

'I may have had a little bit to do with it.'

Nicci flew into his arms. Afterwards, she turned around in a circle taking everything in, before running over to greet her family.

When she got to Sophie and Beth, she pulled them both close. 'I can't believe you did all this for us. Thank you, thank you, thank you!'

Once the wedding meal was served, and everyone's glass had been refilled, Sophie finally began to relax. It had all worked out perfectly on the day.

As usual, Matt and Ryan were like a double act with their pre-rehearsed routine as best men. They had the bride and groom's family and friends roaring with laughter in no time as they relayed anecdote after anecdote about Jay – luckily keeping them all clean. They even managed to remember to thank the bridesmaids as tradition expected them to. Ryan then went on to have the last word.

'And finally, may I say a special thank you to *my* wife.' He raised his glass in salute to Cassie. 'Not only does she do a fantastic job of raising our daughters, she also looks after me – and that's a hell of a thing to ask anyone to do.'

Everyone laughed.

'To Cassie Pellington.'

As family and guests toasted her health, Cassie's smile was tight.

'And what about you, Matt?' Jay shouted up. 'Any special lady in your life?'

'Sure there is.' Matt looked at the other end of the table to where Beth was sitting.

As all eyes in the room followed his gaze, Beth looked on in bewilderment.

When everyone had finished, and Nicci and Jay were doing the rounds chatting to their guests, Ryan joined Cassie at the end of the table where she'd sat with the twins. Sandra had taken them off her hands for a while, no doubt enjoying the opportunity to show the guests what beautiful grandchildren she had.

'Was I good or was I good?' Ryan asked with a smirk as he sat down next to her.

'You're always good, aren't you?' Cassie spoke quietly, not wanting to bring attention to them.

Ryan sat down with a frown. 'What's up?'

'I've had enough of you.'

'Give me a break.' Ryan reached for a half full glass of wine that had been left on the table and took a sip.

'I don't think you understand. I want a divorce,' Cassie hissed. 'And I want you out of the house.'

Ryan was about to take another sip, but stopped, glass in mid-air.

'I know about Jess.' Cassie watched the colour drain from his face. 'I know that it isn't your baby – thank the lord – but it still doesn't excuse the fact that you slept with her.'

'I—'

'Don't you dare think of lying.' She held up her hand.

Ryan gulped. 'It was only the once or twice.'

Cassie laughed inwardly at his choice of words, exactly the same as Jess had chosen earlier. She still didn't want to know exactly how many times it had been. Because, sitting here with him, she realised that she wasn't actually concerned.

'I don't care if you had sex umpteen times all over Somerley, I still—'

'It's over now anyway,' Ryan interjected.

'Yes, it is.' Cassie took the glass from him and knocked back the rest of the wine. She placed it down on the table and stood up. Not wanting to make a scene, her tone was quiet but forceful. 'I want you out of the house by next weekend.'

'Wait!' Ryan grabbed her hand as she began to walk away. 'Please. I can explain.'

Cassie snatched it away. 'I don't want to play happy families anymore. It's too late.'

CHAPTER FIFTY-SEVEN

Around seven thirty, the music started and as evening guests began to filter in, Nicci and Jay took to the floor for their first dance as a married couple. To the sounds of 'Thinking out Loud', by Ed Sheeran, people clapped, oohed and aahed and took more photos. It was a magical moment for everyone involved in the day.

Over at her table, Sophie sat with Reece. She looked around the room to see all the people she worked with, the ones who had made this day possible. Geoff Adams was chatting to Malcolm. Melissa was over at the bar, laughing at something that Duncan, the delivery man, was telling them. Marilyn stood talking to Sally from Cupcake Delights. All in all, it had been flawless.

Beth came over and sat down. 'Why can't I have that?' She pointed at the bride and groom as they slow-danced in the makeshift dance area. By this point, several other couples had taken to the floor too.

'Marriage isn't all it's cracked up to be,' Reece said. Then he glanced at Sophie guiltily. 'I didn't mean to say that out loud.'

Despite his insinuation, Sophie couldn't help but smile. Before she had time to come back with something jokey, Matt raced over, grabbed Beth's hand and pulled her to her feet.

'Come and dance with me.' He led her away.

Sophie realised this might be the right time to speak to Reece.

'It's not working for you, is it?' she asked.

Reece shook his head. 'I'm sorry.'

'Don't be. It's not working for me either.' She smiled, for the first time ever feeling shy around her husband. They sat in silence why they each digested the other's words.

Reece reached for her hand finally and gave it a quick squeeze.

'Will you go back to Sheffield?' Sophie asked. 'Or stay around here?'

'I'm not sure. Is it all right with you anyway?'

She nodded.

'Is it okay if I stay over tonight? I can sleep on the settee, and then in the morning I can go to my parents.'

'I'm hardly likely to kick you out right now.'

Reece leaned across and ever so tenderly kissed her on the cheek. 'I'll miss you,' he said.

'No, you won't.' Sophie smiled.

They sat together for a while, content with each other. Then, feeling buoyed up by the day, the emotion, the champagne or whatever, Sophie reached for her phone. There was nothing stopping her from doing what she wanted to now.

Maybe it was too late, but maybe, possibly, it might not be. She had never really stopped thinking about him, but it hadn't been right to lead him on.

Hey Damien. Just wondering how you are? Sophie x

It took a few minutes but a message came back.

Hi! I'm good, great to hear from you. How are you?

Good, thanks. I was wondering if...

Before she could send that message, another came in.

Still with your old man?

She deleted the message she was writing and wrote something else.

Not anymore

Her phone lit up as it began to ring. She smiled as she picked it up and went outside to take the call.

As Matt twirled Beth around in his arms, she threw her head back and laughed. 'I'm not sure my feet will take much more. These heels are killing me.'

'Then let me sweep you off your feet instead.'

'Ooh, get you, you smooth talker,' she teased.

He led her off the dance floor into a quieter area of the room. 'Maybe it's time I just came out with it.'

Beth frowned. 'What's up?'

'I want to ask you something.'

'I'm not covering for you on the stall while you swan off somewhere on holiday, if that's what you're after. You know I need to stay in Sophie's good books. I've caused her enough trouble lately and—'

'Can you shut up for one minute?' Before she could protest, Matt silenced her with a kiss.

Beth resisted at first, mainly out of surprise, and then melted into his embrace.

Once they stopped, Matt cupped her face in his hands.

'I think I've wasted far too much time just being your friend when I really want more. I want to be a permanent part of your life, right now. I want to wake up with you. I want to fall asleep with you. And everyone knows you need someone to keep you on the straight and narrow. And I want

... Beth, I love you so much. Do you think we could have a go at being a proper couple?'

Beth's mouth gaped open. Then she found her voice and squealed. 'Ohmigod.'

'That's not the answer I was looking for.' But Matt was smiling.

'Yes.' Beth flung her arms around his neck. 'Yes. Yes. One hundred billion trillion times, yes.'

Beth and Matt grinned at each other. Then Matt kissed her again. She vaguely recalled someone shouting 'get a room' before they stopped.

Giddy by the euphoria of the day, she searched out Charley with her eyes. She was by the side of the dance floor with Sarah, waving at them. Beth beckoned her over and she ran into her arms.

'I was waiting for you to finish with the necking first,' Charley shrieked, hugging her tightly.

Beth feigned hurt. 'Didn't you think anyone would have your old mum?'

'I mean that I can't believe after all this time you two have finally got together.' Charley gave Matt a hug too. 'You're meant for each other.'

'But how did you know?' Beth asked.

'Mum, *everyone* knows how you feel about him and everyone knows how he feels about you.'

'Really?'

Charley nodded fervently. 'I suppose I'll get to be a bridesmaid again at *your* wedding next?'

'That's a bit early to assume,' Beth giggled.

'I'm definitely leading up to that,' Matt said.

'Please let me pick my own dress then,' Charley continued. 'I don't want to look like an overgrown fairy at your wedding.'

Behind Charley, Beth spotted Sophie coming into the

room. She rushed towards her as she held out her arms. 'Can you believe he asked me that?' she said, once she told her what she'd missed.

'He should have done it years ago,' Sophie replied. 'I've always thought you were made for each other. But you wouldn't listen to anyone.'

Beth glanced over her shoulder to where Matt was talking to her mum and dad, then back at Sophie.

'Thank you,' she smiled. 'Not for that, but for everything. For being here for me, for putting up with me, for standing by me through thick and thin. I don't know what I would have done without you.'

'It's been a pleasure – well, most of it.' Sophie grinned too. 'And, anyway, that's what friends are for.'

'And you and Reece?' she questioned.

'All done with, I think. Amicably, of course. Time to move on.' She smiled. 'And you and me, no more secrets?'

Beth smiled. 'No more secrets.'

A LETTER FROM MARCIE

First of all, I want to say a huge thank you for choosing to read Secrets, Lies and Love. I hope you enjoyed getting to know Sophie, Beth and Charley as well as I did. I had so much fun writing it. In my next book in The Somerley Series, Second Chances at Love, you'll hear from more characters who live in the fictional market town, Riley, Sadie and Dan. I hope you'll continue to enjoy getting to know them too.

If you did enjoy Secrets, Lies & Love, I would be forever grateful if you'd write a review. I'd love to hear what you think, and it can also help other readers discover one of my books for the first time. Or maybe you can recommend it to your friends and family ...

Many thanks to anyone who has emailed me, messaged me, chatted to me on Facebook or Twitter and told me how much they have enjoyed reading my books. I've been genuinely blown away with all kinds of niceness and support from you all. A writer's job is often a lonely one but I feel I truly have friends everywhere.

Why not join my readers VIP club? I'll send you a free ebook, Coffee with Marcie, with stories you can read on a break. I'll keep you up to date with when the next book will be out, as well as run regular competitions to win books and goodies, and talk about other books I've read and enjoyed.

I'd love to keep in touch,

Marcie x

WHAT'S NEXT IN THE SOMERLEY SERIES?

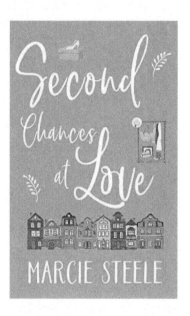

A tale of love, friendship and putting your best foot forward.

All **Riley** wants is to meet someone who makes her happy. But attracting the right kind of man is not easy, and with her heart still hurting from her last break-up, she believes she'll never find love again.

Nearly a year ago **Sadie's** whole world was shattered when her husband died. She has struggled to keep herself together for the sake of their young daughter, but with the anniversary of his death approaching, Sadie finds herself overwhelmed by grief.

Sadie and Riley work at Chandler's Shoes in the market town of Somerley. But when the shop is threatened with closure, the friends are confronted with the loss of not only their jobs, but also their support network - the glue that binds them when they are close to breaking.

As they put together a plan to save their beloved shop, Sadie realises that she might be learning to live again. Could it be that new beginnings are just around the corner? The campaign also finds Riley unexpectedly crossing paths with charming photographer, Ethan. Maybe her second chance at love is right under her feet...

<u>Find out more here</u>

ALSO BY MARCIE STEELE

ACKNOWLEDGMENTS

To my friends Alison Niebierszczanski, Caroline Mitchell, Imogen Clark, Talli Roland, Louise Ross and Sharon Sant. Thanks for all the coffee, cake and chats!

Thanks to my early reader group, who never fail to amaze me with their enthusiasm, their speedy reading and their friendship. You rock!

Many thanks also to anyone who has emailed me, messaged me, chatted to me on Facebook or Twitter and told me how much they have enjoyed reading this book. I've been genuinely blown away with all kinds of niceness and support from you all. A writer's job is often a lonely one but I feel I truly have friends everywhere.

ABOUT THE AUTHOR

Marcie Steele is a pen name. I'm Mel Sherratt and ever since I can remember, I've been a meddler of words. Born and raised in Stoke-on-Trent, Staffordshire, I used the city as a backdrop for my first novel, Taunting the Dead, and it went on to be a Kindle number one bestseller and the overall number eight UK Kindle bestselling book of 2012. Since then, I've written twenty-six books and sold over two million copies.

As Mel, I like writing about fear and emotion – the cause and effect of crime – what makes a character do something. Working as a housing officer for eight years also gave me the background to create a fictional estate full of good and bad characters (think *Brassic* meets *Coronation Street*.)

But I'm a romantic at heart and have always wanted to write about characters that are not necessarily involved in the darker side of life. I like to write about love, romance, friendship, family, secrets and lies in everyday life - feel good factor with humour and heart.

Coffee, cakes and friends are three of my favourite things, hence writing under the name of Marcie Steele too. I can often be found sitting in a coffee shop, sipping a cappuccino and eating a chocolate chip cookie, either catching up with friends or writing on my laptop.

Printed in Great Britain
by Amazon